Harlan Ellison

Strange Wine

fifteen new stories from the nightside of the world

A Warner Communications Company

WARNER BOOKS EDITION

This Warner Books Edition is published by
arrangement with Harper & Row Publishers

Cover art by Leo and Diane Dillon

Warner Books, Inc.,
666 Fifth Avenue,
New York, N.Y. 10103

Printed in the United States of America

First Warner Books Printing: *June, 1979*

Reissued: *January, 1984*

10 9 8 7 6 5 4

Copyright information continued on following page

ACKNOWLEDGMENTS

The author wishes to note the following persons whose kindnesses and support enabled him to write these stories better and more easily than would have been the case without their good offices: Jane Rotrosen; Ray Bradbury; the staff of Words & Music in Charing Cross Road, London; Martin Miller, Director, Marketing Research, Mattel Toys; Vonda N. McIntyre; David Wise and Kathleen Barnes; William Rotsler; Robert Silverberg; Barbara Silverberg; Arthur Byron Cover; Mike Hodel; Lydia Marano; Richard Delap; Don Pfiel; Edward L. and Audrey Ferman; Eric Protter; Arline Inge; Gerard Van der Leun; Terry Carr; Sherry Gottlieb and the staff of A Change of Hobbit in Los Angeles; Stephanie Bernstein; Edward Bryant; Norman Goldfind; Larry Todd; Byron Preiss; Neal Adams; Michael Moorcock; Jill Riches; Jane Gould; the staff of The Portobello Hotel in London; Joe Oles and his family; Haskell, Carol and Tracy Barkin (some of whom are *née* Klotz); Maggie Pierce and Linda Steele; and the former Lori Ellison, wherever she may be.

This one, with love,
for my friends
SHERYL AND TERRY
AND
TERRY AND SHERYL

All men dream . . . but not equally. They who dream by night in the dusty recesses of their minds wake in the day to find that it is vanity; but the dreamers of the day are dangerous men, for they act their dream with open eyes, to make it possible.

T. E. LAWRENCE

Only fantasy has
eternal youth.
What happened nowhere
and never can never
age.

SCHILLER

Contents

Strange Wine

GROTESQUE:

". . . the expression in a moment, by a series of symbols thrown together in bold and fearless connection, of truth . . ."

JOHN RUSKIN

GROTESQUE IN THE CLASSIC SENSE:
"anticke figures"

•

"I write of things which I have neither seen nor suffered nor learned from another, things which are not and never could have been, and therefore my readers should by no means believe them."

LUCIAN OF SAMOSATA

"I sing of places I've never seen, of people I've never been. But savor my songs, because they're free."

PETER ALLEN

•

"Better the illusions that exalt us than ten thousand truths."

ALEKSANDER PUSHKIN

Introduction

Revealed at Last! What Killed the Dinosaurs! And You Don't Look So Terrific Yourself.

It's all about drinking strange wine.

It seems disjointed and jumps around like water on a griddle, but it all comes together, so be patient.

At 9:38 A.M. on July 15th, 1974, about eight minutes into *Suncoast Digest,* a variety show on WXLT-TV in Sarasota, Florida, anchorwoman Chris Chubbuck, 30, looked straight at the camera and said, "In keeping with Channel 40's policy of bringing you the latest in blood and guts in living color, you're going to see another first —an attempt at suicide."

Whereupon she pulled a gun out of a shopping bag and blew her brains out, on camera.

Paragraph 3, preceding, was taken verbatim from an article written by Daniel Schorr for *Rolling Stone.* I'd heard about the Chubbuck incident, of course, and I admit to filching Mr. Schorr's sixty concise words because they *are* concise, and why should I try to improve on precision? As the artist Mark Rothko once put it: "Silence is so accurate."

Further, Mr. Schorr perceived in the bizarre death of Chris Chubbuck exactly what I got out of it when I heard the news broadcast the day it happened. She was making a statement about television . . . *on television!*

The art-imitating-life resemblance to Paddy Chayefsky's film *Network* should not escape us. I'm sure it wouldn't have escaped Chris Chubbuck's attention. Obvious cliché; onward.

I used to know Dan Blocker, who played Hoss Cartwright on *Bonanza.* He was a wise and a kind man, and there are tens of dozens of people I would much rather see dead than Dan. One time, around lunch-break at Paramount, when I was goofing off on writing a treatment for a Joe Levine film that never got made, and Dan was resting his ass from some dumb horsey number he'd been reshooting all morning, we sat on the steps of the weathered saloon that probably in no way resembled any saloon that had ever existed in Virginia City, Nevada, and we talked about reality versus fantasy. The reality of getting up at five in the morning to get to the studio in time for makeup call and the reality of how bloody much FICA tax they took out of our paychecks and the reality of one of his kids being down with something or other . . . and the fantasy of not being Dan Blocker, but of being Hoss Cartwright.

And he told me a scary story. He laughed about it, but it was the laugh of butchers in a slaughterhouse who have to swing the mauls that brain the beeves; who then go home to wash the stink out of their hair from the spattering.

He told me—and he said this happened *all* the time, not just in isolated cases—that he had been approached by a little old woman during one of his personal appearances at a rodeo, and the woman had said to him, dead seriously, "Now listen to me, Hoss: when you go home tonight, I want you to tell your daddy, Ben, to get rid of that Chinee fella who cooks for you all. What you need is to get yourself a good woman in there can cook up some decent food for you and your family."

So Dan said to her, very politely (because he was one of

the most courteous people I've ever met), "Excuse me, ma'am, but my name is Dan Blocker. Hoss is just the character I play. When I go home I'll be going to my house in Los Angeles and my wife and children will be waiting."

And she went right on, just a bit affronted because she *knew* all that, what was the matter with him, did he think she was simple or something, "Yes, I know . . . but when you go back to the Ponderosa, you just tell your daddy, Ben, that I said . . ."

For her, fantasy and reality were one and the same.

There was a woman who had the part of a home-wrecker on a daytime soap opera. One day as she was coming out of Lord & Taylor in New York, a viewer began bashing her with an umbrella, calling her filthy names and insisting she should leave that nice man and his wife alone!

One time during a college lecture, I idly mentioned that I had actually *thought up* all the words Leonard Nimoy had spoken as Mr. Spock on the sole *Star Trek* segment I had written; and a young man leaped up in the audience, in tears, and began screaming that I was a liar. He actually thought the actors were living those roles as they came across the tube.

Why do I tell you all this; and what does it have to do with drinking strange wine?

Chris Chubbuck perceived at a gut level that for too many Americans the only reality is what's on the box. That Johnny Carson and Don Rickles and Mary Tyler Moore are more real, more substantial, more immediately important than the members of their own family, or the people in their community. She knew that her death wouldn't be *real* unless it happened on television, unless it took place where life is lived, there in phosphor-dot Never-Never Land. If she did it decently, in the privacy of her home, or in some late night bar, or in a deserted parking lot . . . it would never have happened. She would have been flensed from memory as casually as a popped pimple. Her suicide on camera was the supreme act of loathing and ridicule for the monkeymass that watched her.

When I was writing my television criticism for the Los Angeles *Free Press,* circa 1968–72, I used *The Glass Teat* columns to repeat my belief that those of us who cared, who had some ethics and some talent, dared not abandon to the Visigoths what was potentially the most powerful medium the world had ever known for the dissemination of education and knowledge. I truly believed that. And I said it again and again.

But it's been five years since I last wrote those words, and I've done so many college speaking engagements that Grand Forks, North Dakota, has blurred with Minneapolis, Minnesota, has blurred with Bethel, Maine, has blurred with Shreveport, Louisiana, and what I've come away with is a growing horror at what television has done to us.

I now believe that television itself, the medium of sitting in front of a magic box that pulses images at us endlessly, the act of watching TV, per se, is mind crushing. It is soul deadening, dehumanizing, soporific in a poisonous way, ultimately brutalizing. It is, simply put so you cannot mistake my meaning, *a bad thing.*

We need never fear Orwell's 1984, because it's here, with us now, nearly a decade ahead of schedule, and has been with us for quite a while already. Witness the power of television and the impact it has had on *you.*

Don't write me letters telling me how *you've* escaped the terror, how *you're* not a slave to the box, how *you* still read and listen to Brahms and carry on meaningful discussions with your equally liberated friends. Stop and *really* take stock of how many hours last week you sat stunned before the tube, relaxing, just unwinding, just passing a little time between the demanding and excoriating life-interests that *really* command your energies. You will be stunned again, if you are honest. Because *I* did it, and it scared me, genuinely put a fright into me. It was far more time than I'd have considered feasible, knowing how much I despise television and how little there is I care to watch.

I rise, usually, between five and seven in the morning, depending how late I've worked the night before. I work like a lunatic all day . . . I'm a workaholic . . . pity me . . . and by five or six in the evening I have to unwind. So I lie down and turn on the set. Where before I might have picked up a book of light fiction, or dozed, or just sighed and stared at the ceiling, now I turn on the carnivorous coaxial creature.

And I watch.

Here in Los Angeles between five and eight, when "Prime Time" begins (oh, how I *love* that semantically twisted phrase) we have the same drivel you have in your city. Time that was taken from the networks to program material of local interest and edification. Like reruns of *Adam-12, The Price Is Right, The Joker's Wild, Name That Tune, I Dream of Jeannie, Bewitched, Concentration,* and *Match Game P.M.*. I lie there like the quadruple amputee viewpoint character of Dalton Trumbo's *Johnny Got His Gun,* never speaking, breathing shallowly, seeing only what flashes before my eyes, reduced to a ganglial image receptor, a raw nerve-end taking in whatever banalities and incredible stupidities they care to throw at me in the name of "giving the audience what they want."

If functional illiterates failing such mind-challenging questions as "What was the name of the character Robert Stack played on *The Untouchables?*" is an accurate representation of "what the audience wants," then my point has been solidly made . . .

. . . and it goes directly to the answer to the question of what killed the dinosaurs and you don't look so terrific yourself!

But I wander. So. I lie there, until my low bullshit threshold is reached, either through the zombie mannerisms of the *Adam-12* cops—dehumanized paragons of a virtue never known by L.A.'s former lunatic chief of police, Weirdo Ed Davis—or because of some yotz on *The Price Is Right* having an orgasm at winning a thirty-year supply of rectal suppositories. And then I curse, snap off the set, and realize I've been lying there for ninety minutes.

And when I take stock of how much time I'm spending in front of that set, either at the five-to-eight break or around eleven o'clock when I fall into bed for another break and turn on *The CBS Late Movie,* I become aware of five hours spent in mindless sucking at the glass teat.

If you're honest, you'll own up to that much time televiewing, too. Maybe more. Maybe a little less. But you spend from three to eight hours a day at it. And you're not alone. Nor am I. The college gigs I do have clearly demonstrated that to me. Clearly. I take show-of-hands polls in the audience; and after badgering them to cop to the truth, the vast bulk of the audience admits it, and I see the stunned looks of concern and dawning awareness.

They never realized it was that much; nor did I.

And the effect it has had on them, on you, young people and old alike; black and white and Hispanic and Oriental and Amerind; male and female; wealthy and impoverished; WASPs and Jews and Shintoists and Buddhists and Catholics and even Scientologists. All of us, all of you, swamped day after day by stereotypes and jingoism and "accepted" life-styles. So that after a while you come to believe doctors are all wise and noble and one with Marcus Welby and they could cure you of *any*thing if only you'd stop being so cranky and irrational; that cops never abuse their power and are somehow Solomonic in their judgments; that, in the final extreme, violence—as represented by that eloquent vocabulary of a punch in the mouth—solves problems; that women are either cute and cuddly and need a strong hand to keep them in line or defeminize themselves if they have successful careers; and that eating McDonald's prefab food is actually *better* for you than *foie de veau sauté aux fines herbes* . . . and tastier, too.

I see this zombiatic response in college audiences. It manifests itself most prominently in the kinds of questions that are asked. Here I stand before them, perhaps neither Melville nor Twain, but nonetheless a man with a substantial body of work behind him, books that express the artist's view of the world (and after all, isn't that why they paid me two grand or better a night to come and speak? Surely it can't be my winsome manner!), and they persist in asking me what it was like to work on *Star Trek* or what Jimmy Caan is *really* like and why did Tom Snyder keep cutting me off on the *Tomorrow* show. I get angry with them. I make myself lots less antic and entertaining. I tell them what I'm telling you here. And they don't like me for it. As long as I'm running down the military-industrial complex or the fat money cats who play sneaky panther games with our lives, they give me many "Right on, brother!" ovations. But when I tell them how shallow and programmed television is making them, there is a clear lynch tenor in the mob. (It isn't just college kids, gentle reader. I was recently rewarded with sullen animosity when I spoke to a dinner gathering of Southern California Book Publicists, and instead of blowing smoke up their asses about what a wonderful thing book publicity through the Johnny Carson show is—because there isn't one of them who wouldn't sacrifice several quarts of blood to get a client on that detestable viewing ground for banal conversationalists—I quoted them the recent illiteracy figures released by HEW. I pointed out that only 8% of the 220,000,000 population of this country buy books, and of that 8% only 2% buy more than a single book a year. I pointed out that 6% of that measly 8% were no doubt buying, as their single enriching literary experience each year, *Jaws* or *Oliver's Story* or the latest Harold Robbins ghastliness, rather than, say, *Remembrance of Things Past* or the Durants' *The Lessons of History* or even the latest Nabokov or Lessing novel. So that meant they were hustling books to only 2% of the population of this country; while the other 98% sank deeper and deeper into illiteracy and functional illiteracy, their heads being shoved under by the pressure of television, to which they were slavishly making obeisance. They were, in effect, sharpening the blade for their executioner, assisting in their own extinction. They *really* didn't want to hear that. Nor do college audiences.)

A *bad* thing. Watching television. Not rationalizing it so that it comes out reading thus: "Television is *potentially* a good thing; it can educate and stimulate and inform us; we've just permitted it to be badly used; but if we could get some *good* stuff on the tube . . ." No, I'm afraid I've gone beyond that rationalization, to an extreme position. The *act* of watching television for protracted periods (and there's no way to insure the narcotic effects won't take you over) is deleterious to the human animal. The medium itself insists you sit there quietly and cease thinking.

The dinosaurs. How they died.

Television, quite the opposite of books or even old-time radio that presented drama and comedy and talk shows (unlike Top Forty radio programming today, which is merely TV without moving parts), is systemically oriented toward stunning the use of individual imagination. It puts everything out there, *right there,* so you don't have to dream even a little bit. When they would broadcast a segment of, say, *Inner Sanctum* in the Forties, and you heard the creaking door of a haunted house, the mind was forced to *create the picture* of that haunted house—a terrifying place so detailed and terrifying that if Universal Studios wanted to build such an edifice for a TV movie, it would cost them millions of dollars and it *still* wouldn't be one one-millionth as frightening as the one your own imagination had cobbled up.

A book is a participatory adventure. It involves a creative act at its inception and a creative act when its purpose is fulfilled. The writer dreams the dream and sets it down; the reader reinterprets the dream in personal terms, with personal vision, when he or she reads it. Each creates a world. The template is the book.

At risk of repeating myself, and of once again cribbing from another writer's perfection of expression (in this case, my friend Dr. Isaac Asimov), here is a bit I wrote on this subject for an essay on the "craft" of writing teleplays:

Unlike televison, films, football games, the roller derby, wars in underdeveloped nations and Watergate hearings, which are spectator sports, a book requires the activation of its words by the eyes and the intellect of a reader. As Isaac Asimov said recently in an article postulating the perfect entertainment cassette, "A cassette as ordinarily viewed makes sound and casts light. That is its purpose, of course, but must sound and light obtrude on others who are not involved or interested? The ideal cassette would be visible and audible only to the person using it. . . . We could imagine a cassette that is always in perfect adjustment; that starts automatically when you look at it; that stops automatically when you cease to look at it; that can play forward or backward, quickly or slowly, by skips or with repetitions, entirely at your pleasure. . . . Surely, that's the ultimate dream device—a cassette that may deal with any of an infinite number of subjects, fictional or non-fictional, that is self-contained, portable, non-energy-consuming, perfectly private and largely under the control of the will. . . . Must this remain only a dream? Can we expect to have such a cassette some day? . . . We not only have it now, we have had it for many centuries. The ideal I have described is the printed word, the book, the object you now hold—light, private, and manipulable at will. . . . Does it seem to you that the book, unlike the cassette I have been describing, does not produce sound and images? It certainly does. . . . You cannot read without hearing the words in your mind and seeing the images to which they give rise. In fact, they are *your* sounds and images, not those invented for you by others, and are therefore better. . . . The printed word presents minimum information, however. Everything but that minimum must be provided by the reader—the intonation of words, the expressions on faces, the actions, the scenery, the background, must all be drawn out of that long line of black-on-white symbols."

Quite clearly, if one but looks around to assess the irrefutable evidence of reality, books strengthen the dreaming facility, and television numbs it. Atrophy soon follows.

Shelley Torgeson, who is the director of the spoken word records I've cut for Alternate World Recordings, is also a mass media teacher at Harrison High School in Westchester. She tells me some things that buttress my position:

1) A fifteen-year-old student summarily rejected the reading of books because it "wasn't real." Because it was your imagination, and your imagination isn't real. So Shelley asked her what was "real" and the student responded instantly, "Television." Because you could see it. Then, by pressing the conversation, Shelley discovered that though the student was in the tenth grade, when she read

she didn't understand the words and was *making up* words and their meanings all through the text—far beyond the usual practice, in which we all indulge, of gleaning an *approximate* meaning of an unfamiliar word from its context. With television, she had no such problems. They didn't use words. It was real. Thus—and quite logically in a kind of Alice-down-the-rabbit-hole manner—the books *weren't* real, because she was making them up as she went along, not actually reading them. If you know what I mean.

2) An important school function was woefully underattended one night, and the next day Shelley (suspecting the reason) confirmed that the absence of so many students was due to their being at home watching part two of the TV movie based on the Manson murder spree, *Helter Skelter*. Well, that *was* a bit of a special event in itself, and a terrifying program; but the interesting aspect of their watching the show emerged when a student responded to Shelley's comparison of watching something that "wasn't real" with a living event that "was real." The student contended it *was* real, he had seen it. No, Shelley insisted, it wasn't real, it was just a show. Hell no, the kid kept saying, it *was* real: he had *seen* it. Reasoning slowly and steadily, it took Shelley fifteen or twenty minutes to convince him (if she actually managed) that he had not seen a real thing, because he had not been in Los Angeles in August of 1969 when the murders had happened. Though he was seventeen years old, the student was incapable of perceiving, *unaided,* the difference between a dramatization and real life.

3) In each classroom of another school at which Shelley taught, there was a TV set, mostly unused save for an occasional administrative announcement; the sets had been originally installed in conjunction with a Ford Foundation grant to be used for visual training. Now they're blank and silent. When Shelley had trouble controlling

the class, getting them quiet, she would turn on the set and they would settle down. The screen contained nothing, just snow; but they grew as fascinated as cobras at a mongoose rally, and fell silent, watching nothing. Shelley says she could keep them that way for extended periods.

Interestingly, as a footnote, when Shelley mentioned this device at lunch, a chemistry professor said he used something similar. When his students were unruly he would place a beaker of water on a Bunsen burner. When the water began to boil, the students grew silent and mesmerized, watching the water bubbling.

And as a subfootnote, I'm reminded of a news story I read. A burglar broke into a suburban home in Detroit or some similar city (it's been a while since I read the item and unimportant details have blurred in my mind) and proceeded to terrorize and rob the housewife alone there with her seven-year-old son. As the attacker stripped the clothes off the woman at knife point, the child wandered into the room. The burglar told the child to go into the bedroom and watch television till he was told to come out. The child watched the tube for six straight hours, never once returning to the room where his mother had been raped repeatedly, tied and bound to a chair with tape over her mouth, and beaten mercilessly. The burglar had had free access to the entire home, had stripped it of all valuables, and had left unimpeded. The tape, incidentally, had been added when the burglar/rapist was done enjoying himself. All through the assault the woman had been calling for help. But the child had been watching the set and didn't come out to see what was happening. For six hours.

Roy Torgeson, Shelley's husband and producer of my records, reminded us of a classroom experiment reported by the novelist Jerzy Kosinski, in which a teacher was set to speaking at one side of the front of a classroom, and a television monitor was set up on the other side of the room, showing the teacher speaking. The students had unobstructed vision of both. They watched the monitor. They watched what was real.

Tom Snyder, of the NBC *Tomorrow* show, was telling me that he receives letters from people apologizing for their having gone away on vacation or visiting with their grandchildren, or otherwise not having been at home so he could do his show—but now that they're back, and the set is on, he can start doing his show again. Their delusion is a strange reversal of the ones I've noted previously. For them, Snyder (and by extension other newscasters and actors) aren't there, aren't happening, unless *they* are watching. They think the actors can see into *their* living rooms, and they dress as if for company, they always make sure the room is clean, and in one case there is a report of an elderly woman who dresses for luncheon with "her friends" and sets up the table and prepares luncheon and then, at one o'clock, turns on the set for a soap opera. Those are her friends: she thinks they can see into her house, and she is one with them in their problems.

To those of us who conceive of ourselves as rational and grounded in reality (yes, friends, even though I write fantasy, I live in the real world, my feet sunk to the ankles in pragmatism), all of this may seem like isolated, delusionary behavior. I assure you it isn't. A study group that rates high school populations recently advised one large school district that the "good behavior" of the kids in its classes was very likely something more than just normal quiet and good manners. They were *too* quiet, *too* tranquilized, and the study group called it "dangerous." I submit that the endless watching of TV by kids produces this blank, dead, unimaginative manner.

It is widespread, and cannot possibly be countered by the minimal level of reading that currently exists in this country. Young people have been systematically bastardized in their ability to seek out quality material—books, films, food, lifestyles, life-goals, enriching relationships.

Books cannot combat the spiderwebbing effect of television because kids simply cannot read. It is on a par with their inability to hear music that isn't rock. Turn the car radio dial from one end to another when you're riding with young people (up to the age of fifty) and you will perceive that they whip past classical music as if it were "white noise," simply static to their ears. The same goes for books. The printed word has no value to them and carries no possibility of knowledge or message that relates to *their* real world.

If one chooses to say, as one idiot I faced on the *90 Minutes Live* talk show over the Canadian Broadcasting Corporation said, that people don't need to read, that people don't like books, that they want to be "entertained" (as if reading were something hideous, something other than *also* entertainment), then we come to an impasse. But if, like me, you believe that books preserve the past, illuminate the present, and point the way to the future . . . then you can understand why I seem to be upset at the ramifications of this epiphany I've had.

Do not expect—as I once did because I saw Senator Joseph McCarthy of Wisconsin unmasked on television—that TV will reveal the culprits. Nixon lied without even the faintest sign of embarrassment or disingenuousness on TV, time after time, for years. He told lies, flat out and outrageously; monstrous lies that bore no relation to the truth. But well over half the population of this country, tuning him in, believed him. Not just that they *wanted* to believe him for political or personal reasons, or because it was easier than having waves made . . . they believed him because he stared right at them and spoke softly and they could *tell* he was telling the truth. TV did not unmask him. Television played no part in the revelations of Watergate. In point of fact, television prevented the unmasking, because Nixon used TV to keep public opinion tremblingly on his side. It was only when the real world, the irrefutable facts, were slammed home again and again, that the hold was loosened on public sentiment.

Nor did television show what a bumbler Gerald Ford was. He was as chummy and friendly and familiar as Andy Griffith or Captain Kangaroo when he came before us on the tube. Television does not show us the duplicitous smirk, the dull mentality, the self-serving truth behind the noncommittal statement of administration policy. It does not deal in reality, it does not proffer honesty, it only serves up nonjudgmental images and allows thugs like Nixon to make themselves as acceptable as Reverend Ike.

And on the Johnny Carson show they have a seven-minute "author's spot," gouged out of ninety minutes festooned with Charo's quivering buttocks, Zsa Zsa Gabor's feelings about fiscal responsibility, John Davidson on recombinant DNA, and Don Rickles insulting Carson's tie. Then, in the last ten minutes they invite on Carl Sagan or Buckminster Fuller or John Lilley to explain the Ethical Structure of the Universe. And they contend this is a rebirth of the art of conversation. Authors of books are seldom invited on the show unless they have a new diet, a new sex theory, or a nonfiction gimmick that will make an interesting demonstration in which Johnny can take part—like wrestling a puma, spinning a hula hoop, or baking lasagna with solar heat.

All this programs the death of reading.

And reading is the drinking of strange wine.

Like water on a hot griddle, I have bounced around, but the unification of the thesis is at hand.

Drinking strange wine pours strength into the imagination.

The dinosaurs had no strange wine.

They had no imagination. They lived 130,000,000 years and vanished. Why? Because they had no imagination. Unlike human beings who have it and use it and build their future rather than merely passing through their lives as if they were spectators. Spectators watching television, one might say.

The saurians had no strange wine, no imagination, and they became extinct. And you don't look so terrific yourself.

This is a collection of fantasies, strange wine. Fifteen draughts your mind can quaff. They lie here, silent, waiting for you to activate them with your imagination.

In writing them, I fulfilled myself. That is why I write. If this book were never to be opened and read they would, nonetheless, have served their purposes for me. I wrote them. But now they belong to you. They were mine only as long as they were unformed and incomplete. That is the nature of the tragedy: the work is mine only when it is being done. Thereafter it must be remanded to the custody of the readers, and the writer can only hope for intelligence, patience, and tender mercies.

I urge those of you who find pleasure or substance in these random dreams to ignore the analyses of academicians and critics. Ignore what they tell you these stories are "about." Surely, *you* will decide what they're about. What they mean and what they meant when I wrote them are quite different. When I wrote them they had personal significance for me. What they will do for you depends on how you feel at the moment you read them, whether or not you feel estranged or loved, what kind of a day you have had, where your emptiness lies on that particular day.

> ". . . People say, 'What does it mean?' *That's* what it means. . . . It would be a bad thing if I could explain the tale better than what I have already said in the tale."
>
> Isak Dinesen

Each story is preceded by a brief note on how I came to write the tale, and is accompanied by a random aphorism, not necessarily illustrative of the story, but merely an epigram I've chanced across that speaks to the general tone and purpose of my work. The introduction to this chrestomathy, the troubled *prolegomena* you have just read, is all the explanation I can give at this time, of who I am and what all this means. At this time.

To end, then, and send you on to the work, just these final words from that mysterious and wonderful woman who wrote under the name Isak Dinesen:

> "Where the storyteller is loyal, eternally and unswervingly loyal to the story, there in the end, silence will speak. Where the story has been betrayed, silence is but emptiness. But we, the faithful, when we have spoken our last word, will hear the voice of silence."

Introduction to Croatoan

On page 33 of *A Reader's Guide to Literary Terms,* "confessional literature" is defined as "a type of autobiography involving the revelation by an author of events or feelings which normally are discreetly concealed." Rousseau's *Confessions* is referred to.

In considerably less polite language—one London newspaper review referred to it as "gut-spilling"—much of my work has been so labeled. It seems to disturb critics that I cannot keep a secret. Like impressionable readers who write me letters that attempt low-level psychoanalysis of the author by their wonky interpretations of what the author has written, critics too closely identify the writer with what he has written.

Well, there certainly is a degree of truth in the charge. I have no secrets and, as is the case with Capote, nothing said to me or seen by me is safe from revelation. It all goes into the stew-pot, to be used in a story if the need arises. Like Isak Dinesen, I owe allegiance to nothing and no one but the story. But further, by having no secrets, I put myself beyond the shadow of blackmail . . . of any kind. By publishers, by friends, by corporations, by governments, even by myself and the cowardly fears to which we are all heir. I cannot be coerced into keeping anything back. I will say it all.

Take for instance, "Croatoan." It is a story about being responsible. Its magazine publication brought howls of outrage from male sexists, feminists, right-to-life advocates, pro-abortion supporters, and even a snotty note from someone in the New York City department of drains and sewers. Apparently they all read it as they chose, not as I intended. Poor things.

All you need to know is that I wrote this story after an affair with a woman who had led me to believe she was on The Pill, who became pregnant, and who subsequently had an abortion. It was far from her first abortion, but that's very much beside the point. The point, which obsessed me, was that if the people whose lives were touched by mine failed to take responsibility for their own lives, then I had to do it for them. I am not anti-abortion, but I *am* anti-waste, anti-pain, anti-self-brutalization. I vowed it would never happen again, no matter how careless they or I became.

Two weeks after writing "Croatoan" I had my vasectomy.

●

"The only abnormality is the incapacity to love."

Anaïs Nin

Croatoan

Beneath the city, there is yet another city: wet and dark and strange; a city of sewers and moist scuttling creatures and running rivers so desperate to be free not even Styx fits them. And in that lost city beneath the city, I found the child.

Oh my God, if I knew where to start. With the child? No, before that. With the alligators? No, earlier. With Carol? Probably. It always started with a Carol. Or an Andrea. A Stephanie. Always someone. There is nothing cowardly about suicide; it takes determination.

"Stop it! Godammit, just *stop* it . . . I said stop . . ." And I had to hit her. It wasn't that hard a crack, but she had been weaving, moving, stumbling: she went over the coffee table, all the fifty-dollar gift books coming down on top of her. Wedged between the sofa and the overturned table. I kicked the table out of the way and bent to help her up, but she grabbed me by the waist and pulled me down; crying, begging me to *do* something. I held her and put my face in her hair and tried to say something right, but what could I say?

Denise and Joanna had left, taking the d&c tools with them. She had been quiet, almost as though stunned by the hammer, after they had scraped her. Quiet, stunned, dry-eyed but hollow-eyed; watching me with the plastic Baggie. The sound of the toilet flushing had brought her running from the kitchen, where she had lain on a mattress pad. I heard her coming, screaming, and caught her just as she started through the hall to the bathroom. And hit her, without wanting to, just trying to stop her as the water sucked the Baggie down and away.

"D-*do* somethi-ing," she gasped, fighting for air.

I kept saying Carol, Carol, over and over, holding her, rocking back and forth, staring over her head, across the living room to the kitchen, where the edge of the teak dining table showed through the doorway, the amber-stained mattress pad hanging half over the edge, pulled loose when Carol had come for the Baggie.

After a few minutes, she spiraled down into dry, sandpapered sighs. I lifted her onto the sofa, and she looked up at me.

"Go after him, Gabe. Please. Please, go after him."

"Come on, Carol, stop it. I feel lousy about it . . ."

"Go after him, you sonofabitch!" she screamed. Veins stood out on her temples.

"I *can't* go after him, dammit, he's in the plumbing; he's in the fucking river by now! Stop it, get off my case, let me alone!" I was screaming back at her.

She found a place where untapped tears waited, and I sat there, across from the sofa, for almost half an hour, just the one lamp casting a dull glow across the living room, my hands clasped down between my knees, wishing she was dead, wishing I was dead, wishing everyone was dead . . . except the kid. But. He was the only one who *was* dead. Flushed. Bagged and flushed. Dead.

When she looked up at me again, a shadow cutting off the lower part of her face so the words emerged from darkness, keynoted only by the eyes, she said, "Go find him." I had never heard anyone sound that way, ever. Not ever. It frightened me. Riptides beneath the surface of her words created trembling images of shadow women drinking Drano, lying with their heads inside gas ovens, floating face up in thick, red bath water, their hair rippling out like jellyfish.

I knew she would do it. I couldn't support that knowledge. "I'll try," I said.

She watched me from the sofa as I left the apartment, and standing against the wall in the elevator, I felt her eyes on me. When I reached the street, still and cold in the predawn, I thought I would walk down to the River Drive and mark time till I could return and console her with the lie that I had tried but failed.

But she was standing in the window, staring down at me.

The manhole cover was almost directly across from me, there in the middle of the silent street.

I looked from the manhole cover to the window, and back again, and again, and again. She waited. Watching. I went to the iron cover and got down on one knee and tried to pry it up. Impossible. I bloodied my fingertips trying, and finally stood, thinking I had satisfied her. I took one step toward the building and realized she was no longer in the window. She stood silently at the curb, holding the long metal rod that wedged against the apartment door when the police lock was engaged.

I went to her and looked into her face. She knew what I was asking: I was asking, *Isn't this enough? Haven't I done enough?*

She held out the rod. No, I hadn't done enough.

I took the heavy metal rod and levered up the manhole cover. It moved with difficulty, and I strained to pry it off the hole. When it fell, it made a clanging in the street that rose up among the apartment buildings with an alarming suddenness. I had to push it aside with both hands; and when I looked up from that perfect circle of darkness that lay waiting, and turned to the spot where she had given me the tool, she was gone.

I looked up; she was back in the window.

The smell of the unwashed city drifted up from the manhole, chill and condemned. The tiny hairs in my nose tried to baffle it; I turned my head away.

I never wanted to be an attorney. I wanted to work on a cattle ranch. But there was family money, and the need to prove myself to shadows who had been dead and buried with their owners long since. People seldom do what they want to do; they usually do what they are *compelled* to do. Stop me before I kill again. There was no rational reason for my descending into that charnel house stink, that moist darkness. No rational reason, but Denise and Joanna from the Abortion Center had been friends of mine for eleven years. We had been in bed together many times; long past the time I had enjoyed being in bed together with them, or they had enjoyed being in bed together with me. They knew it. I knew it. They knew I knew, and they continued to set that as one of the payments for their attendance at my Carols, my Andreas, my Stephanies. It was their way of getting even. They liked me, despite themselves, but they had to get even. Get even for their various attendances over eleven years, the first of which had been one for the other, I don't remember which. Get even for many flushings of the toilet. There was no rational reason for going down into the sewers. None.

But there were eyes on me from an apartment window.

I crouched, dropped my legs over the lip of the open manhole, sat on the street for a moment, then slipped over the edge and began to climb down.

Slipping into an open grave. The smell of the earth is there, where there is no earth. The water is evil; vital fluid that has been endlessly violated. Everything is covered with a green scum that glows faintly in the darkness. An open grave waiting patiently for the corpse of the city to fall.

I stood on the ledge above the rushing tide, sensing the sodden weight of lost and discarded life that rode the waters toward even darker depths. *My God,* I thought, *I must be out of my mind just to* be *here.* It had finally overtaken me; the years of casual liaisons, careless lies, the guilt I suppose I'd *always* known would mount up till it could no longer be denied. And I was down here, where I belonged.

People do what they are compelled to do.

I started walking toward the arching passageway that led down and away from the steel ladder and the street opening above. Why not walk: aimless, can you perceive what I'm saying?

Once, years ago, I had an affair with my junior partner's wife. Jerry never knew about it. They're divorced now. I don't think he ever found out; she would have had to've been even crazier than I thought to tell him. Denise and Joanna had visited that time, too. I'm nothing if not potent. We flew to Kentucky together one weekend. I was preparing a brief, she met me at the terminal, we flew as husband and wife, family rate. When my work was done in Louisville, we drove out into the countryside. I minored in geology at college, before I went into law. Kentucky is rife with caves. We pulled in at a picnic grounds where some locals had advised us we could do a little spelunking, and with the minimal gear we had picked up at a sporting goods shop, we went into a fine network of chambers, descending beneath the hills and the picnic grounds. I loved the darkness, the even temperature, the smooth-surfaced rivers, the blind fish and water insects that scurried across the wet mirror of the still pools. She had come because she was not permitted to have intercourse at the base of Father Duffy's statue on Times Square, in the main window of Bloomingdale's, or on Channel 2 directly preceding *The Late News*. Caves were the next best thing.

For my part, the thrill of winding down deeper and deeper into the earth—even though graffiti and Dr. Pepper cans all along the way reminded me this was hardly unexplored territory—offset even her (sophomoric) appeals to "take her violently," there on the shell-strewn beach of a subterranean river.

I *liked* the feel of the entire Earth over me. I was not claustrophobic, I was—in some perverse way—wonderfully free. Even soaring! Under the ground, I was soaring!

The walk deeper into the sewer system did not unsettle or distress me. I rather enjoyed being alone. The smell was terrible, but terrible in a way I had not expected.

If I had expected vomit and garbage, this was certainly not what I smelled. Instead, there was a bittersweet scent of rot—reminiscent of Florida mangrove swamps. There was the smell of cinnamon, and wallpaper paste, and charred rubber; the warm odors of rodent blood and bog gas; melted cardboard, wool, coffee grounds still aromatic, rust.

The downward channel leveled out. The ledge became a wide, flat plain as the water went down through drainage conduits, leaving only a bubbling, frothy residue to sweep away into the darkness. It barely covered the heels of my shoes. Florsheims, but they could take it. I kept moving. Then I saw the light ahead of me.

It was dim, flickering, vanished for a moment as something obscured it from my view, moving in front of it, back again, dim and orange. I moved toward the light.

It was a commune of bindlestiffs, derelicts gathered together beneath the streets for safety and the skeleton of camaraderie. Five very old men in heavy overcoats and three even older men in castoff army jackets . . . but the older men were younger, they only *looked* older: a condition of the skids. They sat around a waste barrel oil drum filled with fire. Dim, soft, withered fire that leaped and curled and threw off sparks all in slow motion. Dream-walking fire; somnambulist fire; mesmerized fire. I saw an atrophied arm of flame like a creeper of kangaroo ivy emerge over the lip of the barrel, struggling toward the shadowed arch of the tunnel ceiling; it stretched itself thin, released a single, teardrop-shaped spark, and then fell back into the barrel without a scream.

The hunkering men watched me come toward them. One of them said something, directly into the ear of the man beside him; he moved his lips very little and never took his eyes off me. As I neared, the men stirred expectantly. One of them reached into a deep pocket of his overcoat for something bulky. I stopped and looked at them.

They looked at the heavy iron rod Carol had given me.

They wanted what I had, if they could get it.

I wasn't afraid. I was under the Earth and I was part iron rod. They could not get what I had. They knew it. That's why there are always fewer killings than there might be. People *always* know.

I crossed to the other side of the channel, close to the wall. Watching them carefully. One of them, perhaps strong himself, perhaps merely stupider, stood up and, thrusting his hands deeper into his overcoat pockets, paralleled my passage down the channel away from them.

The channel continued to descend slightly, and we walked away from the oil drum and the light from the fire and the tired community of subterranean castoffs. I wondered idly when he would make his move, but I wasn't worried. He watched me, trying to see me more clearly, it seemed, as we descended deeper into the darkness. And as the light receded he moved up closer, but didn't cross the channel. I turned the bend first.

Waiting, I heard the sounds of rats in their nests.

He didn't come around the bend.

I found myself beside a service niche in the tunnel wall, and stepped back into it. He came around the bend, on my side of the channel. I could have stepped out as he passed my hiding place, could have clubbed him to death with the iron rod before he realized that the stalker had become the stalked.

I did nothing, stayed far back motionless in the niche and let him pass. Standing there, my back to the slimy wall, listening to the darkness around me, utter, final, even palpable. But for the tiny twittering sounds of rats I could have been two miles down in the central chamber of some lost cavern maze.

There's no logic to why it happened. At first, Carol had been just another casual liaison, another bright mind to touch, another witty personality to enjoy, another fine and workable body to work so fine with mine. I grow bored quickly. It's not a sense of humor I seek—lord knows every slithering, hopping, crawling member of the animal kingdom has a sense of humor—for Christ sake even dogs and *cats* have a sense of humor—it's wit! Wit is the answer. Let me touch a woman with wit and I'm gone, sold on the spot. I said to her, the first time I met her, at a support luncheon for the Liberal candidate for D.A., "Do you fool around?"

"I don't fool," she said instantly, no time-lapse, no need for rehearsal, fresh out of her mind, "fools bore me. Are you a fool?"

I was delighted and floored at the same time. I went fumfuh-fumfuh, and she didn't give me a moment. "A simple yes or no will suffice. Answer this one: how many sides are there to a round building?"

I started to laugh. She watched me with amusement, and for the first time in my life I actually saw someone's eyes twinkle with mischief. "I don't know," I said, "how many sides *are* there to a round building?"

"Two," she answered, "*in*side and *out*side. I guess you're a fool. No, you may not take me to bed." And she walked away.

I was undone. She couldn't have run it better if she had come back two minutes in a time machine, knowing what I'd say, and programmed me into it. And so I chased her. Up hill and down dale, all around that damned dreary luncheon, till I finally herded her into a corner—which was precisely what she'd been going for.

"As Bogart said to Mary Astor, 'You're good, shweetheart, very very good.' " I said it fast, for fear she'd start running me around again. She settled against the wall, a martini in her hand; and she looked up at me with that twinkling.

At first it was just casual. But she had depth, she had wiliness, she had such an air of self-possession that it was inevitable I would start phasing-out the other women, would start according her the attention she needed and wanted and without demanding . . . demanded.

I came to care.

Why didn't I take precautions? Again, there's no logic to it. I thought she was; and for a while, she was. Then she stopped. She told me she had stopped, something internal, the gynecologist had suggested she go off the pill for a while. She suggested vasectomy to me. I chose to ignore the suggestion. But chose not to stop sleeping with her.

When I called Denise and Joanna, and told them Carol was pregnant, they sighed and I could see them shaking their heads sadly. They said they considered me a public menace, but told me to tell her to come down to the Abortion Center and they would put the suction pump to work. I told them, hesitantly, that it had gone too long, suction wouldn't work. Joanna simply snarled, "You thoughtless cocksucker!" and hung up the extension. Denise read me the riot act for twenty minutes. She didn't suggest a vasectomy; she suggested, in graphic detail, how I might have my organ removed by a taxidermist using a cheese grater. Without benefit of anesthesia.

But they came, with their dilation and curettage implements, and they laid her out on the teak table with a mattress under her, and then they had gone—Joanna pausing a moment at the door to advise me this was the last time, the last time, the very last time she could stomach it, that it was the last time and did I have that fixed firmly, solidly, imbedded in the forefront of my brain? The last time.

And now I was here in the sewers.

I tried to remember what Carol looked like, but it wasn't an image I could fix in my mind half as solidly as I had fixed the thought that this. Was. The. Last. Time.

I stepped out of the service niche.

The young-old bindlestiff who had followed me was standing there, silently waiting. At first I couldn't even see him—there was only the vaguest lighter shade of darkness to my left, coming from around the bend and that oil drum full of fire—but I knew he was there. Even as *he* had known I was there, all the time. He didn't speak, and I didn't speak, and after a while I was able to discern his shape. Hands still deep in his pockets.

"Something?" I said, more than a little belligerently.

He didn't answer.

"Get out of my way."

He stared at me, sorrowfully, I thought, but that had to be nonsense. I thought.

"Don't make me have to hurt you," I said.

He stepped aside, still watching me.

I started to move past him, down the channel.

He didn't follow, but I was walking backward to keep him in sight, and he didn't take his eyes off mine.

I stopped. "What do you want?" I asked. "Do you need some money?"

He came toward me. Inexplicably, I wasn't afraid he would try something. He wanted to see me more clearly, closer. I thought.

"You couldn't give me nothing I need." His voice was rusted, pitted, scarred, unused, unwieldy.

"Then why are you following me?"

"Why've you come down here?"

I didn't know what to say.

"You make it bad down here, mister. Why don't you g'wan and go back upside, leave us alone?"

"I have a right to be here." Why had I said *that?*

"You got no right to come down here; stay back upside where you belong. All of us know you make it bad, mister."

He didn't want to hurt me, he just didn't want me here. Not even right for these outcasts, the lowest level to which men could sink; even here I was beneath contempt. His hands were deep in his pockets. "Take your hands out of your pockets, slowly, I want to make sure you aren't going to hit me with something when I turn around. Because I'm going on down there, not back. Come on now, do it. Slowly. Carefully."

He took his hands out of his pockets slowly, and held them up. He had no hands. Chewed stumps, glowing faintly green like the walls where I had descended from the manhole.

I turned and went away from him.

It grew warmer, and the phosphorescent green slime on the walls gave some light. I had descended as the channel had fallen away deeper under the city. This was a land not even the noble streetworkers knew, a land blasted by silence and emptiness. Stone above and below and around, it carried the river without a name into the depths, and if I could not return, I would stay here like the skids. Yet I continued walking. Sometimes I cried, but I don't know why, or for what, or for whom. Certainly not for myself.

Was there ever a man who had everything more than I had had everything? Bright words, and quick movements, soft cloth next to my skin, and places to place my love, if I had only recognized that it *was* love.

I heard a nest of rats squealing as something attacked them, and I was drawn to a side tunnel where the shining green effluvium made everything bright and dark as the view inside the machines they used to have in shoe stores. I hadn't thought of that in years. Until they found out that the X-rays could damage the feet of children, shoe stores used bulky machines one stepped up onto, and into which one inserted newly shod feet. And when the button was pushed a green X-ray light came on, showing the bones that lay beneath the flesh. Green and black. The light was green, and the bones were dusty black. I hadn't thought of that in years, but the side tunnel was illuminated in just that way.

An alligator was ripping the throats of baby rats.

It had invaded the nest and was feeding mercilessly, tossing the bodies of the ripped and shredded rodents aside as it went for the defenseless smaller ones. I stood watching, sickened but fascinated. Then, when the shrieks of anguish were extinguished at last, the great saurian, direct lineal descendant of Rex, snapped them up one by one and, thrashing its tail, turned to stare at me.

He had no hands. Chewed stumps, glowing faintly green like the walls.

I moved back against the wall of the side tunnel as the alligator belly-crawled past me, dragging its leash. The thick, armored tail brushed my ankle and I stiffened.

Its eyes glowed red as those of an Inquisition torturer.

I watched its scaled and taloned feet leave deep prints in the muck underfoot, and I followed the beast, its trail clearly marked by the impression of the leash in the mud.

Frances had a five-year-old daughter. She took the little girl for a vacation to Miami Beach one year. I flew down for a few days. We went to a Seminole village, where the old women did their sewing on Singer machines. I thought that was sad. A lost heritage, perhaps; I don't know. The daughter, whose name I can't recall, wanted a baby alligator. Cute. We brought it back on the plane in a cardboard box with air holes. Less than a month later it had grown large enough to snap. Its teeth weren't that long, but it snapped. It was saying: this is what I'll be: direct lineal descendant of Rex. Frances flushed it down the toilet one night after we'd made love. The little girl was asleep in the next room. The next morning, Frances told her the alligator had run off.

The sewers of the city are infested with full-grown alligators. No amount of precaution and no forays by hunting teams with rifles or crossbows or flame throwers have been able to clear the tunnels. The sewers are still infested; workers go carefully. So did I.

The alligator moved steadily, graceful in its slithering passage down one tunnel and into another side passage and down always down, steadily into the depths. I followed the trail of the leash.

We came to a pool and it slid into the water like oil, its dead-log snout above the fetid foulness, its Torquemada eyes looking toward its destination.

I thrust the iron rod down my pant leg, pulled my belt tight enough to hold it, and waded into the water. It came up to my neck and I lay out and began dog-paddling, using the one leg that would bend. The light was very green and sharp now.

The saurian came out on the muck beach at the other side and crawled forward toward an opening in the tunnel wall. I crawled out, pulled the iron rod loose, and followed. The opening gave into darkness, but as I passed through, I trailed my hand across the wall and felt a door. I stopped, surprised, and felt in the darkness. An iron door, with an arched closure at the top and a latch. Studs, heavy and round and smelling faintly of rust, dotted the door.

I walked through . . . and stopped.

There had been something else on the door. I stepped back and ran my fingers over the open door again. I found the indentations at once, and ran my fingertips across them, trying to discern in the utter darkness what they were. Something about them . . . I traced them carefully.

They were letters. C. My fingers followed the curves. R. Cut into the iron somehow. O. What was a door doing down here? A. The cuts seemed very old, weathered, scummy. T. They were large and very regular. O. They made no sense, no word formed that I knew. A. And I came to the end of the sequence. N.

CROATOAN. It made no sense. I stayed there a moment, trying to decide if it was a word the sanitation engineers might have used for some designation of a storage area perhaps. Croatoan. No sense. Not Croatian, it was Croatoan. Something nibbled at the back of my memory: I *had* heard the word before, knew it from somewhere, long ago, a vapor of sound traveling back on the wind of the past. It escaped me, I had no idea what it meant.

I went through the doorway again.

Now I could not even see the trail of the leash the alligator had dragged. I kept moving, the iron rod in my hand.

I heard them coming toward me from both sides, and it was clearly alligators, many of them. From side passages. I stopped and reached out to find the wall of the channel. I couldn't find it. I turned around, hoping to get back to the door, but when I hurried back the way I thought I had come, I didn't reach the door. I just kept going. Either I had gone down a fork and not realized the channel had separated, or I had lost my sense of direction. And the slithering sounds kept coming.

Now, for the first time, I felt terror! The safe, warm, enfolding darkness of the underworld had, in an instant, merely by the addition of sounds around me, become a suffocating winding-sheet. It was as if I'd abruptly awakened in a coffin, buried six feet beneath the tightly stomped loam; that clogging terror Poe had always described so well because he had feared it himself . . . the premature burial. Caves no longer seemed comfortable.

I began to run!

I lost the rod somewhere, the iron bar that had been my weapon, my security.

I fell and slid face first in the muck.

I scrabbled to my knees and kept going. No walls, no light, no slightest aperture or outcropping, nothing to give me a sense of being in the world, running through a limbo without beginning, without end.

Finally, exhausted, I slipped and fell and lay for a moment. I heard slithering all around me and managed to pull myself to a sitting position. My back grazed a wall, and I fell up against it with a moan of gratitude. Something, at least; a wall against which to die.

I don't know how long I lay there, waiting for the teeth.

Then I felt something touching my hand. I recoiled with

a shriek! It had been cold and dry and soft. Did I recall that snakes and other amphibians were cool and dry? Did I remember that? I was trembling.

Then I saw light. Flickering, bobbing, going up and down just slightly, coming toward me.

And as the light grew closer and brighter, I saw there was something right beside me; the something that had touched me; it had been there for a time, watching me.

It was a child.

Naked, deathly white, with eyes great and luminous, but covered with a transparent film as milky as a membrane, small, very young, hairless, its arms shorter than they should have been, purple and crimson veins crossing its bald skull like traceries of blood on a parchment, fine even features, nostrils dilating as it breathed shallowly, ears slightly tipped as though reminiscent of an elf, barefooted but with pads on the soles, this child stared at me, looked up at me, its little tongue visible as it opened its mouth filled with tiny teeth, trying to form sounds, saying nothing, watching me, a wonder in its world, watching me with the saucer eyes of a lemur, the light behind the membrane flickering and pulsing. This child.

And the light came nearer, and the light was many lights. Torches, held aloft by the children who rode the alligators.

Beneath the city, there is yet another city: wet and dark and strange.

At the entrance to their land someone—not the children, they couldn't have done it—long ago built a road sign. It is a rotted log on which has been placed, carved from fine cherrywood, a book and a hand. The book is open, and the hand rests on the book, one finger touching the single word carved in the open pages. The word is CROATOAN.

On August 13, 1590, Governor John White of the Virginia colony managed to get back to the stranded settlers of the Roanoke, North Carolina, colony. They had been waiting three years for supplies, but politics, foul weather and the Spanish Armada had made it impossible. As they went ashore, they saw a pillar of smoke. When they reached the site of the colony, though they found the stronghold walls still standing against possible Indian attacks, no sign of life greeted them. The Roanoke colony had vanished. Every man, woman, and child, gone. Only the word CROATOAN had been left. *"One of the chiefe trees or postes at the right side of the entrance had the barke taken off, and 5. foote from the ground in fayre Capitall letters was grauen CROATOAN without any crosse or signe of distresse."*

There was a Croatan island, but they were not there. There was a tribe of Hatteras Indians who were called Croatans, but they knew nothing of the whereabouts of the lost colony. All that remains of legend is the story of the child Virginia Dare, and the mystery of what happened to the lost settlers of Roanoke.

Down here in this land beneath the city live the children. They live easily and in strange ways. I am only now coming to know the incredible manner of their existence. How they eat, what they eat, how they manage to survive, and have managed for hundreds of years, these are all things I learn day by day, with wonder surmounting wonder.

I am the only adult here.

They have been waiting for me.

They call me father.

Introduction to Working with the Little People

One of the half dozen greatest, most original fantasists this country has ever produced said to me once, "It doesn't matter if it's good or bad, if you finish it that day or the next: every day write a story." I try to do that.

I genuinely love writing. I consider myself one of the most blessed persons I know: I'm doing just what I want to do, just what all my good and bad karma got stored up for me to do. I write. Mornings, nights, in-betweens. I'd almost rather write than fuck. Sometimes it's a difficult choice.

Which means that I frequently write in peculiar places. I'll be noting some of them as we go on through this book, but for openers, "Working with the Little People" was written in the front window of a bookstore in London: Words & Music, in Charing Cross Road, directly across from Foyle's. I was doing a promotion for the hardcover publication of two of my books. It was an activity that seemed to unnerve a few conservative critics. Writers, they felt, should "Do It" in an Ivory Tower, not out there in the open, indecently, where everyone could see it being Done. "Doing It," in their view, was akin to that *other* "Doing It."

But writing, like most holy chores, most miracles, needs to be done in the open, so everyone can see that imagination is everywhere, that there are no secrets, no cabals, no runes to be cast.

All you need is talent, and the need to need to do it. If you follow me. And so, to *all* great, original fantasists, I say: Do It!

•

"Produce! Produce! Were it but the pitifullest infinitesimal fraction of a Product, produce it, in God's name! 'Tis the utmost thou hast in thee: out with it, then. Up, up! Whatsoever thy hand findeth to do, do it with thy whole might. Work while it is called Today; for the night cometh, wherein no man can work."

Thomas Carlyle (1795–1881)

Working with the Little People

Nineteen years earlier, Noah Raymond had written his last fantasy. Since that time over four hundred brilliant stories had been published under his byline. All four hundred had come from his typewriter. What no one knew was that Noah Raymond had not written them. They had been written by gremlins.

Success had come early to Raymond. He had sold his first story, "An Agile Little Mind," to the leading fantasy pulp magazine of the period when he was seventeen. It was slug-lined as a *First Story,* and the craft and imagination it displayed made him an instant *cause célèbre.* He sold a dozen more stories in the next two years and came to the notice of the fiction editor of a major slick magazine.

The slick paid twenty times what the pulps could afford; the response was from a much wider readership; and as the fiction editor was sleeping with the anthologist who annually cobbled up the most prestigious collection of The Year's Best Short Stories, Noah Raymond found himself, four months short of his nineteenth birthday, with a novelette on that year's table of contents between a pastiche by Katherine Anne Porter and a slice-of-life by Isaac Bashevis Singer.

His first collection was published when he was twenty.

Knopf. The promotion manager became enthralled with the book and sent it around to Saroyan and Capote and by special messenger to John Collier. The prepublication quotes in the *Times Book Review* section were awesome. The word "genius" appeared eight times in a half page.

By the time he was twenty-five, because he was fecund, he had seven books to his credit and librarians did not file him under "science fiction/fantasy" but in the "modern literature" section. At age twenty-six his first novel, *Every Morning at First Light,* was selected as a Book-of-the-Month Club alternate and was nominated as one of the finalists for the National Book Award.

His personal papers were solicited for preservation in the Archive Library at Harvard and he went on a critically and financially impressive European lecture tour. He was twenty-seven.

In the month of August, on a Friday night—the 20th, to be exact—at twenty-three minutes to midnight, to be tedious about it—Noah Raymond ran dry. That simply, that easily, that directly, that horrifyingly . . . he ran dry.

He wrote the last original word of the last original idea he had, and abruptly found himself flensed of even the tiniest scintilla of an idea for a new story. He had an assignment from the BBC to write an original story that could be adapted for an hour-long dramatic special, and he hadn't the faintest inkling of what he could write about.

He thought for the better part of an hour, and the only idea that came to him was about a mad, one-legged seaman hunting a big white fish. He thrust the idea from him forcibly; it was redolent with idiocy.

For the first time in his life, since the first moment he realized he had the gift of storytelling, the magic gift of stringing words together so they plumbed the human heart, he was empty of new thoughts. No more strange little fables about the world as he wished it to be, the world that lived in his mind, a world peopled by characters full and firm and more real than those with whom he had to deal each day. His mind was a vast, empty plain without structure upon it or roll to its topography . . . with nothing in sight but gray vistas that extended to limitless horizons.

All that night he sat before his typewriter, urging his mind to dream, to go away from him in wild journeys. But the dreams were empty husks and his mind came back from the journeys as devoid of thoughts as an earthworm.

Finally, when dawn came up over the valley, he found himself crying. He leaned across the typewriter, put his head on the cool metal, and wept. He knew, with the terrible certainty that brooks no exceptions, that he was dry. He had written his last story. He simply had no more ideas. That was the end of it.

Had the world ended just then, Noah Raymond would have cheered. Then he would have had no anguish, no terror, no concern about what he would do tomorrow. And the tomorrow after that. And all the seamless, hopeless tomorrows that stretched before him like a vast, empty plain.

Writing stories was Noah Raymond's whole life. He had nothing else of consequence that approached by a million miles the joy of telling a story. And now that the river had run dry, leaving only the silt of ideas he had worked endlessly and the tag-end memories of other people's work, great classics half remembered, seminal treatments of hoary clichés, he did not know what he would do with the remainder of his life.

He contemplated going the Mark Twain route, cashing in on what he had already written with endless lecture tours. But he wasn't that good a speaker and, frankly, didn't like crowds of more than two people. He considered going the John Updike route: snagging himself a teaching sinecure at some tony Eastern college where the incipient junior editors of unsuspecting publishing houses were still in the larval stage as worshipful students. But he was sure he'd end up in a mutually destructive relationship with a sexually liberated English Lit major and come to a messy finish. He dandled the prospect of simply going the Salinger route, of retiring to a hidden cottage somewhere in Vermont or perhaps in Dorset, of leaking mysterious clues to a major novel forthcoming some decade soon; but he had heard that both Pynchon and Salinger were mad as a thousand battlefields; and he shivered at the prospect of becoming a hermit. And all that was left was the realization that what he had written was the sum total, that one year soon some snide bastard at *The Atlantic Monthly* would write a piercing, penetrating piece titled, "The Spectacular Rise and Soggy Demise of Noah Raymond, ex-Enfant Terrible." He couldn't face that.

But there was no exit from this prison of sterilized nothingness.

He was twenty-seven, and he was finished.

He stopped crying into the typewriter. He didn't want to rust the works. Not that it mattered.

He crawled off to bed and slept the day. He woke at eight o'clock and thought about eating, forgetting for the moment that he was finished. But when the knowledge surged back to drown his consciousness, he promptly went into the bathroom and divested himself of the previous evening's dinner, what had not been digested while he slept.

Packing the queen mother of all headaches, he trudged into the tiny office off the living room, fearing to look at the neglected typewriter he knew would stare back at him with its hideous snaggle-toothed qwertyuiop grin.

Before he stepped through the door he realized he'd

been hearing the sound of the typewriter since he'd slid out of bed. Had heard, and had dismissed the sound as a product of nightmare and memory.

But the typewriter *was* making its furious *tack-tack-tack-space-tack* sound. And it was not an electric typewriter. It was a manual, an old Olympia office machine. He did not trust electric typewriters. They continued humming maliciously when one paused to marshal one's thoughts. And if one placed one's hands on the keyboard preparatory to writing some measure of burning, immortal prose, and hesitated the slightest bit before tapping the keys, the insolent beast went off like a Thompson submachine gun. He did not like, or trust, electric typewriters, wouldn't have one in the same house, wouldn't write a word on one of the stupid things, wouldn't—

He stopped thinking crazy thoughts. He *couldn't* write, would never write again; and the typewriter was blamming away merrily just on the other side of the room.

He stared into the office, and in the darkness he could see the typewriter's silhouette on the typing shelf he had built with his own hands. Behind it, the window was pale with moonlight and he could see the shape clearly. What he felt he was *not* seeing were the tiny black shapes that were leaping up and down on the keys. But he stood there and continued staring, and thought he was further around the bend than even the horror of the night before had led him to believe he could be. Bits of black were bounding up and down on the keyboard, spinning up into the pale square of glassed moonlight, then dropping back into darkness, bounding up again, doing flips, then falling into darkness once more. *My typewriter has dandruff,* was his first, deranged thought.

And the sound of the old Olympia manual office machine was like that of a Thompson submachine gun.

The little black bounding bits were working away at

the keys of the typewriter in excess of 150 words per minute.

"How do you spell *necromancy,"* said a thin, tiny, high, squeaky, sharp, speedy, brittle, chirping voice, "with two *c*'s or a *c* and a penultimate *s?"*

There was a muffled "oof!" as of someone bashing his head against a hollow-core door, and then—a trifle on the breathless side—a second voice replied, "Two *c*'s, you illiterate!" The second voice was only slightly less thin, tiny, high, squeaky, sharp, speedy, brittle, and chirping. It also had a faintly Cockney accent.

And the blamming on the keyboard continued.

My life has been invaded by archy the cockroach, was Noah Raymond's second, literary, even more deranged thought. In those days, the wonderful writings of the late Don Marquis were still popular; such a thought would have been relevant.

He turned on the light switch beside the door.

Eleven tiny men, each two inches high, were doing a trampoline act on his typewriter.

The former *enfant terrible* sagged against the doorjamb, and he heard the hinges of his jaw crack like artillery fire as his mouth fell open.

"Turn off that light, you great loon!" yelled one of the little men, describing a perfect Immelmann and plunging headfirst onto the # key while a pair of the little men with another pair of little men on their shoulders weighted down the carriage shift key so the one who had dived would get an upper-case # and not a lower-case 3.

"Off, you bugger; turn it off!" shouted a trio of little men in unison as they ricocheted across each other's trajectories to type p-a-r-s-i-m-o-n-i-o-u-s. They were a blur, bounding and dodging and shooting past each other like gnats around a dog's ear.

When he made no move to click off the light—because

he was unable to move to do *any*thing—the tallest of the little men (2¼″) did a two-step on the space bar and landed on the typewriter carriage housing, arms akimbo and fists balled. He stared straight at Noah Raymond and in a thin, tiny, high, etcetera voice howled, "That's it! Everybody stops work!"

The other ten bounced off their targets and vacated the typewriter *en masse.* They stood around on the typing shelf, rubbing their heads, some of them removing their tiny caps to massage sore spots on foreheads and craniums.

"Precisely *how* to you expect us to get ten thousand words written tonight with you disturbing us?" the little man (who was clearly the spokesman) said with annoyance.

I can't face the future, he thought. *The delusions are starting already and it's not even twenty-four hours.*

Another of the little men, somewhat shorter than the others, yelled, " 'Ey, Alf. Cawnt'cher get this silly git outta f'ere? We'll never 'ave done, 'e don't move on!"

Noah did not understand one word the littler little man had said.

The tallest of the little men glared at the tiniest one and snarled, "Shut'cher yawp, Charlie." His accent was the same as Charlie's, dead-on Cockney. But when he looked back at Noah he returned to the precise Mayfair tones he had first used. "Let's get this matter settled, Mr. Raymond. We've got a night's work ahead of us, you've got a story due, and neither of us will manage if we don't get this perishing explanation out of the way."

Noah just stared. He had hot flashes.

"Sit down, Mr. Raymond."

He sat down. On the floor. He didn't want to, he just suddenly did it; sat down . . . on the floor.

"Now," said Alf, "your first question is: what are we? Well. We might ask the same of you. What are you?"

Charlie started hooting. "Cut out th' malarkey, Alf. Send 'im out an' tell 'im t'leave off annoyin' us!"

Alf glared at the little man. "Y'know, Charlie, you're a right king mixer, you are. You better close up your cake 'ole before I come down there an' pop you a good'un in the 'ooter!"

Charlie made a nasty bratting sound like a Bronx cheer, the time-honored raspberry, and sat down on the shelf, dangling his tiny legs and whistling unconcernedly.

Alf turned back to Noah. "You're a human, Mr. Raymond. The inheritors of the Earth. We know all about you; all there is to know. We should, after all; we've been around a lot longer than you. We're gremlins."

Noah Raymond recognized them at once. Living and breathing and arguing personifications of the mythical "little people" who had become a household word during World War II, the sort of/kind of elf-folk deemed responsible for mechanical failures and chance mishaps to Allied aircraft, particularly those of the British. They had been as famous as Kilroy. The Royal Air Force had taken them on as mascots, laughing with them but never at them, and in the end the gremlins were supposed to have turned against the Nazis and to have helped win the war.

"I . . . I once wrote a bunch of stories about gremlins," Noah said, the words choked and as mushy as boiled squash.

"That's why we've been watching you, Mr. Raymond."

"Wuh-wuh-watching muh-muh—"

"Yes, watching *you.*"

Charlie made the bratting sound again. It reminded Noah of unhealthy bowel movements, a kind of aural Toltec Two-Step, vocalizing Montezuma's Revenge.

"We've been on to you for ten years; ever since you wrote 'An Agile Little Mind.' For a human, it wasn't a half-bad attempt at understanding us."

"There isn't much historical data available on guh-guh-gremlins," Noah said, off-the-wall, having trouble even speaking the magic name.

"Very good lineage. Direct lineal descendants of the afrit. The French call us *gamelin,* brats."

"But I thought you were just something the pilots dreamed up during the Battle of Britain to account for things going wrong with their planes."

"Nonsense," said the little man. Charlie hooted. "The first modern mention of us was in 1936, out of the Middle East, where the RAF was stationed in Syria. We used the wind mostly. Did some lovely things to their formations when they were on maneuvers. Good deal of tricky Coriolis force business there."

"You really are real, aren't you?" Noah asked.

Charlie started to say something. Alf turned on him and snapped, "Shut'cher gawb, Charlie!" Then he went back to Mayfair accents as he said to Raymond, "We're a bit pressed tonight, Mr. Raymond. We can discuss reality and mythology another time. In fact, if you'll just sit there quietly for a while I'll knock off after a bit and let the boys carry on without me. I'll take a break and explain as much to you as you can hold tonight."

"Uh, sure . . . sure . . . go ahead. But, uh, what are you writing over there?"

"Why, I thought you understood, Mr. Raymond. We're writing that story for the BBC. We're here from now on to write *all* your stories. Since you can't do it, I shouldn't think you'll mind if we maintain your world-famous reputation for you."

And he put two minuscule fingers in his mouth and gave a blast of a whistle, and before Noah Raymond could say that he was so ashamed of himself he could cry, they were once again bounding up and down on the typewriter.

My *God,* how they worked!

It was simply the Nietzschean theory all over again. Nietzsche suggested that when a god lost all its worshipers, the god itself died. Belief was the sustaining force. When a god's supplicants went over to newer, stronger gods, belief in the weaker deity faded and so did the deity. So it had been with the gremlins. They were ancient, of course, and they were worshiped in their various forms under various names. Pixies, nixies, goblins, elves, sprites, fairies, will-o'-the-wisps, *gamelins* . . . gremlins. But when the times were hard and the technocrats rode high, the belief in magic faded, and so did they. Day by day they vanished, one after another. Whole families were wiped out in a morning just by a group of humans switching to Protestantism.

And so, from time to time, they came back in strength with a new method of drawing believers to them. During World War II they had changed and taken on the very raiments of the science worshipers. They became elves of the mechanical universe: gremlins.

But the war was over, and people no longer believed.

So they had looked around for a promotional gimmick, and they had found seventeen-year-old Noah Raymond. He was quick, and he was imaginative, and he believed. So they waited. A few stories weren't good enough. They wanted a body of work, a world-acclaimed body of work that could sustain them through this difficult period of future shock and automation. Tolkien had done his share, but he was an old man and they knew he couldn't do it alone.

And so, on the night Noah Raymond went dry, they were waiting, a commando force of typewriter assaultists specially trained for throwing themselves into their work in the most literal sense. Tough, unsentimental gremlins with steely eyes and a fierce determination to save their race. Assault Force G-1. Each gremlin a hand-picked veteran of extra-dangerous service. Each gremlin a volunteer. Each gremlin a specialist:

Alf, who had led the assault on the Krupp munitions factory's toilets in 1943.

Charlie, who had shipped aboard the *Titanic* on its maiden voyage, April 10th, 1912, as sabotaging supercargo.

Billy, who had been head gremlin in charge of London underground subway disruption since 1952.

Ted, who worked for the telephone company.

Joe, who worked for Western Union.

Bertie, who worked for the post office.

Chris, who was in charge of making coffee bitter in the brewing throughout the Western Hemisphere.

St. John (pronounced Sin-jin), who supervised a large staff of gremlins assigned to complicating the syntax in the public speeches of minor politicians.

And the others, and their standbys, and their reserve troops, and their replacements, and their backup support . . .

Ready to move in the moment Noah Raymond went dry.

And so they began.

For the next nineteen years they came to Noah Raymond's typewriter every night, and they worked with unceasing energy. Noah would stand watching them for hours sometimes, marveling at the amount of kinetic energy flagrantly expended in the pursuit of survival-as-art.

And the stories spun out of Noah Raymond's typewriter, and he grew more famous, and he grew wealthy, and he grew more complacent as the total of their works with his byline grew from one hundred to two hundred, from two hundred to three hundred, from three hundred to four hundred . . .

Until tonight, when Alf stood shamefacedly on the Olympia's carriage housing, his cap in his tiny hands, and said to Noah Raymond, "That's the long and short of it, Noah. We've run dry."

"Now wait a minute, Alf," Noah said, "that's impossible. You've got the entire race of gremlins to choose from, to find talent to keep the stuff coming. I simply cannot believe an entire *race* has run out of ideas!"

"Uh, well, it's not quite like that, Noah." He was obviously embarrassed, and had something of special knowledge he was reluctant to say.

"Listen, Alf," Noah said, laying his hand palm up on the carriage housing so the tiny man could step onto it. "We've been mates now for almost twenty years, right?"

The little man nodded and stepped into Noah's palm.

Noah lifted him to eye level so they could talk more intimately.

"And in twenty-years-almost I think we've come to understand each other's people pretty fair, wouldn't you say?"

Alf nodded.

"I mean, I even get along pretty well with Charlie these days, when his sciatica isn't bothering him too much."

Alf nodded again.

"And God knows your stories have made things a lot better for the reality of the gremlins, haven't they? And I've done my share with the lectures and the public appearances and all the chat shows on telly, now haven't I?"

Alf nodded once more.

"So then what the hell is this load'a rubbish you're

handing me, chum? How can *all* of you have run out of story ideas?"

Alf went harrumph and looked at his feet in their solid workman's shoes, and he said with considerable embarrassment, "Well, uh, those weren't stories."

"They weren't stories? Then what were they?"

"The history of the gremlins. They were all true."

"But they sound like fantasies."

"Life is interesting for us."

"But . . . but . . ."

"I never mentioned it because it never came up, but the truth of it is that gremlins don't have any sense of what you call imagination. We can't dream things up. We just tell what happened. And we've written everything that's ever happened to our race, right up to date, and we, uh, er, haven't got any more stories."

Noah stared at him with openmouthed amazement.

"This is awful," Noah said.

"Don't I know it." He hesitated, as if not wanting to say any more; then a look of determination came over his face and he went on. "I wouldn't tell this to just any human, Noah, but you're a good sort, and we've shared a jar or two, so I'll tell you the rest of it."

"The rest of it?"

"I'm afraid so. The program's been working both ways, I'm sorry to say. The more humans came to believe in us, the more we gremlins have come to believe in you. Now it's pretty well fifty-fifty. But without the stories to keep things going, I'm afraid the gremlins are going to start thinking of you again as semireal, and . . ."

"Are you trying to tell me that now the gremlins are responsible for the reality of *humans?*"

Alf nodded nervously.

"Oh, shit," Noah suggested.

"Been having a bit of trouble in that area, as well," Alf lamented.

And they sat there, the tiny man in the human's hand, and the human in the hands of the gremlins, and they thought about getting drunk. But they knew that wouldn't help. At least not for very long. It had been a good ride for nineteen years, but the gravy train had been shunted onto a weed-overgrown siding.

And they stayed that way, sunk in silent despair, for most of the night.

Until about three fifteen this morning, when Noah Raymond suddenly looked at Alf and said, "Wait a minute, mate. Let me see if I have this figured out right: if the gremlins stop believing in humans, then the humans start disappearing . . . check?"

Alf said, "Check."

"And if the humans start disappearing, then there won't be sufficient of us to keep up the reality of the gremlins and the *gremlins* start vanishing . . . check?"

"Check."

"So that means if we can find a way of writing stories for the gremlins that will reinforce their belief in *us,* it solves the problem . . . check?"

"Check. But where do we get that many stories?"

"I've got them."

"You've got them? Noah, I like you, but let's not lose sight of reality, old chum. You ran out of ideas nineteen years ago."

"But I've got a source."

"A source for stories?"

"A unified mythology just like your gremlin history. Full of stories. We can pass them off as the truth."

And Noah went into one of the other rooms and came back with a book, and opened it to the first page and rolled a fresh piece of typing paper into the Olympia, and checked out the ribbon to make sure it was still fresh, and he said to Alf, "This ought to keep us for at least a few years. And in the meantime we can start looking around for another writer to work with us."

And he began to type the opening of the first fantasy he had attempted in nineteen years: a story that would be printed on very small pages in infinitesimal type, to be read by very little people.

And he typed: "In the beginning Kilroy created the heaven and the earth, and the earth was without form and void and you couldn't get a decent mug of lager anywhere . . ."

"I like that part," said Alf, dropping his Mayfair accent. " 'At's bloody charmin', is what 'at is."

Charlie went *blatttt!*

Introduction to Killing Bernstein

There is absolutely nothing startling or terrific to say about this story, and I'll not be badgered into making something up. Except. All of the toys described in this story as being unmarketable (and for the reasons given) are, in actual fact, as opposed to unactual fact, for-real toys that one or another of the major toy manufacturers tried and discarded. (For the reasons given.) This is called in-depth research and you'd damned well better appreciate it.

•

BERENGER: (to JEAN) Life is an abnormal business.
JEAN: On the contrary. Nothing could be more natural, and the proof is that people go on living.
BERENGER: There are more dead people than living. And their numbers are increasing. The living are getting rarer.
JEAN: The dead don't exist, there's no getting away from that! . . . Ah! Ah . . . ! *(He gives a huge laugh.)* Yet you're oppressed by them, too? How can you be oppressed by something that doesn't exist?
BERENGER: I sometimes wonder if I exist myself.

JEAN: You don't exist, my dear Berenger, because you don't think. Start thinking, then you will.

LOGICIAN: (to the OLD GENTLEMAN) Another syllogism. All cats die. Socrates is dead. Therefore Socrates is a cat.

Eugene Ionesco, *Rhinoceros*

Killing Bernstein

If God (or Whoever's in charge) had wanted Dr. Netta Bernstein to continue living, He (or She) wouldn't have made it so easy for me to kill her.

The night before, she had said again, do it again, we can do it once more, can't we; and her thick, auburn hair smelled fresh and clean and it flowed across the pillows like the sunsets we get these days. The kind that burn the eyes they're so beautiful. Our grandparents never saw such wonders of melting copper, flickering at the edges, sliding into darkness at the horizon. Exquisite beyond belief, created by pollution. Smog produces that kind of gorgeous sunset. Grandeur, created by imminent destruction. Her hair burned and slid into darkness and I buried my face in it and we made love and I didn't make any mistakes.

And the next day she acted as if she didn't know me.

Talked to me as though I were one of the test children she had in for her perception analyses. I felt waves of actual dislike coming from her. "Netta," I said, "what's the matter? Did I say something?"

She looked back at me with the expression of someone who has been asked for her driver's license or other identification at a bank where she has had an account for sixteen years. I was a troublesome new teller, a trainee, an upstart stealing her time, impertinent and callow. "Duncaster," she said, calling me by my last name, "I have work to do. Why don't you go on about your business." The night before she had called me Jimmy a hundred times in a minute.

She pretended not to know what I was talking about. I tried to be polite referring to what had happened between us. I didn't want to use the wrong words, but there were *no words* she responded to. It was as if that bed, and the two of us on it, had never existed. I couldn't believe she could be that brutal. I left the office early that day.

And the next day she hung me out to dry. It was even more brutal than the day before. The day before, it had only been obvious dislike, go on about your business, Duncaster. But the next day we were mortal enemies. Like ancient antagonists from some primordial swamp, she was after me, and I knew it. I can't explain *how* I knew, I simply understood somewhere deep in the blood and bones that this woman was determined to rip out my throat.

Or perhaps I *can* explain it.

Take the film they made of *Jaws*. That is a terrifying film. It collapses entire audiences, and not merely because of the cinematic tricks. People in the middle of Kansas, people who've never even *seen* an ocean or a shark, go into cardiac arrest. Why should that be? There are terrors much closer to us—muggers on the streets, a positive biopsy report, being smashed to pudding in a freeway accident—terrors that *can* reach us; why should we be so petrified by that shark? I reject abstractions: the *vagina dentatus*, that paranoid hobgoblin of Freudian shadow-myth; the simplicity of our recoiling from something filled with teeth, an eating machine. I have another theory.

The shark is one of the few life forms that has come

down to the present virtually unchanged from the Devonian. So few: the cockroach, the horseshoe crab, the nautilus, the coelecanth—probably older than the dinosaurs. The shark.

When we were still aquatic creatures . . . there was the shark. And even today, in the blood that boils through us, the blood whose constituency is the same as sea water, in the blood and somewhere deep in our racial memory, there is still the remembrance of the shark. Of swimming away from that inexorable eating machine, of crawling up onto the land to be safe from it, of vowing never to return to the warm seas where the teeth can reach us.

When we see the shark, we understand that *that* is one of the dreadful furies that drove us to become human beings. Natural enemy from beyond the curtain of time, from beneath the killing darkness. Natural enemies.

Perhaps I *can* explain how I knew, that next day, that Netta Bernstein and I were blood enemies.

The moment I walked into the conference room and saw her sitting next to Sloan—a clipboard fat with charts lying on the table in front of her—I knew she was lying in wait for me. The teeth, the warm seas, the eating machines that had followed us onto the land. And in that instant, I now realize, I first decided to kill her.

You have to understand how it is with a major toy company, how it works in the corporate way; otherwise it doesn't make sense . . . the killing of Netta Bernstein.

Fighting my way to the top at the MyToy Corporation had been the commitment of ten years of my life. It wouldn't have been any different at Mattel or Marx or Fisher-Price or Ideal or Hasbro or Kenner or Mego or Playskool or even Creative Playthings. The race is always to make The Big Breakthrough, to come up with the new toy that sweeps the field before the competition can work up a knockoff imitation. Barbie, G.I. Joe, Hot Wheels, they made millions for one man and one company because they were The Big Breakthroughs. In an industry where sixty percent of each year's product is brand-new, *has to be* brand-new because the kids have a saturation/boredom threshold that is not to be believed, it is the guy with The Big Breaththrough who gets to be Vice President of Product Planning, at $50,000 a year.

I was Director of Marketing Research. Gumball, Destruction Derby, Change-A-Face, those had been my weapons in the fight toward the $50,000 plateau. MyToy was one of the big five and I'd been on the rise for ten years.

But the last four ideas I'd hawked to top management had either been rejected or been put into production and bombed. The fashion-doll line had been too sophisticated—and the recession had hit; there was backlash against opulence, conspicuous consumption; and the feminist movement had come out strong against what they called "training little girls to be empty-headed clotheshorses." Dinosaur had been too impractical to produce at a reasonable per-unit cost. Pretesting had shown that kids rejected Peggy Puffin as being "ugly," even though parents found the packaging attractive; they'd buy it, but the kids wouldn't play with it. And the lousy sales reports on Mother's Helper had verified a negative transference; old learning habits had generally inhibited learning new techniques. It was what the president of MyToy, Sloan, had called "disastrously counterproductive." And I'd begun to smell the ambivalence about me. Then the doubts. Then the veiled antagonisms. The dismissals, the offhand rejections of trial balloons I'd floated. And now there was even open hostility. I was at the crunch point.

Everything was tied up in the two new projects I'd worked out with R&D. The Can-Do Chipper and the Little Miss Goodie Two-Shoes doll. Research & Development had gotten the approval to put them into preliminary design, both aimed at preschool development markets, and Netta Bernstein had tested them in the MyToy play therapy facilities.

MyToy was the only major toy company in America to maintain a full-time staff of child and research psychologists. Netta headed the team. The prototypes had been sent to her for live evaluation with test kids. The reports filled that clipboard. Fifty thou filled that clipboard. And I knew she was out to get me.

Sloan wouldn't look at me. I went down the length of the conference table, took an empty seat between Dixon and Schwann; I was bracketed by cost accountants, a pair of minor sales potential vassals. The seat on the right hand of Brian Sloan, God of MyToy, the seat I'd held for almost ten years, was occupied by Ostlander, the hungry little turncoat from Ideal who'd come over, bringing with him design secrets worth a fortune. Not The Big Breakthrough, but enough knockoff data to pay his way to the other side.

And on the left hand of God sat Netta Bernstein.

My future lay before her fastened tight in the clipboard. Her tests with the kids would make or break me. And the night before last she had said she loved me. And the day before she had told me to go away. And today I smelled the killing darkness of the Devonian seas.

The first hour was marking time. Sales reports, prospectus for third-quarter production, a presentation about the proposed Lexington, Kentucky, plant site, odds and ends. Then Sloan said we'd hear Netta's test results on the new designs. She never looked at me.

"I'll begin with the big dolls for preschoolers," she said, releasing the clip and removing the first batch of reports. "They all reach or exceed the expectations projected by prelim. They have the 'kid appeal' Mr. Sloan discussed last Thursday, with one small modification on the shopper doll. The mother model. I found, in giving the dolls to six selected groups of test children—eight in each group—that the pocket on the apron was ignored completely. The children had no use for it, and I think it can be eliminated to the advantage of the item."

Sloan looked at me. "Jimmy," he said, "what would that mean in terms of lowering the per-unit cost of the mother shopper?"

I already had my calculator out and was running the figures. "Uh, that would be . . . three cents per unit on a projected run of—" I looked at Schwann; he scribbled *3 mil* on his pad. "A run of three million units: ninety thousand dollars." It had been a most ordinary question, and an ordinary answer.

Netta Bernstein, without looking at me, said to Sloan, "I believe that figure is incorrect. The per-unit saving would be closer to 4.6 cents, for a total of one hundred and thirty-eight thousand dollars."

Sloan didn't answer. He just looked at Schwann and Dixon. They both nodded rapidly, like a pair of those Woolworth's cork birds that dip their beaks into a glass of water and then sit upright again. It would have been pointless to say the three-cents-per-unit figure had been given to me by prelim the week before and that Netta had obviously gotten more up-to-date stats on the project. It would have been pointless, not only because Sloan didn't like to hear excuses, but because Netta had clearly set out to mousetrap me. Cost stats were not her area, never had been, never should be; yet she had them. Chance? I doubted it. Either way, I looked like a doughnut.

There was a hefty chunk of silence, and then Netta went on to the test results of three other proposals, none of them mine. On one of them the changes would have been impractical, on the second the kids simply didn't like the toy, and on the third the changes would have been too expensive.

Then she was down to the last two sheafs of notes, and I smelled the warm Devonian seas again.

How I killed her was slovenly, sloppily, untidily, random, and rumpled.

As she reached into the clothes closet for her bathrobe I pushed her inside and tried to strangle her. She fought me off and started to come out and I pushed her back. The clothes rack bar fell out of its brackets and we were lying in a heap on the floor. I hit her a couple of times and she hit me back, even harder than I'd hit her. Finally, I grabbed the plastic clothing bag from a dress fresh from the dry cleaners, and suffocated her with it. Then I went into her bathroom and vomited up the prime rib and spinach.

I could feel Sloan's eyes on me as she launched into the recitation of the problems inherent in producing the Can-Do Chipper. The toy was a preschool game that flipped a group of colored chips into the air when the child stomped on a foot pedal. The chips came in four distinct shapes and colors, four of each, with decals on them of bees, birds, fishes, and flowers. The object was for the child to grab as many of his designated decal chips as possible. Some of the squares were yellow with bees, some of the circles were red with flowers, some of the triangles were blue with birds, some of the stars were green with fishes. But some stars had bees on them, some circles had birds on them . . . and so forth. So a child had to identify in that instant the chips were in the air not only its proper decal, but its shape and its color as well.

Netta had given the game to ten groups of four kids each, for "can-do" testing. She had left them alone in the big playroom on the third floor of the Research & Development wing. One needed a yellow color-coded badge to get *onto* the third floor, and a top-clearance red dot in the center of the yellow badge to get into that *wing*.

The children had not responded to the game as I'd indicated they would. They ignored the decals entirely, set up the rules the way *they* wanted to play it, and simply caught shapes or colors. The cost analysis people said we'd save twenty-five thousand dollars by omitting the decals, and I thought I was home free; but Netta added what I thought was a gratuitous observation: "I think the sales potential of this item is drastically reduced by the loss of the decals. There won't be any ready-to-hand advertising lures. In fact, when we gave each child a list of toys they could have for participating in the tests, and this was when we first brought them in, the Can-Do Chipper was in the lowest percentile of choice. And after we observed them through the one-way mirrors playing with the game, and after we showed them the cartoons and the commercials and then told them we'd made an error on the forms and they should *now* pick their prizes, it was the least wanted item on the list."

They scrubbed the project. I was two down for the day.

She went to the Little Miss Goodie Two-Shoes doll, my Big Breakthrough. It was the last sheaf of test notes, and I harbored the foolish hope that Netta had been playing some kind of deadly stupid lovers' game with me, that she had saved my hottest project for last, so she could recommend it highly. She hung me out to dry.

"This is one of the most dangerous toys I've ever tested," she began. "To refresh your memory, it is a baby doll that contains a voice-activated tape loop. When you say to the doll, 'Good dolly, you're a good dolly,' or similar affectionate phrase, the doll goes *mmmmmm*. When you say, 'Bad dolly, you've been a bad dolly,' or similar hostile phrase, the dolly whimpers. Unfortunately, my tests with a large group of children—" and she looked directly at me,

"—which I've cross-checked through our independent testing group at Harvard, clearly show that not only the tape loop is activated by hostile phrases. This toy activates aggression in children, triggering the worst in them and *feeding* it. They were brutal with the dolls, tormenting them, savaging them, tearing them apart when merely spanking them and throwing them against the walls failed to satisfy their need to hear the whimpering."

I was, on the spot, in an instant, a pariah.

I was the despoiler of the children's crusade.

I was the lurking child molester.

I was the lizard piper of Hamelin.

I was, with the good offices of Netta Bernstein, at the end of an auspicious career with the MyToy Corporation.

And the next day she kissed me, surreptitiously, in the elevator; and asked me if I was free to have dinner at her apartment that night.

I left the body in the clothes closet, shoved back in a fetal position under the mound of wrinkled dresses and pants suits. I went out and wandered around the marina till morning, playing the messy murder of Netta Bernstein over and over again. Then I went to work.

I walked past Sloan's office, toward my own, expecting the door to burst open and Sloan to be standing there with a couple of cops. "That's him, officers. The one who wanted us to sell a demon doll. And he killed our research psychologist, a beautiful woman named Netta Bernstein. Take his yellow color-coded badge with the red dot in the center, and get him the hell out of here."

But nothing of the kind happened. Sloan's door stayed closed, I walked past and headed for my office. As I came abreast of Netta's glass-walled office, I glanced in as casually as I had every day and saw Netta poring over a large graph on her desk.

I once visited the Olympic peninsula of Washington

state. I thought it was very beautiful, very peaceful. Up beyond the Seattle-Tacoma vicinity. Virgin wilderness. Douglas fir and alder with whitish bark and brownish-red at the tops of the leaves. It's flat, but you can see the Olympic range and the Cascades and Mt. Rainier when the mist and fog and rain aren't obscuring the view. And even the mist and fog and rain seem peaceful, comfortable; cold, but somehow sanctified. A person could live there, fast and hard away from Los Angeles and the freeway stranglehold. But there was no $50,000 plateau on the Olympic peninsula.

I couldn't accept it. I don't think I even broke stride. I just walked past, well down the corridor, leaned against the wall for a moment, and breathed deeply. Staff walked past and Nisbett stopped to ask me if I was all right; I said I was fine, just heartburn, and he said, "Ain't it the truth," and he walked away. I could feel my heart turning to anthracite in my chest. I thought I would die. And then I realized I'd been hallucinating, projecting my guilt, having a delayed reaction to what had happened the night before, to what lay huddled in that clothes closet till I could figure out how to dispose of it.

I got myself under control, swallowing several times to force down the lump, breathing through my mouth to clear the dark fog that had begun to swirl in like the fog of the Olympic peninsula.

And then I turned back, walked slowly to Netta's office, and looked through the window-wall. She was talking to one of her assistants, a young woman who had worked with Madeline Hunter at UCLA, or had it been Iris Mink at UCLA Neuropsychiatric . . . *what the hell was I thinking!*

I had killed Bernstein the night before, had seen her eyes start from her head and her tongue go fat in her mouth and her skin turn dark blue with cyanosis when the strangling failed and the suffocation succeeded. She was meat, dead meat, lying under a pile of coat hangers. She could not possibly be in there talking to her assistant.

I opened the door and walked in.

They both looked up and the assistant stopped talking. Netta looked at me with annoyance and said, "Yes?"

"I, uh, the report, I, uh . . ."

She waited. They both waited. I moved my hands in random patterns. The assistant said, "I'll check it again, Netta, and show it to you after lunch; will that be all right?"

Netta Bernstein nodded it would be all right, and the assistant took the graph and slipped past me, giving me a security guard's look; when was the last time I'd seen a look like that?

When she was gone, Netta turned to me and said, "Well, what is it, Duncaster?"

Netta Bernstein was thirty-seven. I had checked. Her dossier in personnel said she had attended the University of Washington, had obtained her degree in psychology, and had majored in child therapy. She had been married at the age of eighteen, while still an undergraduate to one of her professors, who had soon after their marriage left the academy for a job with Merck Sharp & Dohme, the drug company, in New Jersey. She had remained with him until he had received a federal grant for a research project (unspecified, probably defense-oriented), and they had moved to a remote part of the Olympic peninsula of Washington state, where they had remained for the next sixteen years. Grays Harbor County. The husband had died three years before, and Netta Bernstein had gone to work in Houston, at the Baylor Medical School, department of biochemistry. Research on the RNA messenger molecules; something related to autistic children. She had left Baylor and come to MyToy, for a startling salary, only thirteen months before.

She was beautiful, with thick auburn hair and the most penetrating cobalt-colored eyes I had ever seen. Eyes that were wide and dead in a clothes closet near the marina. Before I had killed her, she looked no more than nineteen years old, still as young and beautiful as she must have been when she was an undergraduate at the University of Washington. When I left her she looked like nothing human, certainly nothing living.

I stared at her. She looked nineteen again. There were no black bruises on her throat, her color was fresh and youthful, her cobalt-colored eyes staring at me.

"*Well,* Duncaster?"

I ran away. I hid in my office, waiting for the cops to come. But they never did. I went crazy, waiting. I had all the terrors and the guilt of knowing she would turn me in, that she was playing cobra-at-the-mongoose-rally with me. She hadn't died. Somehow she had still been breathing. I'd *thought* she was dead, but she wasn't dead; she was alive. Down the hall, waiting for me to throw myself out a window or run shrieking through the corridors screaming my confession. Well, I wouldn't do it! I'd outsmart her, I'd make sure she never told anyone about the night before.

I left the building by the service elevator, went to her apartment, and used the key I'd stolen the night before in anticipation of returning to dispose of the body. The first thing I did was check the clothes closet.

It was empty. The clothes were hung neatly. The dress with the plastic clothing bag from the dry cleaner was hanging among the others. There was no sign I'd even been there, that we had had dinner together, that we'd made love, that we'd argued over her performance in the conference room, that she'd denied meaning me any harm, that she had professed her love . . . and no sign I had killed her.

The apartment was silent and had never been the scene of a battlefield engagement for possession of the $50,000 plateau. I thought I might, indeed, be going crazy.

But when she got home, I killed Bernstein. Again.

I used a wooden cooking mallet intended to soften meat. I crushed her skull and wrapped her in the shower curtain and tied up her feet and torso with baling twine from under the sink. I attached a typewriter to the end of the cord, an IBM Selectric, and I carried her out to the marina at three a.m. and threw her in.

And the next day, Netta Bernstein was in her office, and she paid no attention to me, and I thought I'd go crazy, perhaps I'd *already* gone crazy. And that night I killed her with a tire iron and buried her body in the remotest part of Topanga Canyon. And the next day . . .

She didn't come to work.

They told me she had taken a leave of absence, had gone to Washington state on family business.

I ransacked the dossier and found the location. I flew up from LA International to the Sea-Tac Airport and rented a car. West from Olympia toward Aberdeen. North on Highway 101. Twenty miles north. I turned west and drove for fifteen miles, and came to the high wire fence.

I could see the long, low structure of the research facility where Netta Bernstein had lived with her husband for sixteen years. I got in. I don't remember how. I got in, that's all.

I circled the building, looking for a way inside, and when a crack of lightning flashed down the slate of the sky I saw my reflection in a window, wild-eyed and more than a little crazy. It was terribly cold, and I could smell the rain coming.

I found a set of doors and they were open. I went into the building. I went looking, wanting only one thing: to find Netta Bernstein, to kill her once again, finally, completely, thoroughly, without room for argument or return.

There was music coming from somewhere far off in the building. Electronic music. I followed the sound and passed through research facilities, laboratories whose purpose I could not identify, and came, at last, to the living quarters at the rear of the building.

They were waiting for me.

Seven of them.

Netta times seven.

The husband had been a geneticist. Fallen in love with an eighteen-year-old, auburn-haired, cobalt-colored-eyed undergraduate he met at a lecture. He had cloned her. Had taken the cutting and run off nine copies that had been raised from infancy, that had grown up quickly as she aged so slowly, so beautifully. Netta times ten. And when they had raised their children, there, far away from all eyes and all interference, he had died and left the mother with her offspring; left the woman with her sisters; left the thirty-four-year-old original with her sixteen-year-old-duplicates. And Netta had had to go out into the world to make a living, to the drug company, to Baylor, to MyToy.

But when she wanted to return to see herself in the mirrors of their lives, she would call one or two or another of the Nettas to come do her work at MyToy.

And one of them had fallen in love with me.

Killing Bernstein was impossible. Killing Netta, because love had made me crazy, was beyond anyone's power, beyond even madness and hatred.

And one of them had fallen in love with me.

I sat down and they watched me. They had removed the body of their sister from the closet, and they had brought her back home for burial. And soon they would return to Los Angeles and drive up into wild Topanga

Canyon and dig up another. And the third they would never see again.

And one of them had fallen in love with me.

Here on the Olympic peninsula, the fog and the mist and the rain are cool and almost sanctified. There is music, and they don't harm me, and some day they may let me leave. They don't bind me, they don't keep me from going out into the night; but this is where I'll stay.

And perhaps some day, when they clone again, perhaps I'll get lucky again.

And perhaps one of them will fall in love with me.

Introduction to Mom

Despite the fact that my mother died recently (8 October 76), and that she was on my mind for quite a while before that, and that I wrote this story in the same year (25 February 76), those who seek seminal and germinal influences for my stories will have to look further. My mother did not speak with a Yiddish accent, nor did she ever once in my entire life fix me up with a female, Jewish or Gentile. This is just a story.

How it came to be, however, is pretty strange.

On Saturday 16 August 75, in company with nineteen friends, I sprang for a thirteen-course Szechuan meal at Golden China on Van Nuys Boulevard in the Los Angeles suburb of that name. Van Nuys, that is. Come on, keep up with me.

There we were, all sitting around these round tables, with Gil Lamont trying to prove he wasn't drunk by making an ass of himself harassing the waitress, with Arthur Byron Cover looking trepidatiously at the kung-pao beef and trying to reconcile it with his limitless capacity for junk food, with Ed Sunden, who had come in from Chicago to bring me a splendid set of tungsten tournament darts, bugging me to write a story in which he was the hero, with David Wise and Kathleen Barnes trying to pour soy sauce on Chick Dowden in an effort to cut off his puns. . . .

And we got into this dumb discussion of ghost stories. And some smartass said, "They've all been written. There're no fresh twists on the ghost story theme."

Which of course was a gauntlet thrown down for a writer who remembers what Hemingway said in 1936: "There is no use writing anything that has been written before unless you can beat it. What a writer in our time has to do is write what hasn't been written before or beat dead men at what they have done."

I thought a minute, then said, "How about a Jewish momma's boy, whose mother has just died, and the ghost comes back to *nuhdz* him?" And everyone broke up.

And I suddenly started screaming, "It's great, it's a natural! Gimme a typewriter! Gimme a typewriter!"

So David leaped up and ran off to his van where he had a Remington Selectric (which I tell everyone was but one of sixteen such machines he and Kathleen had ripped off from a federal office building just that afternoon, whether it's true or not), and he came back and we shoved aside the savaged remains of lemon chicken and pork Lucerne, and I began writing the story you're about to read. While the nineteen friends watched what they thought was a "party trick." And the old friends who own the Golden China—Frank and Blossom and Sherri and their children—stared in amazement at the strangely inscrutable Occidental.

And I did the first two pages; and I finished it in the front window of A Change of Hobbit six months later. And eight months later my mother died.

But there's no connection. Except love.

•

"To be surprised, to wonder, is to begin to understand. This is the sport, the luxury, special to the intellectual man. The gesture characteristic of his tribe consists in looking at the world with eyes wide open in wonder. Everything in the world is strange and marvelous to well-open eyes."

José Ortega y Gasset

Mom

In the living room, the family was eating. The card tables had been set up and *tante* Elka had laid out her famous tiny meat knishes, the matzoh meal pancakes, the deli trays of corned beef, pastrami, chopped liver, and potato salad; the lox and cream cheese, cold kippers (boned, for God's sake, it must have taken an eternity to do it) and smoked whitefish; stacks of corn rye and a nice pumpernickel; cole slaw, chicken salad; and flotillas of cucumber pickles.

In the deserted kitchen, Lance Goldfein sat smoking a cigarette, legs crossed at the ankles, staring out the window at the back porch. He jumped suddenly as a voice spoke directly above him.

"I'm gone fifteen minutes only, and already the stink of cigarettes. Feh."

He looked around. He was alone in the kitchen.

"It wasn't altogether the most sensational service I've ever attended, if I can be frank with you. Sadie Fertel's, now *that* was a service."

He looked around again, more closely this time. He was still alone in the kitchen. There was no one on the back porch. He turned around completely, but the swinging door to the dining room, and the living room beyond, was firmly closed. He was alone in the kitchen. Lance Goldfein had just returned from the funeral of his mother, and he was alone, thinking, brooding, in the kitchen of the house he now owned.

He sighed; he heaved a second sigh; he must have heard a snatch of conversation from one of the relatives in the other room. Clearly. Obviously. Maybe.

"You don't talk to your own mother when she speaks to you? Out of sight is out of mind, is that correct?"

Now the voice had drifted down and was coming from just in front of his face. He brushed at the air, as though cleaning away spiderwebs. Nothing there. He stared at emptiness and decided the loss of his mother had finally sent him over the brink. But what a tragic way to go bananas, he thought. I finally get free of her, may God bless her soul and keep her comfortable, and I still hear her voice *nuhdzing* me. I'm coming, Mom; at this rate I'll be planted very soon. You're gone three days and already I'm having guilt withdrawal symptoms.

"They're really *fressing* out there," the voice of his mother said, now from somewhere down around his shoe tops. "And, if you'll pardon my being impertinent, Lance my darling son, who the hell invited that *momser* Morris to my wake? In life I wouldn't have that *shtumie* in my home, I should watch him stuff his fat face when I'm dead?"

Lance stood, walked over to the sink, and ran water on the cigarette. He carried the filter butt to the garbage can and threw it in. Then he turned very slowly and said—to the empty room—"This is not fair. You are not being fair. Not even a little bit fair."

"What do I know from fair," said the disembodied voice of his mother. "I'm dead. I should know about fair? Tell me from fair; to die is a fair thing? A woman in her prime?"

"Mom, you were sixty-six years old."

"For a woman sound of mind and limb, that's prime."

He walked around the kitchen for a minute, whistled a few bars of "Eli Eli," just to be on the safe side, drew himself a glass of water, and drank deeply. Then he turned around and addressed the empty room again. "I'm having a little trouble coming to grips with this, Mom. I don't want to sound too much like Alexander Portnoy, but why me?"

No answer.

"Where are you . . . hey, Mom?"

"I'm in the sink."

He turned around. "Why me? Was I a bad son, did I step on an insect, didn't I rebel against the Vietnam war soon enough? What was my crime, Mom, that I should be haunted by the ghost of a *yenta?*"

"You'll kindly watch your mouth. This is a mother you're speaking to."

"I'm sorry."

The door from the dining room swung open and Aunt Hannah was standing there in her galoshes. In the recorded history of humankind there had never been snow in Southern California, but Hannah had moved to Los Angeles twenty years earlier from Buffalo, New York, and there had been snow in Buffalo. Hannah took no chances. "Is there gefilte fish?" she asked.

Lance was nonplussed. "Uh, uh, uh," he said, esoterically.

"Gefilte fish," Hannah said, trying to help him with the difficult concept. "Is there any?"

"No, Aunt Hannah, I'm sorry. Elka didn't remember and I had other things to think about. Is everything else okay out there?"

"Sure, okay. Why shouldn't it be okay on the day your mother is buried?" It ran in the family.

"Listen, Aunt Hannah, I'd like to be alone for a while, if you don't mind."

She nodded and began to withdraw from the doorway. For a moment Lance thought he had gotten away clean, that she had not heard him speaking to whatever or whomever he had been speaking to. But she paused, looked around the kitchen, and said, "Who were you talking to?"

"I was talking to myself?" he suggested, hoping she'd go for it.

"Lance, you're a very ordinary person. You don't talk to yourself."

"I'm distraught. Maybe unhinged."

"Who were you speaking to?"

"The Sparkletts man. He delivered a bottle of mountain spring mineral water. He was passing his condolences."

"He certainly got out the door fast as I came in; I heard you talking before I came in."

"He's big, but he's fast. Covers the whole Van Nuys and Sherman Oaks area all by himself. Terrific person, you'd like him a lot. His name's Melville. Always makes me think of big fish when I talk to him."

He was babbling, hoping it would all go away. Hannah looked at him strangely. "I take it all back, Lance. You're not that ordinary. Talking to yourself I can believe."

She went back to the groaning board. Sans gefilte fish.

"What a pity," said the voice of Lance Goldfein's mother. "I love Hannah, but she ain't playing with a full deck, if you catch my drift."

"Mom, you've *got* to tell me what the hell is going on here. Could Hannah hear your voice?"

"I don't think so."

"What do you mean: you don't *think* so? You're the ghost, don't you know the rules?"

"I just got here. There are things I haven't picked up yet."

"Did you find a mah jongg group yet?"

"Don't be such a cutesy smartmouth. I can still give you a crack across the mouth."

"How? You're ectoplasm."

"Don't be disgusting."

"You know, I finally believe it's you. At first I thought I was going over the edge. But it's you. What I still want to know is *why?!?* And why you, and why me? Of all the people in the world, how did this happen to us?"

"We're not the first. It happens all the time."

"You mean Conan Doyle really *did* speak to spirits?"

"I don't know him."

"Nice man. Probably still eligible. Look around up there, you're bound to run into him. Hey, by the way: you *are* up *there,* aren't you?"

"What a dummy I raised. No, I'm not *up there,* I'm down here. Talking to you."

"Tell me about it," he murmured softly to himself.

"I heard that."

"I'm sorry."

The door from the dining room swung open again and half a dozen relatives were standing there. They were all staring at Lance as though he had just fallen off the moon. "Lance, darling," said Aunt Rachel, "would you like to come home tonight with Aaron and me? It's so gloomy here in the house all alone."

"What gloomy? It's the same sunny house it's always been."

"But you seem so . . . so . . . distressed. . . ."

From one of the kitchen cabinets Lance heard the distinct sound of a blatting raspberry. Mom was not happy with Rachel's remark. Mom had never been that happy with Rachel, to begin with. Aaron was Mom's brother, and she had always felt Rachel had married him because he had a thriving poultry business. Lance did not share the view; it had to've been true love. Uncle Aaron was a singularly unappetizing human being. He picked his nose in public. And always smelled of defunct chickens.

"I'm not distressed, Rachel. I'm just unhappy, and I'm trying to decide what I'm going to do next. Going home with you would only put it off for another day, and I want to get started as soon as I can. That's why I'm talking to myself."

They stared. And smiled a great deal.

"Why don't you all leave me alone for a while. I don't mean it to sound impertinent, but I think I'd like to be by myself. You know what I mean?"

Lew, who had more sense than all the rest of them put together, understood perfectly. "That's not a bad idea, Lance. Come on, everyone; let's get out of here and let Lance do some thinking. Anybody need a lift?"

They began moving out, and Lance went with them to the front room where Hannah asked if he minded if she put together a doggie bag of food, after all why should it go to waste such terrific deli goodies. Lance said he didn't mind, and Hannah and Rachel and Gert and Lilian and Benny (who was unmarried) all got their doggie bags, savaging the remains on the card tables until there was nothing left but one piece of pastrami (it wouldn't look nice to take the last piece), several pickles, and a dollop of potato salad. The *marabunta* army ants could not have carried out a better program of scorching the earth.

And when they were gone, Lance fell into the big easy chair by the television, signed a sigh of release, and closed his eyes. "Good," said his mother from the ashtray on the side table. "Now we can have a long mother-son heart-to-heart."

Lance closed his eyes tighter. *Why me?* he thought.

He hoped Mom would never be sent to Hell, because he learned in the next few days that Hell was being a son whose mother has come back to haunt him, and if Mom were ever sent there, it would be a terrible existence in which she would no doubt be harassed by her own long-dead mother, her grandmothers on both sides, and God only knew how many random *nuhdzing* relatives from ages past.

Primary among the horrors of being haunted by a Jewish mother's ghost was the neatness. Lance's mother had been an extremely neat person. One could eat off the floor. Lance had never understood the efficacy of such an act, but his mother had always used it as a yardstick of worthiness for housekeeping.

Lance, on the other hand, was a slob. He liked it that way, and for most of his thirty years umbilically linked to his mother, he had suffered the pains of a running battle about clothes dropped on the floor, rings from coffee cups permanently staining the teak table, cigarette ashes dumped into the waste baskets from overflowing ashtrays without benefit of a trash can liner. He could recite by heart the diatribe attendant on his mother's having to scour out the wastebasket with Dow Spray.

And now, when by all rights he should have been free to live as he chose, at long last, after thirty years, he had been forced to become a housemaid for himself.

No matter where he went in the house, Mom was there. Hanging from the ceiling, hiding in the nap of the rug, speaking up at him from the sink drain, calling him from the cabinet where the vacuum cleaner reposed in blissful disuse. "A pigsty," would come the voice, from empty air. "A certifiable pigsty. My son lives in filth."

"Mom," Lance would reply, pulling a pop-tab off a fresh can of beer or flipping a page in *Oui*, "this is not a pigsty. It's an average semiclean domicile in which a normal, growing American boy lives."

"There's *shmootz* all over the sink from the peanut butter and jelly. You'll draw ants."

"Ants have more sense than to venture in here and take their chances with you." He was finding it difficult to live. "Mom, why don't you get off my case?"

"I saw you playing with yourself last night."

Lance sat up straight. "You've been spying on me!"

"Spying? A mother is spying when she's concerned her son will go blind from doing personal abuse things to himself? That's the thanks I get after thirty years of raising. A son who's become a pervert."

"Mom, masturbation is not perversion."

"How about those filthy magazines you read with the girls in leather."

"You've been going through my drawers."

"Without opening them," she murmured.

"This's got to stop!" he shouted. "It's got to end. E-n-d. End! I'm going crazy with you hanging around!"

There was silence. A long silence. Lance wanted to go to the toilet, but he was afraid she'd check it out to make sure his stools were firm and hard. The silence went on and on.

Finally, he stood up and said, "Okay, I'm sorry."

Still silence.

"I *said* I was sorry, fer chrissakes! What more do you want from me?"

"A little respect."

"That's what I give you. A little respect."

More silence.

"Mom, you've got to face it, I'm not your little boy anymore. I'm an adult, with a job and a life and adult needs and . . . and . . ."

He wandered around the house but there was only more silence and more free-floating guilt, and finally he decided he would go for a walk, maybe go to a movie. In hopes Mom was housebound by the rules for ghost mothers.

The only movie he hadn't seen was a sequel to a Hong Kong kung fu film, *Return of the Street Fighter*. But he paid his money and went in. No sooner had Sonny Chiba ripped out a man's genitals, all moist and bloody, and displayed them to the audience in tight closeup, than Lance heard the voice of his mother behind him. "This is revolting. How can a son of mine watch such awful?"

"Mom!" he screamed, and the manager came down and made him leave. His box of popcorn was still half full.

On the street, passersby continued to turn and look at him as he walked past conversing with empty air.

"You've got to leave me alone. I need to be left alone. This is cruel and inhuman torture. I was never *that* Jewish!"

He heard sobbing, from just beside his right ear. He threw up his hands. Now came the tears. "Mommmm, *please!*"

"I only wanted to do right for you. If I knew why I was sent back, what it was for, maybe I could make you happy, my son."

"Mom, you'll make me happy as a pig in slop if you'll just go away for a while and stop snooping on me."

"I'll do that."

And she was gone.

When it became obvious that she *was* gone, Lance went right out and picked up a girl in a bar.

And it was not until they were in bed that she came back.

"I turn my back a second and he's *shtupping* a bum from the streets. That I should live to see this!"

Lance had been way under the covers. The girl, whose name was Chrissy, had advised him she was using a new brand of macrobiotic personal hygiene spray, and he had been trying to decide if the taste was, in fact, as asserted, papaya and coconut, or bean sprout and avocado, as his taste buds insisted. Chrissy gasped and squealed. "We're not alone here!" she said. Lance struggled up from the depths; as his head emerged from beneath the sheet, he heard his mother ask, "She isn't even Jewish, is she?"

"Mom!"

Chrissy squealed again. *"Mom?"*

"It's just a ghost, don't worry about it," Lance said reassuringly. Then, to the air, "Mom, will you, fer chrissakes, get out of here? This is in very poor taste."

"Talk to me taste, Lance my darling. That I should live to see such a thing."

"Will you stop saying that?!?" He was getting hysterical.

"A *shiksa,* a Gentile yet. The shame of it."

"Mom, the *goyim* are for practice!"

"I'm getting the hell out of here," Chrissy said, leaping out of bed, long brown hair flying.

"Put on your clothes, you *bummerkeh,"* Lance's mother shrilled. "Oh, God, if I only had a wet towel, a coat hanger, a can of Mace, *some*thing, *anything!!"*

And there was such a howling and shrieking and jumping and yowling and shoving and slapping and screaming and cursing and pleading and bruising as had never been heard in that block in the San Fernando Valley. And when it was over and Chrissy had disappeared into the night, to no one knew where, Lance sat in the middle of the bedroom floor weeping—not over his being haunted, not over his mother's death, not over his predicament: over his lost erection.

And it was all downhill from there. Lance was sure of it. Mom trying to soothe him did not help in the least.

"Sweetheart, don't cry. I'm sorry. I lost my head, you'll excuse the expression. But it's all for the best."

"It's not for the best. I'm horny."

"She wasn't for you."

"She was for me, she was for me," he screamed.

"Not a *shiksa.* For you a nice, cute girl of a Semitic persuasion."

"I *hate* Jewish girls. Audrey was a Jewish girl; Bernice was a Jewish girl; that awful Darlene you fixed me up with from the laundromat, she was a Jewish girl; I hated them all. We have nothing in common."

"You just haven't found the right girl yet."

"I HATE JEWISH GIRLS! THEY'RE ALL LIKE YOU!"

"May God wash your mouth out with a bar of Fels-Naptha," his mother said in reverential tones. Then there was a meaningful pause and, as though she had had an epiphany, she said, *"That's* why I was sent back. To find you a nice girl, a partner to go with you on the road of life, a loving mate who also not incidentally could be a very terrific cook. That's what I can do to make you happy, Lance, my sweetness. I can find someone to carry on for me now that I'm no longer able to provide for you, and by the way, that *nafkeh* left a pair of underpants in the bathroom, I'd appreciate your burning them at your earliest opportunity."

Lance sat on the floor and hung his head, rocked back and forth and kept devising, then discarding, imaginative ways to take his own life.

The weeks that followed made World War II seem like an inept performance of Gilbert & Sullivan. Mom was everywhere. At his job. (Lance was an instructor for a driving school, a job Mom had never considered worthy of

Lance's talents. "Mom, I can't paint or sculpt or sing; my hands are too stubby for surgery; I have no power drive and I don't like movies very much so that eliminates my taking over 20th Century-Fox. I *like* being a driving teacher. I can leave the job at the office when I come home. Let be already.") And, of course, at the job she could not "let be." She made nothing but rude remarks to the inept men and women who were thrust into Lance's care. And so terrified were they already, just from the *idea* of driving in traffic, that when Lance's mother opened up on them, the results were horrendous:

"A driver you call this idiot? Such a driver should be driving a dirigible, the only thing she could hit would be a big ape on a building maybe."

Into the rear of an RTD bus.

"Will you look at this person! Blind like a *litvak!* A refugee from the outpatient clinic of the Menninger Foundation."

Up the sidewalk and into a front yard.

"Now I've seen it all! This one not only thinks she's Jayne Mansfield with the blonde wig and the skirt up around the *pupik,* hopefully she'll arouse my innocent son, but she drives backwards like a pig with the staggers."

Through a bus stop waiting bench, through a bus stop sign, through a car wash office, through a gas station and into a Fotomat.

But she was not only on the job, she was also at the club where Lance went to dance and possibly meet some women; she was at the dinner party a friend threw to celebrate the housewarming (the friend sold the house the following week, swearing it was haunted); she was at the dry cleaner's, the bank, the picture framers, the ballet, and inevitably in the toilet, examining Lance's stools to make sure they were firm and hard.

And every night there were phone calls from girls. Girls

who had received impossible urges to call this number. "Are you Lance Goldfein? You're not going to believe this, but I, er, uh, now don't think I'm crazy, but I heard this *voice* when I was at my kid brother's bar mitzvah last Saturday. This voice kept telling me what a swell fellah you are, and how we'd get along so well. My name is Shirley and I'm single and . . ."

They appeared at his door, they came up to him at work, they stopped by on their lunch hour, they accosted him in the street, they called and called and called.

And they were *all* like Mom. Thick ankles, glasses, sweet beyond belief, Escoffier chefs every one of them, with tales of potato *latkes* as light as a dryad's breath. And he fled them, screaming.

But no matter where he hid, they found him.

He pleaded with his mother, but she was determined to find him a nice girl.

Not a woman, a girl. A nice girl. A nice *Jewish* girl. If there were easier ways of going crazy, Lance Goldfein could not conceive of them. At times he was *really* talking to himself.

He met Joanie in the Hughes Market. They bumped carts, he stepped backward into a display of Pringles, and she helped him clean up the mess. Her sense of humor was so black it lapsed over into the ultraviolet, and he loved her pixie haircut. He asked her for coffee. She accepted, and he silently prayed Mom would not interfere.

Two weeks later, in bed, with Mom nowhere in sight, he told her he loved her, they talked for a long time about her continuing her career in advocacy journalism with a small Los Angeles weekly, and decided they should get married.

Then he felt he should tell her about Mom.

"Yes, I know," she said, when he was finished.

"You know?"

"Yes. Your mother asked me to look you up."

"Oh, Christ."

"Amen," she said.

"What?"

"Well, I met your mother and we had a nice chat. She seems like a lovely woman. A bit too possessive, perhaps, but basically she means well."

"You *met* my mother . . . ?"

"Uh-huh."

"But . . . but . . . Joanie . . ."

"Don't worry about it, honey," she said, drawing him down to her small, but tidy, bosom. "I think we've seen the last of Mom. She won't be coming back. Some *do* come back, some even get recorporeated, but your mother has gone to a lovely place where she won't worry about you anymore."

"But you're so unlike the girls she tried to fix me up with." And then he stopped, stunned. "Wait a minute . . . you *met* her? Then that means . . ."

"Yes, dear, that's what it means. But don't let it bother you. I'm perfectly human in every other way. And what's best of all is I think we've outfoxed her."

"We have?"

"I think so. Do you love me?"

"Yes."

"Well, I love you, too."

"I never thought I'd fall in love with a Jewish girl my mother found for me, Joanie."

"Uh, that's what I mean about outfoxing her. I'm not Jewish."

"You're not?"

"No, I just had the right amount of soul for your mother and she assumed."

"But, Joanie . . ."

"You can call me Joan."

But he never called her the Maid of Orléans. And they lived happily ever after, in a castle not all that neat.

•

A MINI-GLOSSARY OF YIDDISH WORDS USED IN "MOM"

bummerkeh (bum-er-keh) — A female bum; generically, a "loose" lady.

"Eli Eli" (á-lee á-lee) — Well-known Hebrew-Yiddish folk song composed in 1896 by Jacob Koppel Sandler. Title means "My God, my God." Opens with a poignant cry of perplexity: "My God, my God, why hast thou forsaken me?" from Psalm 22:2 of the Old Testament. Owes its popularity to Cantor Joseph Rosenblatt, who recorded and sang it many times as an encore during concerts in early 1900s. Al Jolson also did rather well with it. Not the kind of song Perry Como or Bruce Springsteen would record.

fressing (fress-ing) — To eat quickly, noisily; really stuffing one's face; synonymous with eating mashed potatoes with both hands.

latkes (lot-kess) — Pancakes, usually potato pancakes but can also be made from matzoh meal. When made by my mother, not unlike millstones.

Litvak (lit-vahk) — A Jew from Lithuania; variously erudite but pedantic, thin, dry, humorless, learned but skeptical, shrewd and clever; but used in this context as a derogatory by Lance's mom, who was a *Galitzianer*, or Austro-Polish Jew; the antipathy between them is said to go back to Cain and Abel, one of whom was a Litvak, the other a Galitzianer . . . but that's just foolish. I guess.

momser (muhḿ-zer) — An untrustworthy person; a stubborn, difficult person; a detestable, impudent person; not a nice person.

nafkeh (nahf́-keh) — A nonprofessional prostitute; a *bummerkeh* (see above); not quite a hooker, but clearly not the sort of woman a mother would call "mine darling daughter-in-law."

nuhdzing (noooooó-jing) — To pester, to nag, to bore, to drive someone up a wall. The core of the story. Practiced by mothers of all ethnic origins, be they Jewish, Italian, or WASP. To bore; to hassle; to be bugged into eating your asparagus, putting on your galoshes, getting up and taking her home, etc. Very painful.

pupik (píp-ik or puhṕ-ik) — Navel. Belly button.

shiksa (shiḱ-šuh) — A non-Jewish woman, especially a young one.

shmootz (shmootz) — Dirt.

shtumie (shtooḿ-ee) — Lesser insult-value than calling someone a *schlemiel* (shleh-meal'). A foolish person, a simpleton; a consistently unlucky or unfortunate person; a social misfit; a clumsy, gauche, butterfingered person; more offhand than *schlemiel*, less significant; the word you'd use when batting away someone like a gnat.

shtupping (shtoooooṕ-ing) — Sexual intercourse.

tante (tahń-tuh) — Aunt.

yenta (yeń-tuh) — A woman of low origins or vulgar manners; a shrew; a shallow, coarse termagant; tactless; a gossipy woman or scandal spreader; one unable to keep a secret or respect a confidence; much of the *nuhdz* in her. If it's a man, it's the same word, a blabbermouth.

Introduction to In Fear of K

The demons that live within our skins are the worst. From time to time, when I write of the madness of men and women who savage one another, I am pilloried by readers who do not perceive my misery at how little we think of ourselves. They write me and accuse me of holier-than-thou attitudes, denying the demons I say are in them. "Not I!" they cry, and detail their good deeds. "And you're no better than we," they add. How right they are. The same furies reside in me. What they do not seem to understand is that I have a love-hate relationship with the human race. That I revere the nobility and the courage and the friendship in us, and despise the violence, cowardice, and the rapaciousness that motivates us most of the time.

I chuckle at the paper tiger of violence on television, that which provides rallying cries for self-serving petty politicians. We decry violence, and yet the most watched films and television series are those that come closest to satisfying our need for blood. What a duplicitous, mendacious species we are.

The demons within us are only fear.

And living with fear is a miserable way to exist.

There is more violence in *Who's Afraid of Virginia Woolf?* than in an entire season of television cruelty.

And there is more psychic violence in one night of the marriage of two of my dearest friends than in the streets of San Francisco on that same night. This story is an open letter to them. It says: Do not live in fear of K.

•

> "It is precisely at their worst that human beings are most interesting."
>
> H. L. Mencken, 12 Jan 43

In Fear of K

"He who sleeps in continual noise is wakened by silence."

William Dean Howells, *Pordenone,* Act IV

They had been in the pit as long as either could remember; they had discussed it many times; neither could think of a time when they had *not* been in the pit. They had, perhaps, been there forever. It didn't matter.

There was no way out.

Where they lived, in the single chamber, the greenglass walls were smooth and gave off a dull, constant, pale-emerald light; too dim and corrupt to ever see anything clearly or free of disquieting distortion, too bright to ever permit untroubled sleep. The chamber was perfectly circular, and the walls rose up slick and unbroken until they vanished in darkness. If there was an opening far above, it could neither be seen nor reached. They were two prisoners, condemned to live at the bottom of a well.

There was one opening. It was a semicircular hole two heads taller than Noah. The opening looked out on the maze. If Claudia stepped two paces beyond the opening, just outside their living chamber, and looked to her left, she saw a dark rough-stone passage that followed the outside wall of the chamber. To her right was another, vanishing into darkness. Directly in front of her were seven more tunnels whose mouths were black and ominous. The ceiling above her was also rough dark stone, with tiny flecks of brightness that might have been tin.

She had once ventured a few steps down the fourth of the seven tunnels, and two steps further it had branched in three directions. Clearly, what lay beyond the chamber was a maze. A black void of tunnels within tunnels within tunnels.

But it was not the certainty of being lost forever in the tunnel maze that had kept her, or Noah, from venturing into that labyrinth. Even being lost, even to die attempting to find a way out would have been preferable to living alone with such a hated companion. Neither Claudia nor Noah went more than a step or two into the tunnels for another, more important reason. The creature lived in those tunnels. K lived in the tunnels.

More than they despised each other, the man and the woman feared K. The central fact of their lives was fear of K. They had always lived in fear of K. There was nothing more important, nothing that dominated their waking and sleeping thoughts more than their fear of K. Survival, it seemed, depended on their fear of K. The unseen tormentor who roamed freely in those endless tunnels, who waited to kill them, devour them, who left them without peace or thoughts that were free of fear. Of K.

Claudia came through the opening dragging the sheet of black, shining fabric. The ingots of food were stacked on the sheet. She came in backward, digging her bare feet in and yanking the sheet with difficulty.

"You could help," she said, over her shoulder.

Noah looked up from his task. He looked at her, then

went back to winding the oil-soaked rags around the flambeau.

"Stop ignoring me, you sonofabitch! Help me with this!"

He wound the rag tightly, pulling it till the fabric began to rip, tucked the end under to hold it in place, and did not look up. She waited the long moment, to see if he would assist her when his immediate task was finished, but he picked up another torch, selected another rag, and began working intently on the winding.

Her face tightened, then relaxed into innocence as she said, "I only wanted help to get it in because I heard K down the right tunnel."

His head came up sharply, he got to his feet in an instant and grabbed the end of the fabric. With one intense yank he pulled the ingot-laden sheet into the center of the chamber. Without a word he bent to the arms store and lifted out a long metal rod with six propeller-shaped blades dangling from its end. With practiced ease he fitted the rod into an interlocked network of bars and swivel joints that opened into a tripod structure that braced against the walls. The rod with its blades protruded just beyond the chamber opening.

"Give me a hand with this pump," he said, hauling a generator from the pile of equipment. It was a hefty hand-crank generator on a tripod, with handles to crank on either side. He attached it to the end of the metal rod, sat down behind it, and began furiously bicycling the handles till the generator whirred to life. As he pumped faster and faster, the blades lifted and began to spin, forming a deadly circle of sharpened steel just beyond the chamber opening. Sparks leaped off the blades. Anything walking into that swirling circle would be sliced apart.

"I said give me a hand, dammit!" he yelled.

The woman ignored him.

He continued bicycling his arms furiously; then his brow furrowed and he slowed his movements, gradually letting the blades droop. Finally, he stopped the cranking and the sparks died and the blades fell. He turned to look at the woman. She was grinning nastily.

"Thanks for the help, bastard," she said, smiling.

He started to rise, his left hand forming into a fist; she saw the movement and stepped quickly to the arms store, picked up a mace constructed of a hexagonal chunk of greenglass studded with sharp points on its planed surfaces. "You don't want to try that, Noah." He settled back behind the hand generator.

"I should've known," he said. "I didn't hear the song."

"You should've known a lot of things, like how to get out of here. But you never learned." She dropped the mace back into the pile of weapons and returned to the ingots of food. She lifted one in each hand and took two steps toward the depleted pyramid of ingots against the curving rear section of the chamber when Noah rolled out from behind the generator, got his legs under him, and sprang up in her path. Without taking aim he jacked his left fist into her stomach. Claudia staggered backward, the ingots falling to the floor. The force of his blow doubled her over, even as she stumbled away from him. He followed her, moving in from the side, his eyes narrowed; she tried to keep away from him, but he backed her around toward the tangle of woven mats and fiber blankets that served as sleeping area. The pain in her stomach kept her from straightening up, prevented her from taking an offensive stance against him.

Suddenly Noah rushed her, and she tried to pivot out of his way; her feet tangled in the sleeping gear and she went down. As he rocked back to kick her, she scrambled sidewise, flinging the blankets with her feet; they snarled around him and he tried to stamp loose.

Almost casually, Claudia extricated herself as Noah spun about trying to free himself. She got to her feet, set herself with legs apart, and as Noah kicked loose of the blankets she gave a short leap and kicked him with the edge of her foot, squarely in the mouth.

He was lifted off the floor, arms wide, and was driven backward with such force that he hit the wall and crumpled up against it. He sank down, stunned, and lay unmoving, eyes glazed, blankets half-covering him.

"Take a little nap," she said. "I'll wake you when dinner's ready." She went back to the ingots of food.

It had left food. Then it had lounged. Drinking from them. But the greenglass walls came between them. Its thirst could not be slaked. It edged nearer. It drank but could not drink enough. It began to whine with the need.

"I wonder where the food comes from," she said.

"You always wonder where it comes from. It just comes, that's all. Stop talking about it." He ripped loose a warm chunk of the quarter-ingot and shoved it into his mouth. "It's rubbery this time."

"Fat lot I have to talk to you about if I don't talk about where the food comes from. How's your mouth?"

He touched his ripped lip. "It hurts."

She laughed. "Doesn't seem to be interfering with your gorging yourself."

"I have to keep my strength up. K's going to come soon; I can feel it."

She got up and walked around the chamber counterclockwise. She always walked counterclockwise. He walked around the chamber clockwise.

"You're making me nervous," he said, not looking up. "Can't you at least stay seated till I'm done eating?"

"Your strength," she said, walking. "That's fabulous! Who saved your gut the last time? Your strength. Right, Noah: keep it up, so you'll have the wherewithal to scream for help during and cry a lot after." She walked. "Strength," she murmured once more, softly.

"Listen, dammit, if you don't like it here, why don't you just take off. There's a whole world of tunnels out there. Pick any one of them and just *go.*"

She stopped directly in front of him, looming over him as he ate, her hands on her hips, balled into fists, her face reddening. "This is as much my chamber as yours. *You* get out. You're the one with 'strength'! Take your torches—your stupid torches—you've been working on them as long as I can remember—take the damned things and go find a way out of the tunnels yourself!" She was trembling with rage.

Then they heard the song.

From the darkness beyond their living space the sound rose and fell, at first distantly, then nearer, rising and falling in measured cadence, each time climbing to a new level of intensity that made their skin prickle and the roots of their hair itch. They could not move; there was a force, a restraint, a repulsion, an invisible spiderwebbing of tone that froze them where they were. No names for the sound it seemed to be. They had always been in the chamber and they did not have referents. They were held in stasis by the threat of the song . . . a song they could never identify as, perhaps, the shrieking wail of flying reptiles on the wind.

K was coming for them.

Abruptly, as if wrenching themselves from quicksand, they began to move, very quickly now, as the song grew louder and closer.

It drank from their mutual hatred and their fear. A pool dark and thick and bubbling. Without bottom, without the possibility of depletion. It drank and was still thirsty. It had not always been in the labyrinth. It had come from a far place, through a maze of quite another sort; how it had come to be here, it did not understand. There were many things it did not understand, things only vaguely realized, needs that were overwhelming, powerful, all-consuming. How it had come from that far place to this place was beyond its ability to understand, but it knew it could never return, and it had been sad, tormented, lost, and alone; and it had begun to starve. Then it had chanced upon them, and they had fed it as it lay in shadows watching them. And it had taken them, and wiped them, and constructed this place, and they had existed together symbiotically for a very long time. It meant them no harm, but that was something they could never know. If they knew, they would stop feeding it, and it would die. Crying with the need, it came to them periodically, and their terror and their loathing for one another sustained it. At times it gave them dreams, and they began to call it K; that was their interpretation of its concept for itself. And it had come to call itself K, as well. But as time passed, it felt the need for more; for greater draughts of what they felt; and so it came to them, wailing of its need.

"There, down tunnel number two. You can see the light."

"For God's sake, Noah, those knives won't stop it; we've got to lay out the stickys."

He bicycled his hands faster and faster, the knives whirling at the end of the steel rod, their edges emitting sparks, tiny glass-cracks of electricity leaping from the circle of steel to the motes of tin in the ceiling beyond the chamber. Noah had begun to believe they were not tin; he thought he remembered that tin was nonconductive; but he wasn't certain.

"It steps over the stickys," Noah said, breathing raggedly. "It can't get through this."

"What if it isn't solid flesh. What if it's just a gas or light or something elemental?"

"It can't be. If it were, we'd be dead long ago! Help me, here! My arms are getting tired."

He gave it one last furious revolution and leaped away. She slid into the position he had vacated and took up the hand-cranking without losing power. Noah went to the huge pile of torches he had wound with rags and lit one from the flame they always kept burning in the ingot pot. The torch had been soaked in a fluid that burned, a fluid they could not name but which they always found when they went to retrieve supplies left outside their chamber. The flambeau leaped into yellow-blue life and Noah positioned himself just inside the opening, directly behind the whirling circle of knife blades. They could hear K coming.

The light wavered and flickered down the tunnel, coming toward them like a fireball. "Here he comes!" Noah shouted. The song was overwhelming now, thundering against their ears in a rising shriek that was a mixture of pain and hunger and something else: an inarticulate ululation of nameless language, as though something unseen were trying to teach itself to speak with vocal cords that were never meant to form words.

And K rushed toward them.

They screamed, because they could not keep themselves from screaming, and something huge and flaming and shapeless boiled out of the tunnel, burning their eyes till they closed them against the sight, and they could not see K's shape—they had *never* seen K's shape—and the knives whirled as Claudia pumped faster and faster, driven on mercilessly by a fear that rose up in her throat and made her gag. There was nothing *but* fear at that instant, nothing but terror of being overrun by that thing from the second tunnel.

It ran into the blades, there was a timeless instant in which pumping grew more difficult, as though something were actually being chewed by the blades, then a terrible howl of rage and pain, and Noah hurled the flaming torch over the knives, into the very center of the bubbling light that surrounded K, and the light flared up as though dry tinder had caught, there was the whine of power being drained away, and then the boiling light that surrounded K receded quickly, back down the second tunnel.

And K was gone.

For perhaps the millionth time since they had been in the chamber, they had saved themselves. K was gone.

Claudia sank back upon the greenglass floor, her legs folded under her. She lay back and her dark hair, thick and long, formed a pillow for her head. She let her fear drain away in dry sobs that soon became soft crying. She rolled her head and upper body back and forth in helpless frustration. There was no end to this. It went on and on, without relief or hope of relief. She wept softly, but with deep sobs of fright and pitiful frustration.

Noah had slid down the wall to sit staring emptily at the far wall. His hands trembled uncontrollably. He wet his lips and wet them again, then again. His mouth was so dry he could not swallow. The chamber seemed to shrink around him. He could hear the last of the song as it trailed off into darkness, and he wanted to run. But there was no place *to* run. He was here, had always been here, would always *be* here. Without hope, without release, without peace.

He heard her crying and, on hands and knees, crawled to her. She felt his body touching hers and she reached out blindly for him. He came into her arms and they lay there on the warm, smooth greenglass floor, wrapped into one another against the darkness beyond.

After a while, as usual, they made love for a long time; and, as usual, it was very good for both of them.

Dimly, not really comprehending, it knew it had made a mistake giving them the knives and the thing they called a generator. It had lost great chunks of its body, left dripping on the rough stone walls outside the chamber. But it had responded to their thoughts, to their needs, and though it had not understood what the mechanism would do, it had given them the equipment nonetheless. They were linked together. Irrevocably. Eternally. It had to give them what they needed: but never their freedom. Freedom meant death for it, and only their hatred and fear meant life for it. Now it lay pulsing in a dark tunnel, its light dim and fitful. Great pain flowed through its entire bulk. It could not whine in hunger, the sound of flying reptiles on the wind. It could only lie there, heaped, and think of that far place of other colors and warmth that had been forever stolen from it. And it was still hungry. Very hungry. Hungrier than it had ever been before.

"I'm going to find a way out," Noah said. "I can't take any more of this."

"You say that every time K comes. Then you take forever to make torches and you take one step outside, and the dark terrifies you and you come back with some weak excuse why the time isn't right."

"This time I'm going."

"You'll die out there."

"What the hell do you care?"

"I care because it'll be more difficult for me to fight him off if you get killed, that's the only reason I care. I despise you, your weakness, your viciousness, your insensitive stupidity . . . but I can't survive without you."

He stared at her with that bruised look she had come to hate more than any of the others, even the teeth-bared killing rage expression. "I've got to get out of here," he said, very softly.

They did not talk for a long time. If there had been sun or moon or stars or dusk or dawn or light or absence of light it would have been days. There was nothing to say to each other. There was never anything to say. They knew everything there was to know about each other, and there was nothing about each other that was not, in some way, beyond articulation, distasteful to the other.

They found the great drying pieces of K on the floor and walls of the passage outside the chamber. They saw the shining trail, like that left by a slug, that disappeared down the second tunnel. And they knew they had wounded him. For the first time since they had begun trying to keep K from killing them, they had inflicted some of the pain on *him.*

And then, a long time later, they heard the song again.

Sooner than they had expected. The time between attacks was much shorter. And there had been no supplies for a time; so they knew things were changing.

The sound of winged reptiles on the wind.

And they set up their defenses, but the light came more slowly now. It came flickering, and dim, and they were able to watch it without turning away. The sound of the song did not cripple them.

It took a very long time for K to come.

And he came very near the entrance, indistinct but now discernible in his nimbus of light, and he lay on the roughstone floor of the second tunnel, and they were not afraid of him. And they had been silent, without talking, without striking out at each other, for a long time.

So K died. There, in the passage.

And when the light flickered out and was gone, all that remained was a dark gray pulpy mass without feature or form or threat.

They stood staring at it. They said nothing; they knew all there was to know; all they would ever know of K. Then they went back into the chamber and sat silently. Much later, they warmed an ingot and ate.

It was not till *very* much later that they realized they were free.

And even longer for them to do something about it.

They had followed the shining trail K had left. It was a trail of bread crumbs through the forest. A ball of string unraveled through the passages.

They climbed upward and came into light. Real light. There was a sun in the sky. It was bright red. And then they were able to discern an even smaller sun beside it, bright yellow but dwarfed by the nearer red sun.

They had come out on a flat plain. In the distance to the left was an ocean, rolling green and forever toward a golden beach; to the right, far in the distance was a great forest that went on and on to the horizon.

They said nothing to each other. All they wanted, now that they had it, was the future. A future free of each other. Noah did not look back as he started toward the ocean. Claudia stood watching him for a moment, then turned right and went toward the forest.

The plain was flat as a sheet of glass.

They stopped. Not at the same time, but soon. They stopped, the one staring at the ocean, the other at the great trees. Then, without looking directly toward each other, their paths began to alter.

They met in a clear space between the ocean and the

forest, at the end of the flat plain, and keeping their distance, they walked along toward the horizon.

No matter where they would go, beneath the red sun, beneath the yellow sun, they would never hear, nor understand the word karma.

Nor would they ever hear—though it was there—the sound of winged reptiles on the wind.

Introduction to Hitler Painted Roses

The other day Elizabeth asked me, in all seriousness, if I'd heard about how some Middle Eastern oil duchy had towed an iceberg down from the Arctic to water the desert. I told her that not only hadn't I heard about it, but that I hadn't heard about it because it wasn't true. She assured me it *was* true; she'd been sitting around with some rock musicians, and one of them had mentioned it, and two or three others had confirmed their knowledge of the wondrous feat. No, I said again, it was bullshit; it hadn't happened. Liz could not be unconvinced.

So I flew into one of my patented impatience rages, snarling that such a technological miracle was not only currently beyond our fiscal capabilities, but that common sense ought to inform her perception of its unlikelihood, even though they keep talking about trying it.

An iceberg, I told her, depending on its type, can have up to 83 percent of its mass hidden underwater, and unless it has already been calved (separated) from the larger ice mass and is floating toward the Equator, it would take so much explosive to detach a worthwhile chunk that it would probably rend the entire ice sheet or glacier. Not to mention what a hazard it would be to shipping, how enormous would have to be the cables to tow it because the momentum of icebergs is so great that once set in motion they keep going for hours after the wind has abated.

Sure, I screamed, over nineteen percent of the world's water is tied up in icebergs and, if floated to Kuwait or Los Angeles, could solve irrigation problems handily; and it's an idea that's been considered for a long time. But factors of wind effect, breakup, grounding, accessible supply, and controlled melting on delivery have argued convincingly against such a project. Sure, icebergs drift down as far as the North Atlantic (and a few times as far as Ireland or England), but did she have any idea how far it was from the Arctic to the Middle East? Not to mention the small question of how they would get a berg of any unmelted (from the warm currents) size through the Straits of Gibralter.

And even if all of this *were* within our technological reach today, I shouted, and even if there were solid scientific answers to these problems, if anyone had done such a magnificent thing, it would have been in every newspaper, every scientific journal, every popular magazine, on every telecast, on everyone's lips for months before they ever began towing the damned thing. But since I subscribe to *Science News, Time, Esquire, New York, New West, Playboy, Scientific American, Publishers Weekly, New Times, Analog, Natural History, Horizon*, and *The Comic Reader*, and since I hadn't read a word in *any* of them about Anwar Sadat or Hafez Assad or Hussein or the United Arab Emirates or *anybody* shelling out the billions it would take to pull off such a caper, billions which might more easily be spent to the same effect if a desalinization plant were built in this mythical location to pump the wet stuff out of the Red Sea or wherever . . . since all of this was true, it was, therefore, *quod erat demonstrandum*, simply one of those bullshit stories told around the hookah by rock musicians and other scientific illiterates who also believe in Atlantis, green men in flying saucers who built Angkor Wat, Scientology, brown rice, the "fact" that James Dean didn't really die in that car crash but is still alive, hideously disfigured, in an insane asylum somewhere, and other nutso theories mostly propounded by whackos whose names begin with V or Z.

All this I conveyed at one hundred and eighty decibels. (Yes, I know. A soft manner is usually more winning than rank browbeating. I don't necessarily want to win, however. I merely want to express my animosity toward craziness.)

And finally Elizabeth looked at me prettily, not to mention sheepishly, and she said, "I guess I'm pretty gullible, huh?"

Yes, Elizabeth, you are. But don't feel like The Lone Ranger. Most of the population of this country, in one way or another, subscribes to a plethora of freaky rumors and beliefs. Everything from Nazism and endless assassination conspiracies to faith healing and the "fact" that the gas companies have banded together to suppress the distribution of a tiny pill invented by some genius in Indiana which, if dropped into a gallon of water, turns the H_2O into hi-test. It is all detailed in a wonderful book titled *Extraordinary Popular Delusions and the Madness of Crowds* (Charles Mackay, LL.D.). It was first published in 1841 and with only a change of the players' names, the gullibility of our ancestors in flat Earthery, the dancing sickness, and witch burning is not much different. *Plus ça change, plus c'est la même chose.*

People will believe the gah*damnedest* nuttiness. And they don't like to be bothered with facts. They prefer their delusions. And the massed belief of people in anything, in a crazy *de facto* way, makes it true. Whether there is any truth to the conspiracy theory of the death of John F. Kennedy, it *is* true because most people *believe* it's true.

Dwelling on this dichotomy led me to consider poor Lizzie Borden. Ask any ten or twenty people in the street at random what they know about Lizzie Borden, and those who are capable of human speech will probably recite, "Lizzie Borden took an axe/And gave her mother forty whacks;/When she saw what she had done/She gave her father forty-one." Add to that familiar rhyme the recent television special with Elizabeth Montgomery, in which blood covered the walls, and you have a mass belief that Lizzie Borden committed matricide and patricide.

In fact, she did no such thing. The jury acquitted her in just sixty-six minutes. She *couldn't* have done it: She was under medical care at the time, and was knocked out with laudanum, a tincture of opium used widely as a medicine in those days. She was not guilty. But everyone *believes* she did it, and no doubt Lizzie Borden burns in Hell to this day.

That concept, and the injustice of it, were what prompted me to write "Hitler Painted Roses," Elizabeth.

One additional note on how this story was written, omitted from the hardcover edition of this book by inexcusable oversight on the part of the Author. For many years a remarkable man named Mike Hodel hosted a Friday midnight science fiction program over radio station KPFK, the Pacifica outlet in Los Angeles. Until I was ripped-off by KPFK (but never by Mike), I frequently appeared on the *Hour 25* show, and made it a practice to read my latest stories. In August of 1976, Mike suggested that if I could write stories in the middle of parties, in bookstore windows, in busy restaurants . . . why couldn't I write one over the radio, while the audience listened and I described what I was doing?

It seemed like a wild and wonderful idea, and so on 13 August, I went to the station with my typewriter and copy of WORDS MOST OFTEN MISSPELLED AND MISPRONOUNCED and we began what turned out to be an exciting adventure. I had agreed before the broadcast that I would not make notes or begin the actual writing of the story.

Further, I would not even think about it, would not devise a plot. It was to be entirely spontaneous.

To insure that I would maintain the terms of the project, and to reassure the listening audience that such was the case, it was agreed that the beginning of the program would be devoted to taking calls from listeners who would suggest words or phrases that would spark the conception of the plot. Those words and phrases—as many as feasible—would appear in the story as such integral parts that the listeners would know I could not possibly have planned what I was going to write.

Among the words called in and selected were: "autumnal equinox," "megalith," "gillyflowers," "augury," "Jack the Ripper," and one young man proffered the phrase *Hitler painted roses.* (I was not to learn till much later that the young man had lifted the phrase from a published poem.)

The phrase clung, though when I began the story I titled it—I always have a title before I begin to write—"Through the Doorway of Hell." Midway through the on-air writing, it was obvious the story would have to be called "Hitler Painted Roses."

That first night I wrote and explained how and what I was writing . . . reading one and two page progressions as they came off the typewriter there in the tiny broadcast booth . . . for two hours. Then, exhausted, I asked for a break and we talked for an additional hour. The program ran over a full hour, till 3 A.M. During the periods when I was actually typing, the flow of the broadcast was carried by Mike and his co-host, Mitch Harding, in conversation with sf critic Richard Delap and the then-publisher of *Delap's Review,* Frederick Patten.

As I had only gotten halfway through what was to be a 4000 word story, I agreed to come back to finish the work on a later broadcast. The following Friday night, 20 August, had been booked for something that could not be bumped, so I made my second hegira to KPFK on 27 August . . . having set aside the unfinished manuscript and putting all thought of the story from my mind . . . and completed it in another two-hour stint.

On 3 September 1976 I came back for a third time and read the completed story. With only the most minor revisions for grammar and syntax, what you read here is exactly what came off the typewriter in that crowded, pipe-smoke-filled booth, thanks to Mike Hodel and his cohorts.

•

"I cannot but think that he who finds a certain proportion of pain and evil inseparably woven up in the life of the very worms, will bear his own share with more courage and submission."

Thomas Henry Huxley, 1854

Hitler Painted Roses

The precise moment of the opening of the doorway to Hell occurred on a Friday the 13th, apparently ten days earlier than usual for the autumnal equinox to manifest itself. This discrepancy was only superficial, however. To those familiar with the changeover from the Julian calendar to the Gregorian in 1582, the ten-day prematurity was utterly harmonious. As the smoldering sun passed the celestial equator going north to south, numberless portents revealed themselves: a two-headed calf was born in Dorset near the little town of Blandford; wrecked ships rose from the depths of the Marianas Trench; everywhere, children's eyes grew old and very wise; over the Indian state of Maharashtra clouds assumed the shapes of warring armies; leprous moss quickly grew on the south side of Celtic megaliths and then died away in minutes; in Greece the pretty little gillyflowers began to bleed and the earth around their clusters gave off a putrescent smell; all sixteen of the ominous *dirae* designated by Julius Caesar in the First Century B.C., including the spilling of salt and wine, stumbling, sneezing, and the creaking of chairs, made themselves apparent; the aurora australis appeared to the Maori; a horned horse was seen by Basques as it ran through the streets of Vizcaya. Numberless other auguries.

And the doorway to Hell opened.

For just a moment. The macrocosmic maze of the universe proffered exits, and escapes were effected.

Jack the Ripper fled. Caligula slipped away. Charlotte Corday, her hands still reeking with Marat's blood, seized the moment to get away. Edward Teach, beard still bristling but with the ribbons therein charred and colorless, decamped, laughing hideously. Burke and Hare and Crippen (who had become friends in The Foul Place) ran off together. Cain's release was realized. Cesare and Lucretia Borgia elbowed one another in their attempts to break loose, and the sister won her poisonous freedom, leaving the impotent brother behind. George Armstrong Custer galloped up and off on a flaming ghost stallion, his long blond hair trailing fire, hounds baying at his heels. Others.

Hitler found himself directly beside the portal, and could have escaped. But did not. He had found a home; his eternity had been spent painting roses on the walls of Hell; and he could not leave his masterpiece behind.

The doorway closed, and all was as it had been before.

As it closed, a paradoxical whirlpool was created in the megaflow, sucking back all the doomed souls but one.

Margaret Thrushwood escaped undetected. Impossibly, (for the very best records were always kept up to date in Hell), no notice was taken of her absence; and all was as it had been.

But Margaret Thrushwood, recently quartered in Hell, was back in the world.

There had been a multiple slaying in Downieville in 1935.

There had been a house in Downieville that the residents called the Octagon House, because of the shape in which it had been built. Ramsdell had been the name of the family that had built and had lived in the Octagon House. The Ramsdells had been in mining and when the mine had played out they had gone into cattle and farming. Wealthy, friendly, interested in their community, giving and sharing during the Great Depression, they had been both loved and respected in Downieville.

The slaughter at the Ramsdell Octagon House had shocked and infuriated the god-fearing townsfolk.

Margaret Thrushwood, the housekeeper, thirty-one years old, had been the only person left alive in that abbatoir. Covered with blood and crying piteously, she had been found crouched down, half naked, in the dining room clogged with the bodies of the six Ramsdells, three of whom had been children. The townsfolk had dragged her from the house and drowned her in a nearby well. Lynching was commonplace in 1935.

On Friday the 13th, on a day of chill winds and rivers that tried for a moment to run upstream, the burned and ruined shade of Margaret Thrushwood returned to Downieville.

Henry "Doc" Thomas no longer lived there.

He had died in 1961.

The still-smoldering cinder that was the shade of Margaret Thrushwood did not linger long in Downieville; as Midgard, it had not long held the waiting shadow of Henry "Doc" Thomas. She continued searching; and when she realized he was not there, she gave a pitiful wail that made babies cry throughout the town; and she continued searching. He had not gone to Hell . . . she would have met him there and settled accounts between them. Again impossibly, defying all logic, refuting the commonly held belief that the universe balances itself in crystalline purity between good and evil, justice and injustice, Henry Thomas had been taken to Heaven.

Freed from The Foul Place, Margaret Thrushwood crawled to Heaven to find the man who had taken her virginity.

It was near twilight when she reached Heaven. The blessed host moved in slow and stately patterns. Heaven was a great pastel city, suffering from overcrowding. The faces of the residents seemed strained, but the sound of muted laughter was everywhere. It was considerably cooler than Hell had been. There were no birds in the sky. Crickets nattered.

Margaret Thrushwood asked directions and was led by stages to a common square where a pool of pale golden water whispered gently against the coming of evening. And there, at the edge of the pool, she found Henry Thomas with his bare legs dangling in the water.

She came up behind him and her hands clenched into fists without her knowledge. The clenching was painful: her hands were terribly burned. She wanted to *hit* him.

She tried to speak, and found she could not. Was it too much emotion, or that she had not spoken in Hell (save to scream) for so very long? She tried again and managed to speak his name. "Doc."

A tremor passed through him, and he stared straight ahead. She said his name again. He turned his head slowly and looked up at her. As their eyes met, he began to cry.

Hidden in the moment was the memory of that evening.

She sank to her knees beside him and looked at his face. It was twenty-six years older than the face that had compelled her love in 1935. Torment lay like a patina of dust across the fine features. He had not shaved. Perhaps he was not required to shave here. Perhaps he had been unshaved at the moment of his death. She wondered *how* he had died, but the thought was a vagrant breeze. She wanted to take his face in her blackened hands and feel once again the heat that came from him. But it was not possible. Too much time, too many moments in Hell, lay between them, as that evening lay between them.

And he cried.

Helplessly, he stared at her. He was totally and wholly at her command now. He whispered her name, then again. And the hearing of it, twice, so quickly like that, melted all the hatred in her. She leaned forward and put her sooty face against his shoulder. Black marks were left on his white flesh. She made gentle, baby-soothing sounds, even as her own body trembled. She had never seen him like this. The last time she had seen him had been that night as he . . .

Heaven began to run at the edges.

Margaret looked over Doc's shoulder. The sky of Heaven was beginning to smear and drip. She had seen a house run that way once, just the year before, in 1934. Ultraviolet rays and moisture worked rapidly on the linseed-oil binder in paints of the time. Rain would get at the fascia and trim and produce what house painters called "chalking." The colors would run. That was common in 1934, 1935.

There was a trembling in the ground beneath them. The pale golden water of the pool gently swelled to the left, then to the right. It sloshed back and forth, overflowing first at one side, then the other.

It grew much warmer. Margaret thought she heard the cry of a bird, but there were still no birds, no birds in the sky, nowhere in that smeared drizzle of heavenly sky-color running down.

She held onto Doc as tightly as she could.

The silvery light that had no source, that illuminated Heaven, dimmed; and disturbing cancers of darkness appeared here and there in the empty spaces around the square.

Margaret pressed herself more tightly into Doc's body, as she had that night. There in her servant's room at the rear of the Octagon House. Oh. The room. She could see it now in her mind, just as fresh and sharp as it was . . . when? Was it that many years ago, just yesterday, back in 1935, just one real day ago when they dragged her out of the house and tied the well-rope around her ankles, and one of the men doubled his fist and hit her in the side of the head, and another man bounced her face off the bricks of the well, and they hoisted her up, dazed and squirming and crying and now completely naked, so embarrassed at her nakedness, and tipped her head down and threw her over the lip into darkness, way down there, all the way down there to The Foul Place—was it just a day ago in real time, or forty, fifty, a hundred years ago burning always burning? She could see the room, that sweet little room the Ramsdells had given her when she came to work for them, from Dr. Pulney's in Oxnard. Through the big kitchen with the butcher's-block table in the middle and the matched copper-bottom pans hanging from their hooks and the slick sweet smell of freshly-washed-down oilcloth on the breakfast nook table and the wood-burning stove the Ramsdells continued to use even though there was piped-in gas. Through the main pantry, the huge walk-in pantry with the circular staircase at the back wall, the staircase that led up to the second and third floors where the family had their bedrooms, where Mr. Ramsdell slept and could get up quietly in the middle of the night and come downstairs for a snack of some kind or other. And the door to her room, her servant's room, she being the full-time paid-well just-twenty-eight-years-old-when-she-came to-them housekeeper. Under the circular staircase that led up to Mr. Ramsdell who came down very late in the night for snacks, the door to her sweet and clean and neat-as-a-pin room.

The sky ran, the ground trembled, darkness swirled through Heaven and the blessed host ran in random directions trying to escape the increasing warmth; as Margaret Thrushwood clung to the weeping body of Doc Thomas, as she had that evening.

"Don't you want to know where my dream comes from?"

He looked down at her and the smile came to his face even though he fought to contain it. "Why should I want to know where it comes from?"

"Because it's necessary to know that dreams come from someplace close. From someplace dear. Otherwise, they would be no better than wishes for money or great runs of land or all the caviar you could eat."

"So tell me where the dream comes from."

She sat up on the bed in the small room at the rear of the huge pantry. She wore only a slip and her silk stockings. They had been making love on the bed, and her skin was pink from having been pressed; small marks on her breasts and upper arms testified to the intensity of her love; intense enough for her to give herself up to his need to nibble, even when it was risky that someone might see the signs of passion.

"My dream comes from seeing my mother. She was from Birmingham, in England. I told you that, didn't I?"

He smiled, as he had smiled at a child who had brought him a hummingbird with a broken wing just that morning. "Yes, you told me that."

"I knew I had. Come hold me and I'll tell you more."

He slid back onto the bed and they lay side by side. He held her, with her chestnut hair which she had let down till it reached the back of her knees, all her beautiful hair, blanketing his naked body. Her head was pressed into the secret hollow under his chin, and he heard her speaking from far away. "My mother always worked; I cannot remember a time when she wasn't working. My father died when I was very young. My mother told me that."

"But you didn't believe her," he said, softly.

She sat up and stared at him. "Good lord, Doc, how did you know that?"

He motioned her to resume the position. At that moment he coughed. He had been sick, a minor summer cold; but the cough was very loud. She grew alarmed, fell back upon him and put her hand over his mouth. "Shhhh. They're eating dinner. They think I'm meditating. They mustn't know you're here . . . oh, Doc, why did you come here so early . . . ?"

"I couldn't wait to see you." His words were muffled by her hand. He kissed the palm against his lips.

"Oh, you mustn't. Not ever again. Late is the only time. Very very late, Doc." Then she paused, as if considering something, and added, "But sometimes not *too* late at night."

He didn't get a chance to ask her what that meant.

"My father really ran off. Then my mother saved her money and followed him to New York. She got tired of waiting for him to send her the fare. He was a furniture refinisher. So she worked and saved it herself and came without telling him, because I think she *wanted* to catch him living with that girl, and he was, of course, and then he just ran off and left the both of them. My mother became friends with her; that was my Aunt Sally."

He slid her slip up her legs. She tried to push it back down, but his hand was there. "Oh," she said, as if it were the first time, and again, when he had moved over her, "Oh."

The door opened.

She heard the soft sound of the empty cardboard box she had placed against the door, moving across the floor.

She had come to place the cardboard box there as a matter of course. Every night. So she would know, when she was asleep, if she was to be visited. Very, *very* late at night, some nights, Mr. Ramsdell came downstairs for a snack. Of some kind or other.

She looked over Doc's shoulder and *he* was watching them.

He did not stop them.

He watched until Doc was finished, muffling his sounds against the pillow; and then when Doc rose up slightly to look at her, to see if he was ahead or behind, and Doc saw she was staring past him, and he strained around to see what she was looking at, *then* he spoke to them: "I'll have no whores under my roof. Be packed and gone before we're done eating."

He turned, leaving the door open, and walked away, stooping from his six-foot height to pass under the circular staircase that led up to the bedrooms.

Doc was braced with a hand on either side of her seminaked body, staring down at her.

"My mother was in the Triangle Shirtwaist fire in 1911," she said. She spoke as if they had not been interrupted in their conversation, as if he had not made love to her again, as if they had not been discovered, as if Mr. Ramsdell had not looked at them with the burning eyes of God, as if she had not been told to leave within minutes. "She always worked. That was where my dream came from." Then she began to cry.

Henry Thomas rose from her body and from her bed. He looked down at her. Then he looked at the open door and the cardboard box. He had wondered about the cardboard box. It wasn't strong enough or heavy enough to keep anyone out. He had wondered why she had placed it there. And now he knew what she meant by her warning that he not come to visit very *very* late some nights.

He seemed to shrink, then. To grow smaller. He was a tall man, a good and succoring height for a veterinarian who must reassure small children who came to him with the broken-winged hummingbird and the puppy with worms and the cat that had lost an eye in a fight. But he shrank. He withered. He fell in upon himself, making a terrible, heartbreaking, wounded sound.

And then he went mad.

He grabbed her from the bed by her long chestnut hair and threw her through the open door, across the linoleum floor of the pantry. He followed her, now suddenly growing large again, swelling as if filling with poison, and dragged her by the hair across the kitchen linoleum. She tried to turn over, and saw in his hand the cleaver from the rack on the wall. He had taken it, but she did not know when he had put his hand to it first.

And then they were in the dining room, and Doc was screaming about theft and valuables that had been stolen and defilement and other insane things that made no sense, and then he was blood all over, and his hand went up and down in movements too swift to see, and there was blood on the walls and across the damask tablecloth, and there were spots of thick, terrible color on the crystal prisms of the low-hanging chandelier. And there was screaming.

And then she was alone, lying in blood, half-naked, thirty-one years old, the only thing left alive in the dining room of the Octagon House.

Until they came and put her down the well.

Lava filled the Heavenly pool. It had seeped in through fissures at the bottom, and the pale golden water had been dissipated as steam. Now it boiled up, green and black and angry crimson just beneath the crackling, shifting crust.

Margaret Thrushwood clung to Henry Thomas and felt

their bodies trembling in unison. "Why did you leave me?" she said, so softly he could barely hear her above the crackling of the lava.

Then she was pulling him to his feet, and she noticed that though his bare legs had been submerged in the pool, in the lava, they were untouched. In the Foul Place she had been sent to the lava baths. It was not the same. That was probably the chief difference between Heaven and Hell.

She took him away from the pool, and they stood near one of the pastel walls even as it developed jagged lightning-fork rents in its smooth face. The air was thick and charged.

Then God came to them and whatever else was sad or funny or according to legend or cleverly beyond anyone's imagining, there was nothing humorous about God in Their multiplicity. They came to Margaret Thrushwood and the trembling shade that was Henry "Doc" Thomas and They said, "You are an alien flesh here. You cannot stay."

"I won't go back," said Margaret Thrushwood, speaking to Them more boldly than she had ever spoken before either in life or in death, speaking to Them as though They were not God at all, just speaking up boldly. "It was a mistake. I never did anything wrong. He did it all, and then he ran away and I never had a chance. *You* should know that! You keep records, don't you?"

But God insisted, pointing back the way Margaret Thrushwood had crawled.

"Take him down there," she said. Then she caught herself. "No, I didn't mean that. Let him be. He couldn't make it down there."

God was pulling her by the arm. "All right, all right! Don't pull me, I can go on my own, thank you." And God let go of her arm and she said to Them, "Give me a second." And God waited, but not patiently, because Heaven was fracturing at every juncture.

Margaret took Henry Thomas' face in her hands, and looked into his eyes, and she realized he had grown shorter and she had grown taller, just as it had happened that night. She leaned in close to him and murmured, "They did it wrong, Doc. They made mistakes. And they'll keep it this way, just because everyone wants to believe it. They don't want to know the truth, Doc. It's easier for everyone this way. If enough people believe the fantasy, well, then it becomes the reality. But we know, Doc. *We* know who belongs where, don't we?"

And she kissed him gently, and patted his cheek, and shook her head at the stupidity of it all; she looked at God and They looked back at her impatiently. "There are some people who just shouldn't be allowed to fool around with love," she said to God. "He was irrational. What did Mr. Ramsdell matter? What did any of it matter?"

Then God led her away, back toward The Foul Place.

When they reached the doorway, God knocked, and after a little while the doorway opened, loosing a terrible smell. "I can make it by myself from here," Margaret Thrushwood said, drawing herself up regally. She stepped across the threshold, but just as the door was closing, she turned to God and said, "When you see Mr. Ramsdell, give him my regards."

Then she walked inside and the doorway closed again.

And the last thing God saw, as Margaret Thrushwood crawled down into crimson darkness, was a short, shadowy figure just inside the portal. The figure was naked, and smoldering, and held a paint brush and a palette.

Covering the walls of Hell, just inside the portal, was a fresco of roses so painfully beautiful to behold that They could not wait to get back to find Michelangelo, to tell him about the grandeur They had beheld, there in that most unlikely of places.

Introduction to
The Wine Has Been Left Open Too Long and the Memory Has Gone Flat

Because of the widespread intelligence of my intractability with publishers and editors who feel it is their god-given right to revise what an author puts on paper, because of this knowledge throughout the length and breadth of the publishing industry, when someone buys a story from me they know the contract will include a clause that forbids their altering even a comma without my written permission. If it's wrong, I'll no doubt change it when it's pointed out to me. I'm not an amateur. But the indiscriminate and foolish meddling of self-important copyeditors and recent graduates of the Seven Sisters is a kind of literary vampirism I will not tolerate. If there are to be mistakes in a story, let them be mine, for which I assume full responsibility. And as for my style and syntax, well, they may not be Cyril Connolly or Jacques Barzun, but by Crom they're *mine!*

So, like the cranky child I am, as most of us can be from time to time, I get my way . . . or I don't sell the story to that buyer. Which means I seldom write to order. I do a story with what Flaubert called "clean hands and composure" and *then* send it out to market. For the most exorbitant rate I can bleed out of a magazine or television network.

But Terry Carr is a friend of mine, and when he asked me for a story for an upcoming anthology, I amused myself by playing a little game. "What *kind* of story do you want, Terry?" I said over the long-distance phone.

"Whatever you want to write," he replied.

"No, I'm serious," I said. "Let me give you your heart's desire. Tell me what kind of story you like to read, and I'll do that thing."

So Terry expressed a delight at Jack Vance-style stories in which many and variegated aliens appear, in a strange and alien setting, and with a happy ending, which he said I don't often have in my work. He also said it should be the longest title I'd ever written (in a career that has featured some real doozies), because "long titles are in this year."

So I wrote down the title "Out Near the Funicular Center of the Universe the Wine Has Been Left Open Too Long and the Memory Has Gone Flat," which was twenty-two words, beating my next closest by seven entire words. (The title was later shortened at Terry's request to what now appears; I do not think this has anything to do with Mr. Carr and cowardice. However, when the manuscript arrived in Oakland, Mr. Carr's place of residence, the horrified gulp of disbelief registered a full 6.8 on the Richter Scale.)

Serves him right for making me work my weary old brain to figure out a happy ending for a story about the heat death of the universe. Next time he'll ask me for a soft pink-and-white bunny-rabbit story.

•

"Not every end is a goal. The end of a melody is not its goal; however, if the melody has not reached its end, it would also not have reached its goal. A parable."

Friedrich Nietzsche

The Wine Has Been Left Open Too Long and the Memory Has Gone Flat

> "Taking advantage of what he had heard with one limited pair of ears, in a single and isolated moment of recorded history, in the course of an infinitesimal fraction of conceivable time (which some say is the only time), he came to believe firmly that there was much that he could not hear, much that was constantly being spoken and indeed sung to teach him things he could never otherwise grasp, which if grasped would complete the fragmentary nature of his consciousness until it was whole at last—one tone both pure and entire floating in the silence of the egg, at the same pitch as the silence."
>
> W. S. MERWIN, "The Chart"

Ennui was the reason only one hundred and one thousand alien representatives came to the Sonority Gathering. One hundred and one thousand out of six hundred and eleven thousand possible delegates, one each from the inhabited worlds of the stellar community. Even so, counterbalancing the poor turnout was the essential fact that it had been ennui, in the first place, that had caused the Gathering to be organized. Ennui, utter boredom, oppressive worlds-weariness, deep heaving sighs, abstracted vacant stares, familiar thoughts and familiar views.

The dance of entropy was nearing its end.

The orchestration of the universe sounded thick and

gravelly, a tune slowing down inexorably, being played at the wrong speed.

Chasm ruts had been worn in the dance floor.

The oscillating universe was fifty billion years old, and it was tired.

And the intelligent races of six hundred and eleven thousand worlds sought mere moments of amusement, pale beads of pastel hues strung on a dreary Möebius strip of dragging time. Mere moments, each one dearer than the last, for there were so few. Everything that could be done, had been done; every effort was ultimately the fuzzed echo of an earlier attempt.

Even the Sonority Gathering had been foreshadowed by the Vulpeculan Quadrivium in '08, the tonal festival hosted by the Saturniidae of Whoung in '76, and the abortive, ludicrous Rigellian Sodality "musical get-together" that had turned out to be merely another fraudulent attempt to purvey the artist Merle's skiagrams to an already disenchanted audience.

Nonetheless (in a phrase exhumed and popularized by the Recidivists of Fornax 993-λ), it was "the only game in town." And so, when the esteemed and shimmering DeilBo devised the Gathering, his reputation as an innovator and the crush of ennui combined to stir excitement of a sluggish sort . . . and one hundred and one thousand delegates came. To Vindemiatrix Σ in what had long ago been called, in the time of the heliocentric arrogance, the "constellation" of Virgo.

With the reddish-yellow eye of the giant Arcturus forever lighting the azure skies, forever vying with Spica's first magnitude brilliance, Σ's deserts and canyons seemed poor enough stage setting for the lesser glow of Vindemiatrix, forever taking third place in prominence to its brawny elders. But Σ, devoid of intelligent life, a patchwork-colored world arid and crumbling, had one thing to recommend it that DeilBo found compelling: the finest acoustics of any world in the universe.

The Maelstrom Labyrinth. Remnant of volcanic upheavals and the retreat of oceans and the slow dripping of acid waters, Σ boasted a grand canyon of stalagmites that rose one hundred and sixty kilometers; stalactites that narrowed into spear-tip pendants plunging down over ninety kilometers into bottomless crevasses; caverns and arroyos and tunnels that had never been plotted; the arching, golden stone walls had never been seen by the eyes of intelligent creatures; the Ephemeris called it the Maelstrom Labyrinth. No matter where one stood in the sixteen-hundred-kilometer sprawl of the Labyrinth, one could speak with a perfectly normal tone, never even raise one's voice, and be assured that a listener crouching deep in a cave at the farthest point of the formation could hear what was said as if the speaker were right beside him. DeilBo selected the Maelstrom Labyrinth as the site for the Gathering.

And so they came. One hundred and one thousand alien life-forms. From what the primitives had once called the constellations of Indus and Pavo, from Sad al Bari in Pegasus, from Mizar and Phecda, from all the worlds of the stellar community they came, bearing with them the special sounds they hoped would be judged the most extraordinary, the most stirring, the most memorable: ultimate sounds. They came, because they were bored and there was nowhere else to go; they came, because they wanted to hear what they had never heard before. They came; and they heard.

". . . he domesticated the elephant, the cat, the bear, the rat, and kept all the remaining whales in dark stalls, trying to hear through their ears the note made by the rocking of the axle of the earth."

W. S. Merwin, "The Chart"

If she had one fear in this endless life, it was that she would be forced to be born again. Yes, of course, life was sacred, but how *long,* how ceaselessly, repetitiously long did it have to go on? Why were such terrible stigmas visited on the relatives and descendants of those who simply, merely, only wished to know the sweet sleep?

Stileen had tried to remember her exact age just a few solstices ago. Periodically she tried to remember; and only when she recognized that it was becoming obsessive did she put it out of her mind. She was very old, even by the standards of immortality of her race. And all she truly hungered to know, after all those times and stars, was the sweet sleep.

A sleep denied her by custom and taboo.

She sought to busy herself with diversions.

She had devised the system of gravity pulse-manipulation that had kept the dense, tiny worlds of the Neer 322 system from falling into their Primary. She had compiled the exhaustive concordance of extinct emotions of all the dead races that had ever existed in the stellar community. She had assumed control of the Red Line Armies in the perpetual Procyon War for over one hundred solstices, and had amassed more confirmed tallies than any other commander-in-chief in the War's long history.

Her insatiable curiosity and her race's longevity had combined to provide the necessary state of mind that would lead her, inevitably, to the sound. And having found it, and having perceived what it was, and being profoundly ready to enjoy the sweet sleep, she had come to the Gathering to share it with the rest of the stellar community.

For the first time in millennia, Stileen was not seeking merely to amuse herself; she was engaged on a mission of significance . . . and finality.

With her sound, she came to the Gathering.

She was ancient, deep yellow, in her jar with cornsilk hair floating free in the azure solution. DeilBo's butlers took her to her assigned place in the Labyrinth, set her down on a limestone ledge in a deep cavern where the acoustics were particularly rich and true, tended to her modest needs, and left her.

Stileen had time, then, to dwell on the diminished enthusiasm she had for continued life.

DeilBo made the opening remarks, heard precisely and clearly throughout the Maelstrom. He used no known language, in fact used no words. Sounds, mere sounds that keynoted the Gathering by imparting his feelings of warmth and camaraderie to the delegates. In every trench and run and wash and cavern of the Maelstrom, the delegates heard, and in their special ways smiled with pleasure, even those without mouths or the ability to smile.

It was to be, truly, a Sonority Gathering, in which sounds alone would be judged. Impressed, the delegates murmured their pleasure.

Then DeilBo offered to present the first sound for their consideration. He took the responsibility of placing himself first, as a gesture of friendship, an icebreaker of a move. Again, the delegates were pleased at the show of hospitality, and urged DeilBo to exhibit his special sound.

And this is the sound, the ultimate sound, the very special sound he had trapped for them:

On the eleventh moon of the world called Chill by its inhabitants, there is a flower whose roots are sunk deep, deep into the water pools that lie far beneath the black stone surface. This flower, without a name, seems to be an intricate construct of spiderwebs. There are, of course, no spiders on the eleventh moon of Chill.

Periodically, for no reason anyone has ever been able to discern, the spiderweb flowers burst into flame, and very slowly destroy themselves, charring and shriveling and turning to ashes that lie where they fall. There is no wind on the eleventh moon of Chill.

During the death ceremonies of the spiderweb flowers, the plants give off a haunting and terrible sound. It is a song of colors. Shades and hues that have no counterparts anywhere in the stellar community.

DeilBo had sent scavengers across the entire face of Chill's eleventh moon, and they had gathered one hundred of the finest spiderweb flowers, giants among their kind. DeilBo had talked to the flowers for some very long time prior to the Gathering. He had told them what they had been brought to the Maelstrom to do, and though they could not speak, it became apparent from the way they straightened in their vats of enriched water (for they had hung their tops dejectedly when removed from the eleventh moon of Chill) that they took DeilBo's purpose as a worthy fulfillment of their destiny, and would be proud to burn on command.

So DeilBo gave that gentle command, speaking sounds of gratitude and affection to the spiderweb flowers, who burst into flame and sang their dangerous song of death. . . .

It began with blue, a very ordinary blue, identifiable to every delegate who heard it. But the blue was only the ground coat; in an instant it was overlaid with skirls of a color like wind through dry stalks of harvested grain. Then a sea color the deepest shade of a blind fish tooling

through algae-thick waters. Then the color of hopelessness collided with the color of desperation and formed a nova of hysteria that in the human delegates sounded exactly like the color of a widower destroying himself out of loneliness.

The song of colors went on for what seemed a long time, though it was only a matter of minutes, and when it faded away into ashes and was stilled, they all sat humbled and silent, wishing they had not heard it.

Stileen revolved slowly in her jar, troubled beyond consolation at the first sound the Gathering had proffered. For the first time in many reborn lifetimes, she felt pain. A sliver of glass driven into her memories. Bringing back the clear, loud sound of a moment when she had rejected one who had loved her. She had driven him to hurt her, and then he had sunk into a deathly melancholy, a silence so deep no words she could summon would serve to bring him back. And when he had gone, she had asked for sleep, and they had given it to her . . . only to bring her life once again, all too soon.

In her jar, she wept.

And she longed for the time when she could let them hear the sound she had found, the sound that would release her at last from the coil of mortality she now realized she despised with all her soul.

After a time, the first delegate—having recovered from DeilBo's offering—ventured forth with its sound. It was an insect creature from a world named Joumell, and this was the sound it had brought:

Far beneath a milky sea on a water world of Joumell's system, there is a vast grotto whose walls are studded with multicolored quartz crystals whose cytoplasmic cell contents duplicate the filament curves of the galaxies NGC

4038 and NGC 4039. When these crystals mate, there is a perceptible encounter that produces tidal tails. The sounds of ecstasy these crystals make when they mate is one long, sustained sigh of rapture that is capped by yet another, slightly higher and separate from the preceding. Then another, and another, until a symphony of crystalline orgasms is produced no animal throats could match.

The insect Joumelli had brought eleven such crystals (the minimum number required for a sexual coupling) from the water world. A cistern formation had been filled with a white crystalline acid, very much like cuminoin; it initiated a cytotaxian movement; a sexual stimulation. The crystals had been put down in the cistern and now they began their mating.

The sound began with a single note, then another joined and overlaid it, then another, and another. The symphony began and modulations rose on modulations, and the delegates closed their eyes—even those who had no eyes—and they basked in the sound, translating it into the sounds of joy of their various species.

And when it was ended, many of the delegates found the affirmation of life permitted them to support the memory of DeilBo's terrible death melody of the flowers.

Many did not.

> ". . . the frequencies of their limits of hearing . . . a calendar going forward and backward but not in time, even though time was the measure of the frequencies as it was the measure of every other thing (therefore, some say, the only measure) . . ."
>
> W. S. Merwin, "The Chart"

She remembered the way they had been when they had first joined energies. It had been like that sound, the wonderful sound of those marvelous crystals.

Stileen turned her azure solution opaque, and let herself drift back on a tide of memory. But the tide retreated, leaving her at the shore of remembrance, where DeilBo's sound still lingered, dark and terrible. She knew that even the trembling threads of joy unforgotten could not sustain her, and she wanted to let them hear what she had brought. There was simply too much pain in the universe, and if she—peculiarly adapted to contain such vast amounts of anguish—could not live with it . . . there must be an end. It was only humane.

She sent out a request to be put on the agenda as soon as possible and DeilBo's butlers advised her she had a time to wait; and as her contact was withdrawn, she brushed past a creature reaching out for a position just after hers. When she touched its mind, it closed off with shocking suddenness. Afraid she had been discourteous, Stileen went away from the creature quickly, and did not reach out again. But in the instant she had touched it, she had glimpsed something . . . something with its face hidden . . . it would not hold . . .

The sounds continued, each delegate presenting a wonder to match the wonders that had gone before.

The delegate from RR Lyrae IV produced the sound of a dream decaying in the mind of a mouselike creature from Bregga, a creature whose dreams formed its only reality. The delegate from RZ Cephei Beta VI followed with the sound of ghosts in the Mountains of the Hand; they spoke of the future and lamented their ability to see what was to come. The delegate from Ennore came next with the sound of red, magnified till it filled the entire universe. The delegate from Gateway offered the sound of amphibious creatures at the moment of their mutation to fully land-living living vertebrates; there was a wail of loss at that moment, as their chromosomes begged for return to the warm, salty sea. The delegate from Algol C XXIII gave them the sounds of war, collected from every race in the stellar community, broken down into their component parts, distilled, purified, and recast as one tone; it was numbing. The delegate from Blad presented a triptych of sound: a sun being born, the same sun coasting through its main stage of hydrogen burning, the sun going nova—a shriek of pain that phased in and out of normal space-time with lunatic vibrations. The delegate from Iobbaggii played a long and ultimately boring sound that was finally identified as a neutrino passing through the universe; when one of the other delegates suggested that sound, being a vibration in a medium, could not be produced by a neutrino passing through vacuum, the Iobbaggiian responded—with pique—that the sound produced had been the sound *within* the neutrino; the querying delegate then said it must have taken a *very* tiny microphone to pick up the sound; the Iobbaggiian stalked out of the Gathering on his eleven-meter stilts. When the uproar died away, the agenda was moved and the delegate from Kruger 60B IX delivered up a potpourri of sounds of victory and satisfaction and joy and innocence and pleasure from a gathering of microscopic species inhabiting a grain of sand in the Big Desert region of Catrimani; it was a patchwork quilt of delights that helped knit together the Gathering. Then the delegate from the Opal Cluster (his specific world's native name was taboo and could not be used) assaulted them with a sound none could identify, and when it had faded away into trembling silence, leaving behind only the memory of cacophony, he told the Gathering that it was the sound of chaos; no one doubted his word. The delegate from Mainworld followed with the sound of a celestial choir composed of gases being blown away from a blue star in a rosette (nebula) ten light-years across; all the angels of antiquity could not have sounded more glorious.

And then it was Stileen's turn, and she readied the sound that would put an end to the Gathering.

> "And beyond—and in fact among—the last known animals living and extinct, the lines could be drawn through white spaces that had an increasing progression of their own, into regions of hearing that was no longer conceivable, indicating creatures wholly sacrificed or never evolved, hearers of the note at which everything explodes into light, and of the continuum that is the standing still of darkness, drums echoing the last shadow without relinquishing the note of the first light, hearkeners to the unborn overflowing."
>
> W. S. Merwin, "The Chart"

"There is no pleasure in this," Stileen communicated, by thought and by inflection. "But it is the sound that I have found, the sound I know you would want me to give to you . . . and you must do with it what you must. I am sorry."

And she played for them the sound.

It was the sound of the death of the universe. The dying gasp of their worlds and their suns and their galaxies and their island universes. The death of all. The final sound.

And when the sound was gone, no one spoke for a long time, and Stileen was at once sad, but content: now the sleep would come, and she would be allowed to rest.

"The delegate is wrong."

The silence hung shrouding the moment. The one who had spoken was a darksmith from Luxann, chief world of the Logomachy. Theologians, pragmatists, reasoners *sans appel,* his words fell with the weight of certainty.

"It is an oscillating universe," he said, his cowl shrouding his face, the words emerging from darkness. "It will die, and it will be reborn. It has happened before, it will happen again."

And the tone of the Gathering grew brighter, even as Stileen's mood spiraled down into despair. She was ambivalent—pleased for them, that they could see an end to their ennui and yet perceive the rebirth of life in the universe—desolate for herself, knowing somehow, some way, she would be recalled from the dead.

And then the creature she had passed in reaching out for her place on the agenda, the creature that had blocked itself to her mental touch, came forward in their minds and said, "There is another sound beyond hers."

This was the sound the creature let them hear, the sound that had *always* been there, that had existed for time beyond time, that could not be heard though the tone was always with them; and it could be heard now only because it existed as it passed through the instrument the creature made of itself.

It was the sound of reality, and it sang of the end *beyond* the end, the final and total end that said without possibility of argument, *there will be no rebirth because we have never existed.*

Whatever they had thought they were, whatever arrogance had brought their dream into being, it was now coming to final moments, and beyond those moments there was nothing.

No space, no time, no life, no thought, no gods, no resurrection and rebirth.

The creature let the tone die away, and those who could reach out with their minds to see what it was, were turned back easily. It would not let itself be seen.

The messenger of eternity had only anonymity to redeem itself . . . for whom?

And for Stileen, who did not even try to penetrate

the barriers, there was no pleasure in the knowledge that it had all been a dream. For if it had been a dream, then the joy had been a dream, as well.

It was not easy to go down to emptiness, never having tasted joy. But there was no appeal.

In the Maelstrom Labyrinth, there was no longer ennui.

Introduction to From A to Z, in the Chocolate Alphabet

Nine years ago, letting my mind idle one day, I typed up a group of titles I thought I'd sometime like to write stories around. One of them was "The Chocolate Alphabet." I had no idea what that meant; it just sounded good. I typed ten titles in all on that piece of paper. Over nine years I wrote nine of the ten stories. "The Chocolate Alphabet" was the last title on that sheet. The paper was torn off as I wrote each story until all I had left was a yellowing corner of paper with those three words on it. Fade out; fade in: Three years ago I was visited by San Francisco underground comix magnate Ron Turner and the extraordinary artist Larry Todd. You will remember Todd as the man who worked with the late Vaughn Bodé on so many projects, as the man who developed his own remarkable talent, and who now is considered one of America's premier visual technicians. They visited for the day, and asked me if I would write an eight-page comic story to be used in one of the books Larry was doing for Ron at Last Gasp Eco-Funnies. As Larry was the man who created the dynamite strip "Dr. Atomic," I said I'd be pleased to take a stab at it. Larry then gave me a four-color cover painting and suggested I write the story around it. (You will find that segment of the Chocolate Alphabet I wrote to go with the cover as *N is for NEMOTROPIN*.) The title of Larry's painting was "2 Nemotropin." Well, one thing and another happened, and the cover painting stood against the wall in my office for two years, and I never wrote the story. Fade out; fade in: in February of 1976, I offered to try something that had never been done before. . . . I like doing that kind of thing . . . it upsets people. What I offered to do was to sit in the front window of a bookstore for a full week, and to attempt to write a complete story each day for six days. The store I offered to do this gig for is the famous sf shop in Los Angeles, *A Change of Hobbit* (1371 Westwood Blvd., dial 213-GREAT SF), owned and operated by Sherry Gottlieb and a staff of bright, enthusiastic young sf fans. The promotional gimmick was that anyone who bought over $10 worth of books on any given day that I was in the window, would get an autographed copy of that day's story. Six days, six stories, sixty bucks' worth of merchandise. Gift certificates could be purchased against future merchandise. On the sixth day, Sherry scheduled a big Saturday autograph party at which all six of the *original* manuscripts would be offered for auction. The stories were bound together with whatever source material had first prompted me to think of each story, and the entire package would go to the highest bidder, proceeds to help support the store. (We here in Los Angeles who work in the genre feel very protective about A Change of Hobbit, and we like to help out when we can.) The first day I wrote a 300-word story titled "Strange Wine," which appeared in the 50th Anniversary issue of *Amazing Stories*. That was Monday, February 23rd. As I prepared to leave my home for the store on Tuesday morning, February 24th—with no idea what I would write that day—I saw the painting Larry Todd had left with me two years before. Flashback: Two weeks earlier, LA had had the worst rainstorm in years, after many months of drought. Because I was having an addition to my office built and because they had ripped out the footing around my office (which is in my home) so they could break out a wall to extend the room, my office was flooded and everything resting on the carpet was soaked. Larry's painting was one of those items. So I wanted to write the story and get the painting back to Larry as quickly as possible for repair. I took the now-waterlogged and furled painting with me to the store, climbed up in the front window, and stared at the two alien creatures having a duel. That was what "2 Nemotropin" was—a pair of lobsterlike aliens banging away at each other. I knew that would be Tuesday's story, but I had no idea what it would be. I sat for an hour and a half before the idea came to me that I couldn't think of an eight-page story that could be visually adapted to an underground comix book, that would also hold together as a publishable story, written around that damned cover (which I was now coming to despise). Suddenly, I remembered that title, "The Chocolate Alphabet." I have no idea why it came to me just then. But it did. And I knew instantly that though I couldn't write a long story about those warring aliens, I *could* do a sort of Fredric Brown short-short, a pastiche. And then I carried the thought a little further and thought *Why not 26 pastiches?* And I typed on the cover sheet of the manuscript, "From A to Z, in the Chocolate Alphabet." Sadly, the idea was too big for one day. I was scheduled to sit in the Hobbit's window from 10:30 A.M., when the store opens, till 5:00 when Sherry Gottlieb goes off duty (though the store stays open till 9:00). I wrote all that day, and by 5:00 I was up to H. Sherry went home. I kept on writing. By 11:00 that night, with the cops cruising past and shining their spots into the window trying to figure out what that idiot was doing in there, I was up to R. I couldn't keep my eyes open. My back was breaking. Cramped in that damned window, I was spacing out. A day of having pedestrians gawking, of customers bugging me when I wanted to write, of having to think up a complete story for each letter of the alphabet had taken its toll. I crapped out and went home. I worked on another project I had in my typewriter at the office, a fantasy film script for ABC-TV, and finally got to bed about 2:30 A.M. I got up at 8:00 the next morning, went back to the typewriter to work on the script, and about 9:30, when I should have gone in to take my shower and get ready to go to the store, I suddenly thought what S should be. I didn't get in to the Hobbit till 11:30 but I was on U at that point. I finished the story on Wednesday, the 25th of February, a little after 1:30 P.M., and sent it off that night to Ed Ferman for publication in *The Magazine of Fantasy and Science Fiction,* as well as copies to Larry Todd and Ron Turner for translation into a comix book. Instead of giving Larry a story, I'd given him the crazy problem of illustrating *twenty-six* stories. And that, peculiar as it may seem, is how this story was written.

Since that first writing-in-the-maelstrom stint, I've found occasion to repeat the practice. It's becoming a filthy habit, but damned if I don't get a lot of work done. I'm frequently asked how I can work under such conditions; conditions that other writers would find impossible to produce under. I wasn't equipped to give a competent answer for quite a while. As Irwin Shaw put it once, "Honesty is not the issue. Understanding is." I just shrugged and said, "I like to write, and when I write, the world I go into, the world of the story, is more real to me than the one where I sit doing the writing." Then I ran across a quote from Barzun, and it explained the sensibility better than I could myself. I offer it here to answer all those who think one should, or can, only work in the Ivory Tower.

"[It is not] enough to pay attention to words only when you face the task of writing—that is like playing the violin only on the night of the concert. You must attend the words when you read, when you speak, when others speak. Words must become ever present in your waking life, an incessant concern, like color and design if the graphic arts matter to you, or pitch and rhythm if it is music, or speed and form if it is athletics. Words, in short, must be *there*, not unseen and unheard, as they probably are and have been up to now. It is proper for the ordinary reader to absorb the meaning of a story or description as if the words were a transparent sheet of glass. But he can do so only because the writer has taken pains to choose and adjust them with care. They were not glass to him, but mere lumps of potential meaning. He had to weigh them and fuse them before his purposed meaning could shine through."

Jacques Barzun, 1975

From A to Z, in the Chocolate Alphabet

A is for ATLANTEAN

Their science predicted the quake. There had been two centuries of warning temblors. With the acid of genetic engineering they began a return to the ocean. It would not be a lost continent; it would be an abandoned continent. And throughout the ages that followed, humankind would search for "lost" Atlantis, never realizing that when the earth split and the fires of the underworld seared the land, the Atlanteans would already have developed gill breathing and useful membranes. See, then: Krenoa, capital city of undersea Atlantis. Snug and secure at the bottom of the Maracot Deep. Towers of porphyry and malachite, lit with lambent flames from within; walls of seaweeds and kelp, altered by chemical means to retain their flexibility yet suitable for buildings; flying bridges and causeways all hollow and shimmering. Krenoa, beautiful beyond belief. And lying in a public square, an enormous lead cannister, split open and holding darkness. An alien object dropped into Krenoa from above. See, now: the Atlanteans. Pale blue and great-eyed, gentle expressions and wisdom in their open, staring, dead eyes. What God and Nature could not destroy, the inheritors of the Earth did.

B is for BREATHDEATH

It's waiting for them when they reach space. It grows on virtually every world but the Earth. It is common as weed. The little black flower with the soft red bulb in its center. Its spores fill the atmosphere of gray planets circling yellow stars and burned-out cinders. When the last of the atmosphere has been drawn off into space, the spores will settle. But they will still kill. It is a lovely flower. If one stares into its center one can see many things, disturbing things. Until the aneurisms stop the visions and the blood bursts forth. There is a race on a far star that believes the breathdeath can be ground up and cut with various juices and consumed, and it will give eternal life. No one has ever tried the recipe. It waits.

C is for CUSHIO

When he was ten, he was savaged by a forest creature they had thought extinct thousands of years before. They killed the beast and put it on display in the largest museum of their world. The boy was taken to Regeneration and they rebuilt him with machine parts and soft things that had been flesh in other bodies. He grew up half-human, and thus never understood what humans wanted. He killed his first when he was fifteen. By his twenty-first year he ruled the continent with a guard of mercenaries as ruthless as himself. He went into space with an armada at the age of thirty and left behind him a route of road markers that had been lives and cities and thriving markets. The route of embers and mass graves. They stopped him near Aldebaran and space was littered with wreckage beyond the range of even the most sensitive sensors. They took him alive, and they encased him in amber and they imbedded him in the earth of the homeworld, with cameras that never shut down and never let him out of their sight. And there he stayed, forever. The Regenerators of his world had done their work well. He would live forever. And mothers of the homeworld, who desired their children to go to sleep, invoked the name of Cushio. They said, "Cushio will take you if you don't do good." And the children were too young to know that could never be.

D is for DIKH

He is sick. He writes his books in the lowest level of a deep labyrinthine grotto. His books are filled with things no one ever wanted to know. Unsettling things. He became part mushroom many years ago, but even the small lizards who come and feed off his body never realize he was once a man. If he were on a desert island he would write his awful stories and send them out in bottles. But there, deep in the grotto, no one will ever read a word he has written; written with shards of sharpened stone in the blood of lizards; written on walls that go deep into the earth. But one day they will need fossil fuels, and they will break through a wall of his grotto, and they will find the books, written on endless walls. And they will find the thing with a tormented face, growing in the moist soil of the underworld.

E is for ELEVATOR PEOPLE

They never speak, and they cannot meet your gaze. There are five hundred buildings in the United States whose elevators go deeper than the basement. When you have pressed the basement button and reached bottom, you must press the basement button twice more. The elevator doors will close and you will hear the sound of special relays being thrown, and the elevator will descend. Into the caverns. Chance has not looked favorably on occasional voyagers in those five hundred cages. They have pressed the wrong button, too many times. They have been seized by those who shuffle through the caverns, and they have been . . . treated. Now they ride the cages. They never speak, and they cannot meet your gaze. They stare up at the numbers as they light and then go off, riding up and down even after night has fallen. Their clothes are clean. There is a special dry cleaner who does the work. Once you saw one of them, and her eyes were filled with screams. London is a city filled with narrow, secure stairways.

F is for FLENSER

Among all the paranormals, the flensers are the most kind. They read minds, they are empathic, and they see all the anguish in those they pass. They wipe clean the slates of the minds they encounter. And for this, they suffer a great isolation. They are the pale people whose socks fall down, the ones you see standing on street corners. They are the ones with pimples and odd conversation. Theirs is a terribly lonely existence. Every day they crucify themselves, endlessly, over and over. Be kind to the pale old ladies and the mumbling scrawny boys you pass in the drugstore. They may save you from the terrors of your past.

G is for GOLEM

Golems are *goyim* that always wanted to be Jewish. But they never suffered enough guilt.

H is for HAMADRYAD

The Oxford English Dictionary has three definitons of hamadryad. The first is: a wood nymph that lives and dies in her tree. The second is: a venomous, hooded serpent of India. The third definition is improbable. None of them mentions the mythic origins of the word. The tree in which the Serpent lived was the hamadryad. Eve was poisoned. The wood of which the cross was made was the hamadryad. Jesus did not rise, he never died. The ark was composed of cubits of lumber from the hamadryad. You will find no sign of the vessel on top of Mt. Ararat. It sank. Toothpicks in Chinese restaurants should be avoided at all costs.

I is for ICE CRAWLER

When the exit from the polar icecap was sealed by nukes and thermite, a few of them managed to escape. They were tracked by land and by air, but their thick white skins concealed them from all but chance discovery. With the end of the supply of good skins, the fashion died quickly and the return of stripped corduroy-and-velour soon followed. Those that had escaped found channels in the permafrost and tried to return to their land. They had never known violence, it had come to them slowly, only as a desperate last measure; and only a few had learned the lesson well enough to crawl back to their blasted domain. The hunting parties that had come after them had slaughtered thousands before there was the slightest retaliation. At first they had believed the warm people from the light had come to establish relations. But when their piping language fell on deaf ears, and the harpoons were thrown, they knew they had been discovered to their ultimate undoing. Those who survived crawled back and ate out burrows for their dead. Then they slithered away from that place to a deeper level and began to breed. They would teach their children what they had learned. And perhaps one day they would wear fashionable skins . . . in four or five different colors.

J is for JABBERWOCK

India conceals many secrets. In the Hindu Kush there is a monastery far back in the low mountains where a sect of monks worship the last Jabberwock. It is a fearsome creature: much smaller than one would expect from reading *Alice.* It has bat wings whose membranes between the struts are tattered and torn. It is morbidly bloody in color and covered with bristly fur from its shoulders to its buttocks. It resembles a bat-eared, winged jackal with incredibly sharp teeth and one good eye. The other eye has two pupils and is a most malevolent thing to behold. Its claws can tear rock, and it screams constantly. The monks are the holiest of holy men. They have tried to mate the Jabberwock to preserve its presence in their midst. They have mated it with a pig and produced a thing that can neither walk nor see. They have mated it with a camel and the offspring was born dead but would not decay. They mated it with swans, with ibis, with auks, and with jackals. The monks keep the children of these unions in glass cages, but they seldom go to look. They mated it with a young girl, a virgin stolen from a small village. The girl died but the child still lives. They must change the soft cloth in the bottom of its nest three times a day. It sweats blood. The holy monks hope they will be able to find a mate for the Jabberwock before another hundred years passes. What they do not know is that the Jabberwock has sentience, it is a thinking, feeling creature for all its awesome menace. What they do not know is what the Jabberwock thinks, what it wishes. The Jabberwock wishes it were dead.

K is for KENGHIS KHAN

He was a very *nice* person. History has no record of him. There is a moral in that, somewhere.

L is for LOUP-GAROU

Had Śasa Novácek's parents come to America from Ireland or Sweden or even Poland, he would not have realized that the woman next door was a werewolf. But they had come from Ostrava, in Czechoslovakia, and he recognized the shape of the nostrils, the hair in the palms of her hands when she loaned him a cup of nondairy creamer, the definitive S-curve of the spine as she walked to hang her laundry. So he was ready. He had bought a thirty-aught-six hunting rifle and he had melted down enough twenty-five-cent pieces to make his own silver bullets. And the night of the full moon, when the madness was upon her, and she burst through the kitchen window in a snarling strike of fangs and fur, he was ready for her. Calmly, with full presence, and murmuring the names of the very best saints, he emptied the rifle into her. Later, the coroner was unable to describe the condition of Śasa Novácek's body on a single form sheet. The coin of the United States of America, notably the twenty-five-cent piece, the quarter, has less than one percent pure silver in it. Times change, but legends do not.

M is for MUU MUU

One should always wear one if one has more than six or seven arms.

N is for NEMOTROPIN

Irl and Onkadj were the last to enter the Tunnel of Final Darkness. The competition had been more fierce this Contest than any nemotropin could remember. The gladiators had fallen, spears in their thoracic vitals, mandibles shattered, eyestalks ripped out, claws sliced off . . . until only Irl and Onkadj had survived. Now they were closed off in the Tunnel to decide which of them would have to suffer the penalty. The Contest among the nemotropin was the only way they had to rid themselves of undesirables. And as the nemotropin were universally judged the most evil, warlike race in the galaxy, the level of undesirability was a marvel even to the most vicious brigands and hellspawned marauders. They were forced to produce everything they needed for their existence; no other planet or confederation of planets would undertake to trade with them. They were staked off-limits and permitted to breed and kill and live as best they could. But they could not leave their nameless world. With one exception. Thousands of years before, a mission from the Heart Stars Federation had come to their world and had tried to civilize the nemotropin. Just before the missionaries had been slaughtered and masticated, they had been granted the right to send one of the nemotropin off-world. The mission had no way of knowing that time and ritual would alter this grant as an excuse for the nemotropin to weed out those even too despicable for existence in a society of killers and reavers. The nemotropin were at least sane enough never to reveal the nature of their awful duplicity. And so, periodically, they would hold the Contest, and the worst of their number would slaughter and slay and attack each other till only one was left standing. And he would be sent to the shape-changing satellite the Federation maintained, and would be sent to the pilgrim world where he could do no more harm among the nemotropin. And so Irl and Onkadj went into the Tunnel of Final Darkness with their shell shields covering the soft vulnerable spot beneath which rested the gliomas of their brains. Irl wielded a pair of cutters, and a brace of poison bags was strapped to his right side, protecting his wounds from earlier battles. Should Onkadj strike in that area, the bags would spurt poison and kill the attacker. Onkadj was the younger of the combatants, and without peer in use of the broiler spear. Helmeted, their hooves coated with retardant to keep them from slipping on the mossy stones of the Tunnel, they faced each other and the final combat began. It raged for three days and three nights, and on the morning of the fourth day, Onkadj emerged without one of his four arms, but carrying Irl's lower mandible. He was sent to the shape-changing satellite, made malleable, altered into the form of the superior indigenous life form of the host planet, and sent away. On the host planet, Onkadj did quite well. It was a very different world than that of the nemotropin, and Onkadj functioned well in the body. He became a prominent figure. There *is* an explanation for Attila, for Haman, for Cortez, for Cesare Borgia, for Christie and Specht and Manson and Nixon. For Torquemada. But only the nemotropin know the explanation. And they smile as best they can with bloody mandibles.

O is for OUROBOROS

Banished from the Earth, the great worm coiled ever so tightly and went to sleep. One day he will awake. The moon will writhe.

P is for POLTERGEIST

Essentially very well-coordinated. Very few people remember, because of the Black Sox scandal, but in 1919 the Chicago White Sox carried a pitcher named Fred Morris who won thirty games; pitched seven perfect no-hit, no-run games; struck out twenty-five batters in one contest; and replaced every divot in the outfield without moving from home plate. He played only one season; his heart was broken when Shoeless Joe Jackson turned up a creep, and he inexplicably vanished from whence he came. He was a poltergeist with a whole lot of love for the sport. Hardly anyone today remembers Fred Morris.

Q is for QUETZALCOATL

He did not come from space. He was not an alien. He did not build Toltec or even Aztec pyramids as landing beacons for flying saucers. His most obvious bad habit was a rather nasty appetite for freshly excised, still-pulsing hearts. It is not true what they say about Quetzalcoatl and the virgins. Take it or leave it.

R is for ROQ

The flying city of Detroit (it's up there) was in the midst of its Founder's Day celebration when the great golden roq came to feed. It settled down over the Caliph's Dome (where the roller derby semifinals were in progress) and thrust its ebony beak through the formed plastic and steel girdering. It dipped again and again, bringing up masses of writhing spectators (and blocker "Rumpy" Johansson), their screams feeding into the p.a. system and causing an overload. The great bird's appetite could hardly be satisfied with a few sports fans, however. It rose on enormous, beating pinions, its pink tongue vibrating and its shriek of joy shattering all the facets of the Esso Tetrahedron. The roq's shadow swam across the gigantic flying metropolis as the bird dove on the Servitor Factory. What could have made it seek out such an inedible attraction no one in Detroit (or even Bombay, floating over there a little way off) could ever say. But it settled and began to eat the entire plant, robot parts and all. And when it had finished consuming the Factory, and the millions of individual bits of incipient robot, it slaked its thirst in the Crystal Falls for the better part of a day. And when, hours later, it fell (crushing a whole lot of stuff), and it died, the residents of Detroit were stunned and waxed extremely wroth. The great golden roq of the sky had rusted itself to death and the meat wasn't worth a damn thing, not even for hot-dog casings.

S is for SOLIFIDIAN THE SORCERER

I was an invited guest at the elegant fund-raising party where Solifidian performed his miracles. I'd received the engraved invitation to the party several weeks earlier, but had not planned to RSVP because I knew they'd be hitting us up for contributions to the political war chest of a city councilman whose position on rapid transit I considered really fucked. But Penny Goldman called first, and tried to embarrass me into coming, and when that didn't work Leslie Parrish called and said it had been so long since she'd seen me, why didn't I stop being a poop, and just come to the party; and I wanted to see Leslie again, so I went. It was held at Larry Niven's new home out in Tarzana, and Larry and Marilyn had really outdone themselves in setting up the buffet and hiring the caterers to erect the big party tent on the grounds out back. The minute I came through the door, a committee worker for the councilman handed me a pledge card, which I promptly folded and put in my side jacket pocket. I'd probably give the slob some bucks, but I'd make damned sure I spent a few minutes telling him if he didn't get off his ass and start formulating plans for a new rapid transit district in Los Angeles he was going to find himself facing a *new* committee . . . one I'd form to beat his backside at election time. So I wandered around and made smalltalk with people I knew, and tried to corner Leslie, who was buzzing around doing organizational things; and finally the entertainment started in the tent. George Carlin and Richard Pryor took turns ruining my mind, and then they got together and did an ad lib routine in tandem, which had to be the funniest thing since Jack Lemmon delivered the line "Leslie the Great escaped with a *chicken!?!*" in *The Great Race*. Then there was a break while Tom Hensley got set up with the Roto-Rooter Good Time Christmas Band, and I saw Solifidian for the first time. He looked just like Mandrake the Magician. He was about seven feet tall and as thin as a Watergate alibi; he had one of those hairline mustaches that always made me think of Simon Legree in a stage production of *Uncle Tom's Cabin;* and he had the slimmest, whitest, most beautiful hands I'd ever seen. Brain surgeon fingers with polished nails. He wore a tux with tails, and a top hat. If I'd owned a diner, I'd have hired him on the spot as a sandwich-board man. And after Tom's band had blown everyone away, Solifidian was introduced by "the Candidate" himself, and the sorcerer—because that was what he clearly was—asked the audience to tell him their most secret desires. Nothing big, just something that was personally important to each person. At first no one would speak up, but finally a woman said, "I have a very painful, difficult period every month. Can you do anything about that?" Everyone was startled, and a little embarrassed, but when I realized it was Georgina Voss I smiled; she'd say *any*thing. But Solifidian didn't seem to think it was outrageous, and he pointed a long white finger at her and said, "I think you'll find it all better now." Querulously, Georgina looked at him, and then a big smile came over her face, and she stood up and said, "Oh, my *God!*" and, laughing like a loon, she rushed off into Larry's house, presumably to the bathroom, to check herself. But no one in the crowd doubted that Solifidian had rearranged her parts so she wasn't in pain. Then I heard a man's voice say, "I can't get a decent shave. My beard is like barbed wire and my skin is like a baby's instep," and I suddenly recognized the voice as my own. "When I even use an electric razor I cut myself and get ingrown hairs and then I look like a forty-two-year-old kid with acne. Can you take care of that, sir?" Solifidian nodded, pointed a finger at me and, as everyone gasped in awe (and not a little horror), every follicle on my face wormed its way out of my skin, carrying with it the root and whatever it is that makes the hair grow back. It all fell on my jacket, and I brushed it off, and rubbed my jaw, and I was as smooth as if I'd just come from the barber at the Plaza Hotel in New York. I led the applause. There was more, much more. He performed a dozen similar miracles in the space of mere minutes. He gave one woman a sensational nose job, made a talent agent's penis larger, cured one guy's color blindness, gave Bill Rotsler back the sense of smell, and restored hair to the bald pate of the Candidate. He was amazing, this *miracle worker*. Never saw anything like it. He was in the middle of performing a vasectomy on Marty Shapiro when a stout woman wearing an improbable hat came stalking into the midst of the crowd. She stood there staring at him, this *miracle worker,* with her chubby hands on her hips until he was finished. And when he looked around to see who was next and he saw her, his face fell. "So this is where you are, you asshole," she snarled. He began to fumfuh and wave his hands around helplessly. "Harry Solifidian, get your lazy ass in gear! There's work to be done at the house, and no time for you to be fooling around with these schmucks! Now come *on!*" He looked sheepish, this *miracle worker,* but he followed her docilely.

They walked through the crowd, which parted for them without a murmur, and in a moment they were gone. And that was that. And I never saw him again. But, you know, to this day I'm always amazed at the magic hold some men have over some women . . . and the magic hold some women have over some men.

T is for TROGLODYTE

They live under the city dump and they can eat almost anything except plastic containers. If it weren't for the troglodytes, we'd be *tuchis*-deep in garbage. There is a whole lot to be said for returnable glass bottles.

U is for UPHIR

Demon chemist and doctor, well-versed in knowledge of medicinal herbs, responsible for the health of demons, official apothecary and surgeon to the Court of Satan, Uphir recently had a rather unpleasant experience. Semiazas, chief of the fallen angels with Azazel (no need to go into the subject of office politics), came down with a serious charley horse in his tail. Uphir was called in, diagnosed the problem, and applied the traditional incantations and a poultice of mole paws and liverwort. Just to be on the safe side, he gave Semiazas a shot of penicillin. How was he to know the demon was allergic to mole paws. An unlovely reaction, made even worse by the penicillin. Without volition, Semiazas began to make it snow in Hell. Instantly, hundreds of thousands of foolish promises, idle boasts, dire threats, and contracts Satan had made containing the phrase "It'll be a cold day in Hell" (on which he never thought he'd have to deliver) came true. Uphir was punished by being submerged to his nose in a lake of monkey vomit, while a squad of imps raced motorboats around him, making waves. California is not the only place where it's difficult to get malpractice insurance.

V is for VORWALAKA

Count Carlo Szipesti, a *vorwalaka,* a vampire, having long since grown weary of stalking alleyways and suffering the vicissitudes of finding meals in the streets, hied himself to a commune in upstate New York where, with his beard, his accent, and his peculiar nocturnal habits, he fit right in with the young people who had joined together for a return to the land. For the Count, it was a guaranteed fountain of good, healthy blood. The young people in the commune were very big on bean sprouts and hulled sunflower seeds. They were all tanned from working in the fields and the blood ran hot and vibrant in their veins. When the Count was found dead, the coroner's inquest did not reveal that he had been a creature of darkness, one of the dread vampires of the old country; what it *did* reveal was that he had died from infectious hepatitis. As the *Journal of the American Medical Association* has often pointed out, health is inextricably involved with morality.

W is for WAND OF JACOB

Alfred Jacobi, seventy-two years old and nearly blind, was accosted at one o'clock in the morning on the Sheridan Square station platform of the IRT subway. His grandchildren, Emily and Foster and Hersch, had been yelling at Alfred for years: "Why do you go out walking in this awful city late at night? Crazy old man, you'll be mugged, killed. What's the matter with you?" But Alfred Jacobi had lived in New York for sixty of his seventy-two years, and he believed in the God of his forefathers, and—miraculously it seemed—he had never suffered even a moment's unpleasantness in the streets. Even though New York had become a prowling ground for the most detestable human predators urban America had ever produced, Alfred Jacobi was able to walk where he wished, even in Central Park at midnight, *kene hora,* tapping his way gently with his specially carved cane, painted white to indicate he could not see. But neither the cane nor his age deterred the gang of young toughs with cans of spray paint who paused in their systematic defacement of white tile walls and poster advertisements to attack the old man. They came at him in a bunch, and he extended his cane, and there was a bright flash of light. And Alfred Jacobi was alone on the platform once more. The Wand of Jacob, the stick which preceded the magic wand, that forces spirits to appear or repulses them as did Moses' rod, his Wand of Jacob was still fully charged. If one ventures down onto the Sheridan Square platform of the IRT, one can see a most marvelous example of native artwork. It is a frieze, apparently rendered by an unsung urban Michelangelo in spray paint, in many colors, extremely lifelike, of a gang of young men, screaming in horror. It's a refreshing break from all the obscenities and self-advertisements for CHICO 116 one finds in the New York subway system.

X is for XAPHAN

Demon of the second order. At the time of the rebellion of the angels, *he* proposed that the heavens be set on fire. For his perfidy he has forevermore stoked the furnaces of Hell. It is never good to have dissatisfied help working in one's company. Xaphan is steadily overloading the boilers. Pay attention to stories about the melting polar ice cap. Xaphan is programming for Armageddon, and there's not a damn thing we can do about it.

Y is for YGGDRASIL

The legendary Nordic ash tree with its three roots extending into the lands of mortals, giants, and Niflheim, the land of mist, grows in Wisconsin. Legend has it that when the tree falls, the universe will fall. Next Wednesday, the State Highway Commission comes through that empty pasture with a freeway.

Z is for ZOMBIE

Howard Hughes did not die in 1976, no matter *what* they tell you. Howard Hughes died in 1968. It was not a spectacular death, down in flames in the *Spruce Goose* or assassinated by his next-in-command or frightened to death by an insect that found its way into his eyrie. He choked to death on a McDonald's greaseburger during dinner one night in July of 1968. But wealth has its privileges. Johns Hopkins and the Mayo Clinic and the Walter Reed in Maryland sent their teams. But he was dead. DOA, Las Vegas. And he was buried. Not in 1976, in 1968. And Mama Legba, with whom Hughes had made a deal twenty years earlier in Haiti, came to the grave, and she raised him. The corporate entity is mightier than death. But the end is near: at this very moment, training in the Sierra Maestra, is an attack squad of Fidel Castro's finest guerrillas. They know where Hughes went when he evacuated Nicaragua one week before the earthquake. (Zombies have precognitive faculties, did you know that?) And they know the 1976 death story is merely misdirection like all the other death rumors throughout the preceding years. They will seek him out and put him to *final* rest by the only means ever discovered for deanimating the walking dead. They will pour sand in his eyes, stuff a dead chicken in his mouth, and sew up the mouth with sailcloth twine. It would take a mission this important to get the fierce Cuban fighters to suffer all the ridicule: bayonet practice with dead chickens is terribly demeaning.

Introduction to Lonely Women Are the Vessels of Time

Had this really weird, essentially ugly evening at the University of Rochester (New York) last April. Several persons of a genetically female persuasion had maneuvered the otherwise sane and exemplary U. of Rochester Women's Caucus into an attempt to ban the film version of my story "A Boy and His Dog" on the grounds that it was violently sexist and anti-female.

I'm not going to go into all that. It was a night that only reaffirmed my conviction that the mass of humans, male and female alike, are what the late Bruce Elliott called "genetic garbage." Ugly statement. I won't argue the point. All I wish is that *you* had been there. Kee-*rist!* Madness.

It's mentioned here solely to keynote the point that for a writer in Our Time, trying to write as honestly and even-handedly as he or she can, it is impossible to write *anything* that doesn't infuriate one pressure group or another, large or small. Even if one cares passionately and believes in the validity of some Movement, one can be, at best, only a fellow traveler; and that smacks of sycophancy. So either the writer avoids writing any damned thing that might affront, or gets past a kind of universal knee-jerk Liberalism and cops to the truth that we are all pretty much alike, male and female, black and white, young and old, ugly and lovely. Pretty much alike in our ownership of human emotions, needs, drives, failings. And tries to write about the human heart in conflict with itself as truly as one can.

And if that means stomping on the feet of men or women belonging to this ethnic or cultural group or that . . . well, I've never thought for a moment I was going to die with the reputation of being one of America's most beloved figures. It ain't in the cards. I'd rather be honest than chic, anyhow. (He said, looking over his shoulder.)

•

"The arts serve purposes beyond themselves; the purposes of what they dramatize or represent at that remove from the flux which gives them order and meaning and value; and to deny these purposes is like asserting that the function of a handsaw is to hang above a bench and that to cut wood is to belittle it."

Richard P. Blackmur, *A Critic's Job of Work*

Lonely Women Are the Vessels of Time

After the funeral, Mitch went to Dynamite's. It was a singles' bar. Vernon, the day-shift bartender, had Mitch's stool reserved, waiting for him. "I figured you'd be in," he said, mixing up a Tia Maria Cooler and passing it across the bar. "Sorry about Anne." Mitch nodded and sipped off the top of the drink. He looked around Dynamite's; it was too early in the day, even for a Friday; there wasn't much action. A few dudes getting the best corners at the inlaid-tile and stained-glass bar, couples in the plush back booths stealing a few minutes before going home to their wives and husbands. It was only three o'clock and the secretaries didn't start coming in till five thirty. Later, Dynamite's would be pulsing with the chatter and occasional shriek of laughter, the chatting-up and the smell of hot bodies circling each other for the kill. The traditional mating ritual of the singles' bar scene.

He saw one girl at a tiny deuce, way at the rear, beside the glass-fronted booth where the d.j. played his disco rock all night, every night. But she was swathed in shadow, and he wasn't up to hustling anybody at the moment, anyhow. But he marked her in his mind for later.

He sipped at the Cooler, just thinking about Anne, until a space salesman from the *Enquirer,* whom he knew by first name but not by last, plopped himself onto the next stool and started laying a commiseration trip on him about Anne. He wanted to turn to the guy and simply say, "Look, fuck off, will you; she was just a Friday night pick-up who hung on a little longer than most of them; so stop busting my chops and get lost." But he didn't. He listened to the bullshit as long as he could, then he excused himself and took what was left of the Cooler, and a double Cutty-&-water, and trudged back to a booth. He sat there in the semidarkness trying to figure out why Anne had killed herself, and couldn't get a handle on the question.

He tried to remember *exactly* what she had looked like, but all he could bring into focus was the honey-colored hair and her height. The special smile was gone. The tilt of the head and the hand movement when she was annoyed . . . gone. The exact timbre of her voice . . . gone. All of it was gone, and he knew he should be upset about it, but he wasn't.

He hadn't loved her; had, in fact, been ready to dump her for that BOAC hostess. But she had left a note pledging her undying love, and he knew he ought to feel some deep responsibility for her death.

But he didn't.

What it was all about, dammit, was not being lonely. It was all about getting as much as one could, as best as one could, from as many different places as one could, without having to be alone, without having to be unhappy, without having them sink their fangs in too deeply.

That, dammit, was what it was all about.

He thought about the crap a libber had laid on him in this very bar only a week ago. He had been chatting-up a girl who worked for a surety underwriters firm, letting her bore him with a lot of crap about contract bonds, probate, temporary restraining orders and suchlike nonsense, but never dropping his gaze from those incredible green eyes, when Anne had gotten pissed-off and come over to suggest they leave.

He had been abrupt with her. Rude, if he wanted to be honest with himself, and had told her to go back and sit down till he was ready. The libber on the next stool had laid into him, whipping endless jingoism on him, telling him what a shithead he was.

"Lady, if you don't like the way the system works, why not go find a good clinic where they'll graft a dork on you, and then you won't have to bother people who're minding their own business."

The bar had given him a standing ovation.

The Cutty tasted like sawdust. The air in the bar smelled like mildew. His body didn't fit. He turned this way and that, trying to find a comfortable position. Why the hell did he feel lousy? Anne, that was why. But he wasn't responsible. She'd known it was frolic, nothing more than frolic. She'd known that from the moment they'd met. She hadn't been fresh to these bars, she was a swinger, what was all the *sturm und drang* about! But he felt like shit, and that was the bottom line.

"Can I buy you a drink?" the girl said.

Mitch looked up. It seemed to be the girl from the deuce in the rear.

She was incredible. Cheekbones like cut crystal; a full lower lip. Honey hair . . . again. Tall, willowy, with a good chest and fine legs. "Sure. Sit down."

She sat and pushed a double Cutty-&-water at him. "The bartender told me what you were drinking."

Four hours later—and he still hadn't learned her name—she got around to suggesting they go back to her place. He followed her out of the bar, and she hailed a cab. In the back seat he looked at her, lights flickering on and off in her blue eyes as the street lamps whizzed past, and he said, "It's nice to meet a girl who doesn't waste time."

"I gather you've been picked up before," she replied. "But then, you're a very nice-looking man."

"Why, thank you."

At her apartment in the East Fifties, they had a few more drinks; the usual preparatory ritual. Mitch was starting to feel it, getting a little wobbly. He refused a refill. He wanted to be able to perform. He knew the rules. Get it up or get the hell out.

So they went into the bedroom.

He stopped and stared at the set-up. She had it hung with white, sheer hangings, tulle perhaps, some kind of very fine netting. White walls, white ceiling, white carpet so thick and deep he lost his ankles in it. And an enormous circular bed, covered with white fur.

"Polar bear," he said, laughing a little drunkenly.

"The color of loneliness," she said.

"What?"

"Nothing, forget it," she said, and began to undress him.

She helped him lie down, and he stared at her as she took off her clothes. Her body was pale and filled with light; she was an ice maiden from a far magical land. He felt himself getting hard.

Then she came to him.

When he awoke, she was standing at the other side of the room, watching him. Her eyes were no longer a lovely blue. They were dark and filled with smoke. He felt . . .

He felt . . . awful. Uncomfortable, filled with vague terrors and a limitless desperation. He felt . . . lonely.

"You don't hold nearly as much as I thought," she said.

He sat up, tried to get out of the bed, the sea of white, and could not. He lay back and watched her.

Finally, after a time of silence, she said, "Get up and get dressed and get out of here."

He did it, with difficulty, and as he dressed, sluggishly

and with the loneliness in him growing, choking his mind and physically causing him to tremble, she told him things he did not want to know.

About the loneliness of people that makes them do things they hate the next day. About the sickness to which people are heir, the sickness of being without anyone who truly cares. About the predators who smell out such victims and use them and, when they go, leave them emptier than when they first picked up the scent. And about herself, the vessel that contained the loneliness like smoke, waiting only for empty containers such as Mitch to decant a little of the poison, waiting only to return some of the pain for pain given.

What she was, where she came from, what dark land had given her birth, he did not know and would not ask. But when he stumbled to the door, and she opened it for him, the smile on her lips frightened him more than anything in his life.

"Don't feel neglected, baby," she said. "There are others like you. You'll run into them. Maybe you can start a club."

He didn't know what to say; he wanted to run, but he knew she had spread fog across his soul and he knew if he walked out the door he was never going to reclaim his feeling of self-satisfaction. He had to make one last attempt . . .

"Help me . . . please, I feel so—so—"

"I know how you feel, baby," she said, moving him through the door. "Now you know how they feel."

And she closed the door behind him. Very softly.

Very firmly.

Introduction to Emissary from Hamelin

Like "Killing Bernstein," earlier in this series of tiny fables, there is nothing deep or profound to say about it beyond what the story says for itself. As Mark Rothko put it: "Silence is so accurate."

•

"Civilization is an active deposit which is formed by the combustion of the Present with the Past. Neither in countries without a Present nor in those without a Past is it to be discovered. Proust in Venice, Matisse's bird-cages overlooking the flower market of Nice, Gide on the seventeenth-century quais of Toulon, Lorca in Granada, Picasso by Saint-Germain-des-Pres: that is civilization, and for me it can exist only under those liberal regimes in which the Present is alive and therefore capable of combining with the Past. Civilization is maintained by a very few people in a small number of places, and we need only a few bombs and some prisons to blot it out altogether. "The civilized are those who get more out of life than the uncivilized, and for this the uncivilized have not forgiven them. One by one, the Golden Apples of the West are shaken from the tree."

Cyril Connolly, *The Unquiet Grave*

Emissary from Hamelin

July 22nd, 2076 . . .

Exclusive to the Going Nowhere News Service . . .

Mike Strathearn reporting . . .

My second wife once told me I'd write if I were strapped into a straitjacket in the deepest, moldiest dungeon cell of the most remote lunatic asylum in the world. She said I'd probably write news releases on the insides of my cheeks with my wet tongue-tip. She's probably right, wherever she is. I'm a compulsive. Stranded on the most remote peak of K2 (Mt. Godwin-Austen or Dapsang, 8,611 meters, second highest mountain in the world: in the Himalayas, the Karakorams), I would fold the dispatches in the shape of a glider and skim them off the peak in hopes a Sherpa herdsman or a *yeti* or *some*one would find them. Marooned on a desert island, I would use notes in bottles. No one has ever figured out how someone marooned on a desert island came up with bottles to cast into the sea, but if there weren't a convenient case of empty liquor bottles already there, I'd slip the dispatches into the mouths of dolphins, hoping they had a nice sense of direction. I was born in 2014, little more than a decade after the turn of the century, which makes me sixty-two now, and my mother once ventured that the difficulty she'd had giving birth to me was probably due to my having written all over the walls of her womb. I had a pretty happy childhood and by the time I was . . .

I'm rambling.

That's lousy reportage.

I've always despised personal journalism. I try to be dead-on factual. But there isn't much to do here, and I have this damnable need to *communicate!*

I'll try to keep to the subject.

The child. That kid. The emissary from Hamelin.

I got the word he wanted to meet me from the night desk. They called me at home and said, "There's a kid says he's got the biggest story in the history of the world, says he'll only give it to you."

I stared at the face of the guy in the phone. It was a new guy from the Bombay office, wearing a lot of pancake makeup and glitter on his eyelids. I didn't know him except by sight, and I confess I didn't like him. I guess I didn't much like any of the new breed of reporters. Back when I was a kid, back around '27 and '28, I was greatly impressed by all the wacky film comedies of the nineteen thirties, the ones that took place in the old-style newspaper offices. Wisecracking guys and gals getting the beat on all the other papers, phoning in their leads on phones that just talked, didn't have holo or even sight. Boy, what times those must have been! "Hello, Sharkey? This's Smoke Farnum, hold the presses! I've got a doozy! Gimme rewrite. Hello, rewrite, take a lead for the dead dog final . . ."

I'm rambling again.

That kid. Yeah, I got to stick to telling about that kid.

Well, I looked at this yo-yo from Bombay, and I said, "What the hell are you talking about?"

Glitterlids just stared at me like he wanted to buzz me off, and finally he said, "The cops've got a kid up on a power wand tower out in Westwood. They don't know how he got up there, and they don't much give a damn; but they can't get him down."

"Why not?"

"Says he wants to talk to Strathearn of the Newsservice."

"I asked you why not?"

"Because every time they send up a cop with a flitterpak on, the unit bypasses fail-safe and the cop falls on his ass, that's why not!"

"And what's all this about him having a story?"

"Look, Strathearn," he said, "what the hell am I supposed to be, your grapevine? I've got other things to do; stop annoying me; either take the call or don't. As far as I'm concerned, you can chew mud!" And he buzzed me off before I could ask him why the kid wanted to talk to me and nobody else.

I floated there for a while, just revolving and thinking nothing in particular, just resting. I was half drunk to begin with, and not particularly interested in going out to cover some dumb kid up on a wand. But the more I thought about it, the more curious I got about him, and I must admit my ego was massaged thinking the kid wanted to talk to me and nobody else. It reminded me of the nineteen twenties, when Haldeman or Manson or Pretty Boy Floyd, one of those mobsters, gave himself up to Walter Winchell. *Hold everything, Sharkey,* I thought. *Stop the presses! I got a five-star final for you. Banner headline! Eighty-point Railroad Gothic! Crazed killer kid on a wand with the biggest story in the world!*

I had to laugh at myself, but before I knew what I was doing I was peeling the wrapper off a clean suit, blowing it up, putting it on and skitting for Westwood.

What the hell. Maybe it *was* the biggest story in the world. How often does *that* happen?

I can answer that now. I wish I couldn't, but I can. It only happens once. Damn it.

They fitted me out with a flitterpak. I couldn't believe it when the cops said they blamed the kid up there on the power wand tower for the failure of their units. I planned to do something with *that* bit of self-serving alibi when I put together my story. *If* there was a story.

I kicked the unit on, it hummed prettily, and I took off. Up I went, without any problem. *What noodles, those cops,* I thought.

I went up, 210 meters. Thank God I'm not afraid of heights. And there he was.

It wasn't a crazed teenager. It was a little boy, about ten years old. He was walking around the maintenance platform. Limping. He was dressed in some soft furry kind of jacket and pants, wearing a pointed cap of the same fur, with a feather in it. He had a striped red and yellow scarf around his neck, and at the end of the scarf he had a flute of intricately carved wood attached by a leather thong. I recognized the flute as wood, and the thong as leather. Do you know how long it's been since we had any wood or leather around? Do you know how long it's been since anyone wore fur? Oh, there was a story here, all right.

The kid watched me as I floated up over the guard rails and dropped onto the platform. I kicked off the unit, but I didn't take it off. He was only about 120 centimeters tall, but I wasn't taking any chances on his suddenly going wild and doing something unexpected. It was, after all, more than two hundred meters to a messy finish.

He looked at me. I looked at him. Neither of us said anything. Finally I said, "It's pretty cold up here, son. Don't you want to come down?"

He spoke very quietly, and it wasn't *just* that what he said was so adult, so reasoned; his voice was that of a little man. No, I don't mean a *little man,* I mean what they used to call a young chap when he was being plucky and brave and grown-up. "You're a plucky little man." That's what I mean.

"No thank you, sir. I can come down whenever I choose. I'm sorry you had to come up here to see me, but I'm a child and I knew if I asked to see you on the ground, someone bigger would have stopped me. Or just laughed."

My God, I thought, *it's The Little Prince.* This kid was 120 centimeters tall and fifty years old. What a cute little guy. Very serious. And he looked at me with the steadiest gaze I'd ever encountered. I had the fleeting thought that if a politician could get that steady look down correctly, he'd be a dead shot for the Presidency Commissarship of the whole damned planet.

"Well, uh, what's your name?"

"My name is Willy, sir. And I've come a very long distance to speak to you."

"Why me, Willy?"

"Because you like children, and you remember many things that happened long ago, and you know the poem."

"The poem?"

"Yes, sir, the poem about the Pied Piper who took the children when the Mayor of Hamelin would not pay him what he had promised to pay him for ridding the town of rats."

I hadn't the vaguest idea what the kid was talking about. Yes, I'd memorized Browning's "The Pied Piper of Hamelin" off one of the obscure-search scanner fiches when I was just a child, but that had been many, many years before. And what had Browning's poem to do with this child? And where had he come from? And how had he managed to scale a two-hundred-meter wand? And if he was able to jam the cops' flitterpaks, as they had said, then why had he let *me* fly up? And what was this big story he was supposed to have for me? And where had he gotten fur and wood and leather?

And then I ran Browning through my mind.

> "But when they saw 'twas a lost endeavor,
> And Piper and dancers were gone forever,
> They made a decree that lawyers never
>   Should think their records dated duly
> If, after the day of the month and year,
> These words did not as well appear:
> 'And so long after what happen'd here
>   On the twenty-second of July,
> Thirteen hundred and Seventy-six;'
> And the better in memory to fix
> The place of the children's last retreat,
> They call'd it the Pied Piper's Street . . ."

"In one week it'll be exactly seven hundred years to the day," I said to the child. He did not look happy when I said it. He sighed and looked over the edge of the platform, out across the endless expanse of San Frangeles stretching from what long ago had been Vancouver, all the way down to what had been Baja California. And I thought I saw him crying; but when he turned back, his eyes were only moist.

"Yes, sir, that is correct. We feel more than enough time has been allotted for you. And that is why I was sent out. But I try to be fairer than my ancestor, and that is why I asked for you. You can understand; you will be able to tell them, warn them, so I won't have to . . ."

He didn't finish. He just left it hanging, and up there on the wand, as cold as it was, I felt a deeper chill wash through me, as if someone had walked over my grave.

I asked him what he meant to do.

And he told me. It was the biggest story in the history of the world, if it was true.

I said people would need proof.

He said he was willing to provide that proof. A small demonstration.

So I pulled my communication console out of my breast pocket and linked in with Newsservice, and told them I had something; I told Central in Boise to put me on record and instantly felt the sensor pressure as the units imbedded in my throat and ears and eyes were activated.

"July 15th, 2076," I said. "Exclusive to the World Newsservice. Mike Strathearn reporting. I'm standing atop the power wand tower in Westwood, Greater San Frangeles. With me is a little boy with the most bizarre story I have ever heard . . ."

And I made a prelim they could edit down when they 'cast it.

"Willy has agreed to give us a demonstration, and for that on-the-scene I transfer you now to our remote in Times Square, New York, state of Manhattan."

I watched the console in the palm of my hand. The screen flickered and I was staring down at 42nd and Broadway. Beside me, the child put the pipe to his lips and began to play.

The song made no sense to me, but it apparently made sense to the cockroaches. If there is a scientific explanation for how a tune played softly on a flute can be heard a continent away by cockroaches, it is an explanation that exists within the bounds of a science we do not yet understand. A science we will probably *never* understand.

But as I watched, the cockroaches of Manhattan began to come out. *"And the muttering grew to a grumbling and the grumbling grew to a mighty rumbling and out of the houses the rats came tumbling."* Browning would have written it very differently had the Pied Piper called out the cockroaches. At first there was a low twittering sound and the twittering grew to a clittering and the clittering grew to a mighty clattering as their claws skittered and scuttled across the plastic streets and slidewalks. And they came in a trickle and then a mass and then a wash and then a flood. They came from the underground and they came from the walls and they came from the rotting rusting rafters and the garbage-laden hallways and they came out and covered the streets so there was nothing but a carpet of carapaces, a black carpet of evil little shapes.

And the screen showed them heading toward the East River and as I watched they all scrabbled across the island that had been made the state of Manhattan, and they plunged into the East River and were drowned.

Then remote came back to me.

I turned to the child.

"Willy, tell the audience watching us what it is you want them to do."

He turned to me and looked at me, and my sensors held him. "We want everyone to stop what they are doing to make this a bad place, or we will take this place away from you."

And that was all.

He didn't explain it. He clearly didn't feel he should set the method. But it was clear what he intended. Stop paving over the green lands with plastic, stop fighting, stop killing friendship, have courage, don't lie, stop brutalizing each other, value art and wisdom . . . in short, make over the world or lose it.

I was with him all that next week, as he went from town to town and city to city. They laughed at him, of course. They laughed and they ignored him and several times they tried to take him into custody, but the child stopped them.

And yesterday, when time was almost up, we sat on the bank of a filth-filled stream and Willy toyed with the flute as if he wished it were not there, and he said to me, "I am sorry for you."

"You're going to do it, aren't you?"

"Yes," he said. "We have given you seven hundred years. That is enough time. But I am sorry you will go with them. I like you, you are a nice person."

"But not nice enough to spare me."

"You are one with all the others. They did nothing. You did nothing. You are not a bad person; you just did not care enough."

"I wasn't strong enough, Willy. I'm not sure anyone is."

"They should have been. They are not stupid."

And so, today, Willy began walking, and as he walked he played. And this time I heard the song. It was of finer times and cleaner lands, and I followed him. And everyone else followed him. They came out of the houses and the condos, the towers and the undergrounds. They came from far away and from nearby. And they followed him to an empty field where he piped open the air, and it was black inside. As black as a collapsed star, a black hole. And they marched inside, one after another, all the adults in the world. And as I stepped across the threshold I looked at Willy and he was staring at me, even though he did not stop playing his pipe. His eyes were moist again.

And here we are. There is nothing here, but it doesn't seem to matter. Willy and the children of Hamelin meant us no harm, they just couldn't put up with us any longer. We will stay here forever, I'm sure; and perhaps we will die and perhaps this place will keep us as we are now. But here, nonetheless, forever.

And I would tell you what the world is like today, on July 22nd, 2076, but I don't know. It's out there somewhere. Peopled by children.

I hope Willy is right. I hope they will make a better showing than we did. God knows we had long enough to try.

Introduction to The New York Review of Bird

What's the point of lying about it? I am supposed to be Cordwainer Bird. No, correct that: I *am* Cordwainer Bird. Uh. Well, I *am* Cordwainer Bird and I am *not* Cordwainer Bird. Hmmm. This will take some explaining.

Back in 1950, the final issue of a short-lived magazine (a mere six issues between 1947 and 1950) called *Fantasy Book,* published by William Crawford, one of the pioneering sf fans who risked everything to put science fiction between hard-covers, featured a story titled "Scanners Live in Vain." It was written by someone using the obviously pseudonymous byline "Cordwainer Smith." It was a super story, and it attracted some small attention in the microcosm of sf fandom, even at that time. But it was not to achieve "overnight fame" until 1952 when Frederik Pohl, editing a now-almost-forgotten Permabooks paperback anthology called *Beyond the End of Time,* exhumed the story and reprinted it. This time, for some odd, unexplained reason, the moment to appreciate it had arrived, and the superior imaginative qualities of the story, and the undeniable craft of its author, caused a minor whirl-wind in the genre of imaginative literature. Everyone wanted to know who "Cordwainer Smith" was. Clearly, he or she was no amateur. This was the polished, wildly inventive work of a literary professional: wholly integrated, suggesting a new universe of stories lying just behind this first effort, filled with depths and tensions that no first-time writer could have manipulated so stunningly. I remember well the belief, common coin at that time that "Smith" was in reality A. E. Van Vogt or George O. Smith.

But no one stepped forward to claim credit. If Bill Crawford ever really knew who Smith was, he never said. (As John J. Pierce has noted, in his excellent introduction to *The Best of Cordwainer Smith* [Nelson Doubleday, 1975; available through the SF Book Club], the story was written in the mid-Forties, was submitted to every sf market and rejected by every sf market, and was finally submitted to *Fantasy Book*, in the "slush pile," or unsolicited submissions manner. The magazine was such a marginal enterprise that Crawford never paid for it. And so it is possible Crawford never knew "Smith's" real identity. Pohl no doubt found out who lurked behind the *nom de plume* when he paid the reprint fee for his anthology; and that brings us logically to the next step in the mystery story.)

A mystery. One of those great unsolved literary mysteries to which the science fiction in-crowd would make references when they were sitting around juicing, just talking all those hip things in-crowds talk about.

Then, in the September 1955 issue of *Galaxy* magazine, editor Horace L. Gold announced he would publish, the following month, a *new* Cordwainer Smith story, "The Game of Rat and Dragon." The waves of astonishment went out and for the next thirty days the greatest treasure any fan of sf could buy, beg, or steal was an advance issue of the October *Galaxy*. I was blessed: I was in New York at that time, having only recently been thrown out of Ohio State University, having gone to Manhattan to begin my professional career as a writer; and I copped a copy. With fear that I'd find it a bad story, I opened the issue and began to read.

It was as miraculous as "Scanners Live in Vain." And I was a devout worshipper of "Cordwainer Smith," whoever that might be.

In the next few years Gold (and his successor, Frederik Pohl) published a score of Smith stories, all of them brilliant; and *everyone* became a fan of his/her work. But neither Horace nor Fred ever revealed who Smith really was, and conjecture rose.

But in 1956, when I was beginning to be published here and there, the conjecture was partially tinged with amusement because many of us writing and fanning in the sf medium thought it might be another pen-name trick of Pohl or Lester del Rey or Cyril Kornbluth or someone equally as talented. And so, as a tribute and as a friendly bit of joshing, when it was necessary for me to use a pen name on a story in the July 1957 issue of *Fantastic Universe* ("Song of Death," the editor's retitling) and the August 1957 issue of *Super-Science Fiction* ("Invasion Footnote"), because I had more than one story in each of the books and it was considered poor form to have the same name twice on a single contents page, I came up with "Cordwainer Bird." Ironically, the editor of *Fantastic Universe*, Hans Stefan Santesson, thought there might be some confusion with the names, so it appeared on the title page as "C. Bird," and Bill Scott, editor of *S-SF* got the spelling wrong and it turned out as "Cortwainer Bird."

It was not till many years later that it was revealed that "Cordwainer Smith" had been Dr. Paul Myron Anthony Linebarger (1913–1966). There isn't room here to go into a full recounting of the amazing life and career of Linebarger, and I commend to your attention Mr. Pierce's introduction in the aforementioned *Best of* volume for a full detailing of same; but suffice to say by the time it was no longer a secret that Smith had been a famous and distinguished world traveler, professor of Asiatic politics, writer on Far Eastern affairs, and even presidential advisor . . . "Cordwainer Bird" had become a fact of life.

He was the author of numerous extremely soft-core stories in such magazines as *Adam, Knight, Adam Bedside Reader* and other Los Angeles-based girlie journals. Between 1963 and 1969 he had his by-line on the following sensational winners: "The Girl with the Horizontal Mind," "The Man on the Juice Wagon," "Walk the High Steel," "Tramp," "Goodbye, Eadie!" and "The Hungry One," "The Bohemia of Arthur Archer," "God Bless the Ugly Virgin," "The Fine Art of the 15¢ Pick-Up," "The College Bohemian," "Make it an 'L' and It's Luck," and "Portrait of the Artist as a Zilch Writer." Many of those were reprints of stories I'd written in the late Fifties, and while they could bring me a desperately needed two or three hundred dollars per appearance, they were—how shall I put it—less memorable works than what I was at that time building my dubious reputation on. And so Cordwainer became the author of record.

It was not till 1964 that Cordwainer switched to television writing, and had it not been for Irwin Allen, the King Croesus of the Disaster Flicks (in many senses of the word *disaster*), good old Cordwainer might well have passed into the musty files of old magazine collectors.

But Irwin hired me to write a segment of *Voyage to the Bottom of the Sea* during its pre-airing stages, and though I was one of the first scenarists to work that show, Uncle Irwin managed to confuse himself so thoroughly as to what the direction of the series should be that he collapsed the minds of all intelligent writers unfortunate enough to fall within his sphere of influence. In the process he managed to collapse the quality of my script, and I, in one of my well-known and *wholly* justified fits of pique, invoked the clause in the Writers Guild contract whereby a scenarist can use a preregistered pseudonym on any script he feels has been butchered.

When the time came to tell Irwin what name I wanted on it, almost without thinking I said, "Cordwainer Bird." The bird, of course, is a double-denigrating reference to "for the birds" and "flipping the bird," which is the fine American equivalent of the Sicilian two-fingered "horns," guaranteed to turn milk sour, cause your cow to have a two-headed calf, raise a mustache on your wife, make your husband impotent, turn your fields to dust, and in general make you aware that the invokee doesn't like you a lot.

(For those who are unfamiliar with "flipping the bird," I suggest you make a left turn from a right-hand lane on a six-lane street as soon as possible, and you will see excellent examples of the art form proffered by the drivers of the five other cars you cut off.)

In short, it was my way of saying, "This script sucks."

It was also a way of establishing that I had been rewritten. I followed up the use of the pseudonym with as much bad publicity as I could muster.

And so, Cordwainer Bird moved smoothly from writing cruddy sf and men's magazine garbage to writing cruddy television garbage.

I've used the pseudonym only three times in the thirteen years I've been writing films and television. Once on *Voyage* (the segment titled "The Price of Doom," aired originally over the ABC network on Monday, October 12th, 1964); once on *The Flying Nun* (the segment titled "You Can't Get There from Here," aired originally over the ABC network on Thursday, April 11th, 1968) . . . and how Bird came to write *The Flying Nun* is a weirder story than even *this* book could contain, and it will have to wait for another time; and finally, as the author of the pilot segment of a nasty little short-lived (thank god) series called *The Starlost*. Bird was also featured on the credits of *The Starlost* each week of its 16-episode life, as its creator. That was in the fall of 1973.

I'd go into the full story of Cordwainer's most famous awfulness, *The Starlost*, but I've told it in explicit and defamatory detail as the introduction to a wonderful, terrific book called *Phoenix Without Ashes* (available from another publisher for a paltry $1.50). This incredibly great book to which I make humble and merely passing reference is a novelization of the original version of the pilot script, the one that won the Writers Guild award as the Most Outstanding Dramatic-Episodic Script of the 1973–74 season. I wrote the introduction about how the morons who produced the show screwed it up, forcing me to put the Bird monicker on it, and the talented young sf writer Edward Bryant did the novel. And if you want to read the original version of that script, the one Ellison wrote, not the one that got aired with Bird's name on it, you can read it in an anthology called *Faster than Light*, edited by Jack Dann and George Zebrowski (Harper & Row, 1975). And if you want to read a funny novelization of the shit I went through in Toronto during the period when I worked on the series before walking out on it, try Ben Bova's comic novel, *The Starcrossed* (Chilton, 1975; Pyramid, 1976). In fact, Ben even dedicated the book to Bird. So that's as much cross-reference as you'll need and further than that I don't want to go into it. Besides, the publisher of *this* book will start charging me for advertising if I go into it any further.

Which brings us to the story you're about to read.

A couple of years ago, Philip José Farmer, one of the *great* fantasists of our time, wrote me saying he was in the process of doing stories by famous fictional writers who were characters in stories by real writers. Hemingway's Nick Adams, Kurt Vonnegut's Kilgore Trout, Jack London's Martin Eden, Conan Doyle's Dr. Watson, Thomas Mann's Gustave von Aschenbach, Barry Malzberg's Jonathan Herovit . . . that whole crowd. And he said he wanted to do a Cordwainer Bird story.

At approximately the same time, dashing and debonair young Byron Preiss, editor of a lunatic series of paperbacks called *Weird Heroes*, got in touch and wanted me to write a story about a new American pulp hero who was a writer. I suggested Cordwainer. He thought that was super.

The next thing I knew, Phil and Byron had gotten together and were *nuhdzing* me almost weekly to write the story for the book. Phil even integrated Cordwainer into the genealogy of Doc Savage in the revised chart to be found in the paperback edition of *Doc Savage: His Apocalyptic Life*. Now, let me make one point perfectly, uh, let me say this: I had never *ever* given any thought to who or what Cordwainer Bird might be. It was just a pen name, just a throwaway, a device to let those who knew my work and the standards of craft I try to maintain know that I had been jerked around, that the result was for the birds and I wasn't the one responsible.

But. Here comes that damned Farmer with letters, one after the other, wanting to know this about Bird, wanting to know that, wanting to know how tall he was, and how he wore his hair, and what color his eyes were, and what stories he'd written. Then the phone calls! Between Preiss and Farmer, I was driven bats. The one calling to find out if I'd even started writing the bloody story yet, and the other calling to tell me Bird was a nephew of The Shadow and The Spider and G-8, for God's sake! And it all started ballooning and mushrooming, and the next thing I knew others had found out that Bird was going to take on The New York Literary Establishment, that inarticulated conspiracy of writers, editors, critics, and publishers who get fat while so many fine writers starve in back rooms and Quonset huts across the country. And they started suggesting why didn't Bird kill this one in the story, and why didn't Bird wipe out that one in the story, and why didn't Bird get all the brain-damaged copyeditors who fuck up literate copy in their hell-bent drive to make it conform to Smith or Bryn Mawr type-style and machine-gun them in the lobby of the Plaza.

And I must confess that while Bird's activities in this story are a tot bloodier than any I've engaged in (though I did once send a dead gopher and a recipe for dead gopher stew to the comptroller of a publishing house that was messing me over), there is just the faintest tot of wish fulfillment in the work.

So as you can see, I *am* Cordwainer Bird and I am *not* Cordwainer Bird. I am, when I'm forced to put a pen name on work that's been ruined by other hands; but I'm not the guy in the story, because he's a vigilante and I'd *never* do that sort of thing.

Further, my hair is brown, and Bird's is black; I'm 5'5" and Bird is exactly four feet tall; Bird has Uncle Kent, The Shadow, for a relative, and the best I've got is my Uncle Lew up in Larchmont, who dabbles in stocks . . . I think. (Come to dwell on it, what *does* Lew do for a living?)

In any case, the story you're about to read is a fable. A myth. It ain't true. And if the names of real persons have managed to creep into it, why, it's just literary tomfoolery. I've never even met any of the book-buying staff of Brentano's, and while something like what Skippy Wingwalker talks about in the story happened to me when I was being published by Avon, I'd *never* throw even a creep like Skippy's real-life counterpart out a window. So that disclaims it, and we can all settle back in the assurance that Cordwainer Bird is merely a creature of the imagination. Honest he is. Would I lie to you?

"The one important thing I have learnt over the years is the difference between taking one's work seriously and taking oneself seriously. The first is imperative and the second disastrous."

Dame Margot Fonteyn, 1976

The New York Review of Bird

"Bird, Bird! That's all I hear from you creeps! Bird! I don't give a damn *who* he is, or where he's hiding! The great City of New York has no room in it for vigilantes; I'll find this goddam Bird no matter *where* he's holed up! My men and I, the whole goddam department, in fact, are working on this Bird thing a full twenty-four hours a day! All leaves have been canceled, special 'tac squads have been laid on, we've got our people in the streets following up every possible lead! We expect an arrest within twelve hours! Twenty-four at the very latest! Thirty-six at the most extreme outside estimate! You can quote me! And will you, fer chrissakes, learn to spell my name right in your goddam papers! It's *Pflockian,* not "Fallopian"! Now get the hell out of here and go down to the morgue and take some more pictures of that dead publisher, if that's your idea of fun and games; and let me get back to work! I'll have this Cordwainer Bird by the heels within fifty-two hours, you can quote me!"

Excerpt of interview
with NYPD
Chief of Detectives
Irving L. Fallopian;
New York Times;
29 January 1976

"Oh, the poor little thing," the woman with the silver-blue hair said. "Arthur, give him a dollar."

The portly gentleman in the belted cashmere overcoat and caracul astrakhan shifted the ziggurat of packages in his arms, managed to free his left hand, and reached into his pants pocket. "Hurry, Arthur," the woman said, "it's snowing." He looked at her. He shook his head with mild annoyance. Of *course* it was snowing. It was coming down in great, wet, skimming flakes and covering Fifth Avenue in a coverlet of downy whiteness that meant—without argument—fourteen hundred pedestrians would slip and bust their asses by morning. Of *course* it was snowing!

And that was one of the reasons the woman with the silver-blue hair had stopped before the wretched creature at the edge of the sidewalk. He looked so pathetic. A little man, wearing only an open imitation leather vest, soaking wash'n'wear slacks, and sandals. No shirt, no hat, no socks, no topcoat. His glasses were wet with snow, and a tiny mound of melting snow rested on the bridge of his nose. He looked like a beggar. To the woman with the silver-blue hair.

The formidable, portly gentleman continued trying to fumble a dollar from his pocket, juggling packages. Taxis shushed through the slush, making virtually the only sounds on Fifth Avenue. No horns, no sirens, no jackhammers, no police whistles, no conversation; the aluminum sky had closed down over the city and everything was hushed.

In the silence, the poor little thing spoke.

"Madam, why don't you take your fat-ass husband, your ghastly hairdo, your conspicuous consumption of the Gross National Product, not to mention the certainly ill-gotten dollar he's trying to pry out around his obesity, and insert them vertically where they'll do you simply a *world* of good. And then, if you carefully light them, you can provide yourselves with instant jet-assisted takeoff back to New Rochelle. In short, get the hell away from me before I dropkick you through the window of that bookstore."

The bookstore to which he referred was Brentano's.

Even though lacking four legs each, in precisely the manner of the langouste, or European rock lobster, the woman with the silver-blue hair and her pet Arthur with its hand still doing p.o.w. time in its pants pocket, scuttled sidewise, away down Fifth Avenue, away from the wretched little man with the naked chest and the fierce glow in his robin's-egg blue eyes. "Anarchist!" the Arthur murmured, and then he suddenly slipped and busted his ass on the sidewalk.

The little man with the straight black hair and the face of a handsome eagle had dismissed them from his world view immediately he had verbally savaged the woman. His attention was now, once again, electrically fastened on the front window of Brentano's.

There were eight stacks of books in the window, each stack having been faced with full cover display of the title forming the shaft. The titles were *The Pasha* by Harold Robbins; *Retreat and Regroup* by Allen Drury; *Asimov's Guide to Senescence* by Isaac Asimov; *Pismire's Pique* by Morris L. West; *The Unpublished Letters of Judy Garland* edited by Gerold Frank; *Living Forever* by David Reuben, M.D.; *Beyond Redemption* by Jacqueline Susann, posthumously completed by Erich Segal; and *Say Howdy-do to God, Charlie Brown!* by Charles M. Schulz.

He stood staring into the window as an early dusk settled over the disenfranchised city. A Puerto Rican trying to look like a Czech refugee in stocking cap pulled down over ears, and plaid duck-hunter's jacket pushed a hot-cart of redolent chestnuts and millstone *bialies* past him, behind him, in the gutter. His galoshes made slurping sounds. The little man thought of Campbell's New England style Clam Chowder.

Then, quite suddenly, at precisely ten minutes to five, the little man left his position. He broke out of the mound of snow that had formed around his legs, stamped his blue feet in their sandals, and walked across the sidewalk, elbowing pedestrians to either side. He entered Brentano's.

A slim, polite young man wearing a name tag that said "Mr. Ingham" approached the little fellow, now standing in an ever widening pool of water. He looked down at him. The customer was exactly four feet tall. "And may I help you, sir?"

The little man looked around. Everywhere he looked there were tables of books, stacks of books, pyramids of books. All eight of the titles in the window could be seen prominently exhibited on a counter, surmounted by a sign that read CURRENT BEST SELLERS. "Sir? Was there something you wanted particularly?"

The little man raised his eyes to Mr. Ingham. "Do you have *Bad Karma & Other Extravagances?*"

Mr. Ingham's brow resolved itself into a topographical map of the Indus Valley. *"Backgammon* and *whom?"*

"Not *backgammon,* you thug. *Bad Karma. & Other Extravagances*. It's a book of stories."

"And the author?"

"Cordwainer Bird," the little man said, with just the vaguest echo of sackbut and lyre in his voice.

"Oh," said Mr. Ingham, a thin smile fluttering to rest on his lips like the faintest touch of dragonfly wings. "That would be downstairs in the rear, in the sci-fi section."

"The *what?"* The little man's face tightened, a muscle or possibly a nerve jumping at the hinge of his strong jaw. On the left. "The *what* section?"

"Sci-fi," Mr. Ingham said again, looking a trifle discomfited. "Just beyond the gothics, the nurse novels, and the we-have-been-visited-by-aliens sections."

The little man's tone of voice abruptly altered. Where before it had been commanding and stern, it now became very nearly menacing. "It isn't a science fiction book," he said. "And it *certainly* isn't 'sci-fi,' whatever *that* nauseating neologism might signify. Why isn't it up here with the current best sellers?"

Mr. Ingham began to edge away.

The little man moved toward him. "Where the hell are you going?"

"I have a carton of books to unpack. *The Joy of Cooking*. They have to be handled gingerly or they won't rise." Jerkily, he kept moving away. The little man kept after him. In a moment Mr. Ingham was back-pedaling and the little man was closing in on him inexorably. The salesman found himself, finally, wedged into the corner where ART HISTORY and SELF-HELP confluenced. He had no idea how it had happened; the little man hadn't even raised his voice. It was as though he had been . . . *driven* . . . into the corner. By some palpable force.

A wash of terror brought tears to Mr. Ingham's eyes. He flattened against the wall bookcases, his back pressed so tightly against the barrier he could feel each vertebra through his skin. There was something relentless about the little man, something utterly overwhelming, as if he possessed an arcane gift of inducing fear, a power acquired in the Orient, where, it is said, one can acquire the ability to cloud men's minds so they cannot see you. But that was ridiculous! He could see the little man clearly; and the terror of the sight rendered Mr. Ingham helpless.

The little man stood close, very close. He stepped up onto Mr. Ingham's shoes as a small child might when asking her daddy to dance with her at an older sister's wedding. He put his prominent nose close to Mr. Ingham's chin and said, very softly, "Look at me." Mr. Ingham lowered his gaze. His eyes met those of the little man.

There is a scene in the 1939 Alexander Korda version of *The Thief of Bagdad* in which Ahbhu, the little thief, played with considerable ingenuousness by Sabu, finds himself inside a great stone idol in a forbidding temple set atop the highest mountain peak in the world. He is climbing up a monstrous spiderweb. He looks down and sees, far below, an enormous pool in which swim giant octopi. They are lit by an unholy light and they writhe and swirl in a terrifying manner.

Mr. Ingham looked into the robin's-egg blue eyes of the little man standing on his shoes. He saw writhing octopi.

"Tell me you aren't one of *them*," the little man said softly.

"I'm not one of them," Mr. Ingham said, in a croaking voice.

"Do you know who *they* are?"

"N-no sir, I don't."

"Then how do you know you aren't one of *them?*"

"I'm not a joiner, sir. I'm even a trifle embarrassed to belong to the Book-of-the-Month Club."

The little man stepped off Mr. Ingham's shoes. He appraised him carefully. Finally, he said, "No, clearly you're just another wretched victim. I'm sorry I was rude."

Mr. Ingham smiled nervously. He said nothing.

"How do I get to that section with the name that will never pass my lips again?"

Mr. Ingham pointed to the rear of Brentano's, to a stairway almost hidden by cartons of stock. The little man nodded and started away. "Uh . . . sir?" Mr. Ingham was capable of bravery.

The little man stopped and turned his head. "Would you, uh, would you be Mr. Bird, by any chance?"

The little man stared at him coldly for a long moment. "Bird is a pseudonym. Native Americans have a sensible belief that it isn't necessary for others to know their real name. Knowing someone's real name gives *them* a weapon. Who I am, really, is something you or *they* will never know. But the pseudonym will suffice. Yes, I am Cordwainer Bird." And with that he turned back and moved toward the stairs.

The steps led down into a disturbing semidarkness. Bird thought of the Castle of Otranto. He stayed close to the moist, slimy stones of the wall. Far below he could see the basement section of the bookstore, lit feebly by twenty-five-watt bulbs nakedly protruding from the ceiling. Their withered illumination barely reached the display bookcases ranged in precise rows back and back into the darkness. The floor of the basement section was packed dirt and cobwebs hung everywhere in festoons like Belgian lace. As he reached the bottom, Bird heard the squeaking and scuttling of rats and, from somewhere far back in the hidden depths of the basement, what sounded like the syncopated cracking of a bullwhip.

He paused a moment, shivering with distaste, and approached the first section of bookcases. He was startled to discover they weren't actually bookcases, but orange crates, stacked one atop the other, with hardcover and paperback books jammed in carelessly, dust jackets torn, packed as closely as files in a government office. Bird thought of Jews crammed belly-to-butt in boxcars, on their way to Belsen.

Genre designations had been scribbled on the sides of the orange crates with magic marker. He could barely read the handwriting. He finally deciphered *miztornz* as "westerns" and *slouglles* as "slaughter." The former of the orange crates were filled with paperbacks by people with such first names as Al, Lee, Brace, Prong, and Luke. The latter crates seemed to be an endless series of novels about people called the Butcher, the Executioner, the Tormenter, the Bloodluster, and the Fink.

He kept walking.

Finally, at the extreme rear of the basement, beneath water pipes dripping into pits and pools formed by the continuous patter of rusty droplets of sewer overflow, he found a dozen orange crates hastily identified as "sci-fi."

And there, between a copy of *The Giant Rutabaga That Performed Unspeakable Obscenities on Pittsburgh* and the Ballantine paperback edition of *The Best of Ed Earl Repp,* he found one copy of *Bad Karma & Other Extravagances*. He bent toward the book and reached for it with the reverence of a supplicant at Lourdes. A spider clambered over the spine of the volume and raced away into the darkness.

Bird withdrew the hardcover book from the orange crate. It was covered with mildew. Silverfish had performed unspeakable obscenities on the pages no giant rutabaga could ever have imagined in its kinkiest moments.

Alone in the basement of Brentano's, Cordwainer Bird began to sob softly. He held the book to his naked chest and rocked it back and forth like a mother with a Thalidomide baby.

Then, in the cryptlike confines of that basement, there was a soft trilling sound; an ominous note sustained beyond measuring; almost unhuman, certainly not mechanical; the warning sound of powers about to be unleashed.

The blue of Bird's eyes seemed to darken.

Clutching the book, he spun on his heel and moved swiftly toward the staircase. By the time he reached the steps he was running. He took the steps three at a time, seeming to bound from riser to riser with the ease of an astronaut on a moonwalk. He reached the top at full speed and paused only a moment, legs apart, fist clenched, head turning this way and that as if seeking *them.*

Coming toward him, down an aisle from the ADULT GAMES and PLACE MATS section, an elderly woman leading a group of large, muscular men sporting eyepatches and tattoos approached rapidly. "That's him!" the woman yelled. The heavyweights moved past her and bore down on Bird. He recognized her: Brentano's book buyer!

Instantly, he dropped into what seemed to be an incredibly relaxed posture. He placed the book on a counter nearby and permitted his now open hands to fall to his sides. But his eyes were the color of the Bay of Mexico just off Madeira Beach, Florida, at evening, with a squall approaching.

The first of the muscled men reached Bird and clapped a hand the size of home plate at the Polo Grounds on his shoulder. "I got 'im, Miz Jararacussu," the behemoth said gutturally.

What happened next happened so quickly, no one was later able to describe the actual motion. But it *seemed* as if Bird laid his fist against the attacker's sternum, bent at the knees, and *twitched* his hips. The behemoth was suddenly catapulted backward through the air, a scream torn from his throat. He flailed helplessly as his trajectory carried him over two tables of books of poetry by Rod McKuen. He thundered through the merchandise—which fluttered into the air as light as *beignets* from the Café du Monde in New Orleans had settled like faerie snowflakes on a February morning in Vermont—and, still screaming, he hit the far wall. He lay there in a hideously twisted pile of arms, legs, and trailing visceral material. The surgeon's report later verified that the impact of Bird's movement had shattered the spleen, liver, gallbladder, pancreas, kidneys, and pylorus. The heavyweight had also, inexplicably, contracted sugar diabetes. An intern suggested it was from the exposure to McKuen.

But at that moment, in Brentano's, no one laughed. The elderly woman began shrieking. "Take him! Take him!" And then three of her side-boys converged on Bird from three different aisles. He stood waiting, still loose-limbed in that relaxed posture preceding the flight of the phoenix.

"Huey, Dewey, and Louie," Bird said, smiling tightly.

Dewey reached the little man a fraction of a second before his associates. With a windmilling motion so swift no actual pattern could be discerned, Bird broke *both* his arms. Huey and Louie came at him from either side even as Dewey staggered away sidewise, flapping his broken arms like a VFW poppy salesman. As they careened toward him, Bird gave a bound and rose above their heads. The two heavyweights crashed into each other and Bird came down on their shoulders.

Locking his legs in a scissors grip that pressed the faces of Huey and Louie together like young lovers, Bird tipped backward and applied pressure. The two attackers thrashed this way and that, trying to free themselves from Bird and from each other. Bird squeezed. In a moment both men turned blue and their legs gave out. As they fell, limp and gagging, Bird bounded free.

The other eleven thugs took one look and ran shrieking. In their flight they knocked the elderly Mrs. Jararacussu to the floor. When she looked up, Bird was standing over her.

"Permit me to assist you, madam," he said.

He lifted her overhead with one hand and held her there with her Lord and Taylor pantsuit jacket wrapped tightly within his fist.

"Explain to me why this book," Bird said, carrying her a few feet to the counter where he had placed *Bad Karma & Other Extravagances,* "is not stocked in the hundreds of copies, why it isn't up front near the door where the best sellers can be found, and why it doesn't appear with banners in your miserable front window?"

Mrs. Jararacussu's mouth tightened down into a thin black line. Bird thought of Helen Gahagan Douglas as *She-Who-Must-Be-Obeyed* in the 1934 Merian C. Cooper-Ernest B. Schoedsack film; the best of the seven remakes of Haggard's *She.*

"It isn't a best seller," Mrs. Jararacussu said. It was the first time Bird had ever seen someone speak and sneer at the same time. It was fascinating.

"Who says?"

"*The New York Times* Best Seller list says so. *Publishers Weekly* says so. *The New York Review of Books* says so. Rex Reed says so. George Plimpton says so. Candida Donadio says so. Michael Korda says so. And *I* say so."

Bird's nostrils quivered. Unwittingly, in rage at being held aloft like a Hebrew National salami being inspected for mold or a *shochet*'s illegible signature, she had named some of *them.* For the first time since the fever had taken him, he had a clue to their names, to their secret identities, their holiest invocations.

Actually, she was only Helen Gahagan in those days. She later *married* into the name Douglas.

"Tell your secret masters their days are numbered," Bird said. His eyes were as black as raven wings. No longer a sweet robin's-egg blue. "Tell them one of the slighted and snubbed has finally risen from the dust heaps of great wasted talent. Tell them to buy Fox Locks for their eyries. Tell them today is only the beginning. Go back to your puppet masters and warn them that no matter where they hide or run, Bird will seek them out and gift them with terrible justice!"

"Rodomontade," Mrs. Jararacussu sneered, saying.

Bird reddened. She hung there from his fist, staring at him with nasty little wrinkles around her eyes. Cordwainer Bird. Four feet tall, thick black hair, eyes of robin's-egg blue radiating the charisma of a Napoleon Bonaparte, the face of a handsome eagle. "You think I indulge in mere shabby braggadocio, eh?" He carried her, swinging, toward the front of the store. It was after hours. She had made sure everyone was gone. The doors were locked. Brentano's was silent. "Then you shall see . . . and believe!"

"Do your worst," she said. "Whatever technique you used on those simpleminded thugs won't phase me. I'm made of sterner stuff, as you'll see."

Bird carried her to an eleven-foot-high replica of Giacometti's "Man Pointing" and hung her from the scythe-shaped left arm. "No," Bird said, "*jeet kune do* would hardly be appropriate for the likes of you, a willing mind-slave of *them.* You've probably been conditioned against simple physical pain." The scrawny arm of the Giacometti began to bend away from the body of the sculpture with the weight of the woman. Bird unhooked her and carried her across to a sturdier hook: Auguste Rodin's "St. John the Baptist Preaching." He hung her on the upthrust forefinger of the extended right hand.

"When Bruce Lee and I studied together," Bird said, "he made it clear to me that even the advanced techniques of *jeet kune do* might not work against the true emissaries of darkness. We sat together many a night in that little treehouse in Beverly Glen and discussed alternatives.

"But first, before I extract from you the information I

need, here is a demonstration of how Bird will cut the throat of the monstrous conspiracy you serve. . . ."

He went to the glass case on the wall that held the fire hose, the fire alarm, and the huge double-headed ax. With one sharp blow he shattered the glass and withdrew the ax.

She watched him with growing horror as he moved toward her, past her, and stopped at the door that led to the front window. He used one of the blades of the ax to spring the lock. The door swung open. "You wouldn't dare!" she yelled.

But he would. As she screamed her hatred and defiance, the little man bounded up into the window of Brentano's and with the skill of a Matawatchan, Ontario tree topper swung the fearsome ax over his head and buried it in a stack of Harold Robbins novels. There was an abortive shriek of pain as the blade cleaved the top half-dozen volumes. A strange sound, akin to that of a blood-gorged Amazonian killer plant being cut in half. As though they had a life never granted by the Supreme Deity, the Robbins novels groaned and howled and spurted pages as Bird hacked them to pieces. Mrs. Jararacussu set up a sympathetic wailing as he went from stack to stack, killing the Peanuts books, the necrophiliac Susann/Segal collaboration, the West bibble-bibble, the tomb-robbing exploitation of the Frank privacy invasions. Mrs. Jararacussu's eyes rolled up in her head, and from the front window came the gurgle and cacophony of dying trash.

And when he was done, and his sweat dripped to mingle with the green slime and ichor the books had spurted, Bird threw down the double-bladed ax and came to her. She was only semiconscious now, but a dash of cold water from the drinking fountain brought her around.

Now she stared at the little man with fear: a full and swamping realization that she faced a power as strong as the one she served.

"Now," Cordwainer Bird said. "Now you'll tell me where their headquarters is located. Not the mind-slaves, not the puppets like yourself . . . but the leaders. The head of the conspiracy."

"Never . . ." she whispered.

"Oh, yes. Now." And he went and searched out what he needed and came back to her, and held it up for her to see. Deadlier than any martial art, capable of extracting information from Mt. Rushmore. "Tell me." She said nothing, and he opened the book and began to read.

Within a page, she was babbling, begging him to stop.

Bird hated to sink to their level, hated to use weapons this vile and unholy; the effect on the mind of the victim was so pronounced, so clearly debilitating that only under the most severe conditions would he even contemplate such horror. He laid aside the copy of *The Prophet* by Kahlil Gibran and gave Mrs. Jararacussu another drink of water.

She was very nearly incoherent.

Finally, by speaking softly and reading passages from W. S. Merwin and Joyce Carol Oates and William Kotzwinkle and Randall Jarrell, he was able to bring her back to a semblance of rationality.

"Now," he said, "where are they hidden?"

She tried to speak, but her lips were dry and cracked. A mad coruscation of lights flashed in her eyes. Kahlil Gibran could do that to an unstable personality.

Bird searched behind a counter until he found a pack of Kleenex. He moistened a handful of tissues and wet her lips. She began speaking, but Bird could barely hear her. He leaned close as she hung there from the Rodin, and after a moment he was able to make out her words.

"I never knew. I never actually read any of it. They promised me I'd never have to read any of it. This is the first time I've . . . it . . . it was horrible. Is *this* what I've been making people buy? I'm so ashamed . . . so terribly ashamed, Mr. Bird."

For an instant Cordwainer Bird's chill expression softened. "I understand. Consider this the first moment of your new life. Now, quickly, where do *they* headquarter themselves?"

"You'll find them under the lady—"

The first burst of machine-gun fire tore away her throat. Bird threw himself sidewise, skidded through the snowflake mound of McKuen booklets, and came up running. Behind him he could hear the thunder of assault boots on the floor; he tried to separate the sounds and made an estimate of at least half a dozen attackers. There was nothing he could do for Mrs. Jararacussu. Her own people had silenced her. He dashed for the front window of Brentano's, leaped up into the display case, grabbed the great ax, and swung it at the glass. He needn't have bothered. A rain of machine-gun bullets shattered the front window to his left and began tracking right to him. He flung himself down and rolled, under the trajectory of the slugs, straight out through the window and into the snow-filled avenue.

He cast one quick glance behind him. Yes, six of them. Hooded, carrying Brens and machine pistols, dressed in black-and-white. And Bird saw one other thing.

But the moment was done; he raced away down the silent, darkened length of Fifth Avenue.

When the hooded assassins leaped from the shattered window, scattering shredded, slime-dripping chunks of best sellers onto the sidewalk, Fifth Avenue was empty. It was as though the little man had levitated or dematerialized himself. But he still loomed large in their thoughts; they would remember him.

And Cordwainer Bird would remember the other sight he'd glimpsed in that stolen moment: the sight of *their* agent, the demonic Mrs. Jararacussu, hanging like a slaughtered carcass from the forefinger of Rodin's masterpiece.

"Cordwainer Bird's genealogy is in the inset (upper right-hand corner). E. B., as noted on the main chart, is the Earl of Burlesdon, Robert Rassendyll, the fifth earl. Two of his descendants were Ralph Rassendyll and Rudolf Rassendyll (of *The Prisoner of Zenda* and *Rupert of Hentzau*). Ralph and Rudolf were cousins. Ralph married R. D., or Rhoda Delagardie. Rhoda's descent is more detailedly traced in the chart and Addendum 2 of *Tarzan Alive*. Her first, and brief, marriage to Lord John Roxton (of Doyle's *The Lost World, et al.*) resulted in one child, Richard Wentworth or R. W., The Spider. She remarried, to Ralph, and the Rassendylls moved to New York, where Ralph managed the American affairs of a giant British firm. She bore him Allard Kent Rassendyll (A.K.R., The Shadow) and Bruce Hagin Rassendyll (B.H.R., G-8 of G-8 and his Battle Aces). Her youngest child, Rhonda, did not engage in flamboyant outlawry, but she was a family black sheep. Despite her parents' objections, she married Jason Bird, a part-Jewish acrobat and vaudeville night-club comedian. . . . "Jason's father was Richard Cordwainer Bird, an Irish photographer. His mother was Millicent, daughter of a Dublin Jew, Leopold Bloom. (See James Joyce's *Ulysses* for a perhaps overly detailed account of Bloom. See also *Tarzan Alive* for his relationship to the Greystokes, of whom Tarzan is the most outstanding member.)

"Jason and Rhonda's only child was Cordwainer Bird. Cordwainer was born in 1934 in Painesville, Ohio, in a rooming house near a theater. (Not, as some maintain, in the women's room of the theater.) Cordwainer grew up in Ohio, though not very far. His growth stopped when he reached the height of four feet. . . .

"When TV producers and directors ruined his scripts, he punched them in the mouth and went on to write science fiction. He has gathered together more awards, Hugos and Nebulas, in that field than any other writer. He has won the Edgar Allan Poe award from the Mystery Writers of America. He . . . then became a mainstream novelist and a militant foe of evil. Though he is nowhere near as tall as his ancestors and relatives, the Scarlet Pimpernel, Rudolf Rassendyll, the Shadow, Doc Savage, *et al.*, he has their heroic spirit and their dedication to fighting wickedness. But, unlike these heroes of an earlier age, who fought to preserve The Establishment, he fights to *destroy* The Establishment. One of the Establishments anyway."

Excerpt from *Doc Savage: His Apocalyptic Life* by Philip José Farmer (revised paperback edition; Bantam Books, 1975)

He needed help, advice; that was paramount and obvious. He decided to call on his Uncle Kent. The old man was still lucid, from time to time, and this *had* to be one of those times. He took the IRT uptown, spending his time in transit breaking the nose of a female dip whose hand kept wandering into his hip pocket, and reading the arcane messages left in orange, purple, black, and green by RIKKI TIKKI 101 on the walls, deck, overheads, and windows of the subway car. He disembarked at 116th Street, bounded up the stairs of the station, pausing only momentarily to kick senseless three Pedestrians of the Apocalypse who were mugging a seventy-year-old arthritic washerwoman, charged out of the subway kiosk, crossed Broadway through the speeding traffic, and headed for his uncle's apartment building.

Allard Kent Rassendyll, who had long ago changed his name to Kent Allard, and then changed it again a hundred times—depending on what case he was involved in—but who had always been just one man—The Shadow—was now eighty-one years old, and fallen on hard times. On several occasions, when his nephew Cordwainer discovered that the old man had hocked his fire opal ring, the mysterious Girasol, he had scraped together the money necessary to reclaim it, and had returned it, taking special care to leave it in a drawer or under a sofa pillow so the old man would not realize how much in Cordwainer's debt he was. He was a proud old man, and deserved—Bird firmly believed—nothing but honor and dignified twilight years, in return for the decades he had spent as America's foremost archenemy of evil. It was fortunate his memory was spotty: pawning and finding the ring ten times in six years might otherwise have seemed odd to that once razor-sharp analytical mind.

Under the name Phwombly, a variation on one of the aliases he had employed in the Thirties, he lived in one awful room in an apartment building on West 114th Street between Broadway and the Henry Hudson Parkway. About this building, the kindest description that could be summoned was, perhaps, that it had known less crummy days.

In the early Twenties it had been an elegant example of gracious Uptown West Side Manhattan living. Ten stories high, four huge apartments to a floor, with a common foyer decorated in the then-stylish manner of *L'Exposition des Arts Decoratifs* in Paris, it had been a residence of wealthy and graceful society *mavens* whose descendants had inevitably moved downtown to Gracie Mansion and other loci of power.

Now, as Bird approached the structure, it looked like nothing so much as the fever-dream of an architectural Quasimodo. It was dark and weathered, beaten down, street-level windows boarded and barred. What had once been a canopy was now a tattered battle flag of a war no one had even known was being waged. But the impecunious Columbia students, the penniless Puerto Rican immigrants, the frustrated blacks, and the gone-to-rot septuagenarians in what The Great Society called "their sunset years" had won that war. Uncle Kent's building was a wreck. A shambles. A prison of dead dreams.

As Bird stepped into the dingy lobby through a leaded glass door hanging by one ornate hinge, he was assaulted by the piping shrieks of old women. *A stridency of termagants,* he thought. *A daisy chain of shrews. A spike of shrikes.*

The lobby was jammed with ancient, withered, tiny little women, all of them in bedroom slippers and faded wrappers. Their voices crackled and shattered against the marble walls of the lobby. They seemed to be knotted up around one man, a figure in blue, wearing a cap. It took a moment for Bird's eyes to adjust to the dimness of the lobby—all light bulbs in the ceiling had been broken out eternities earlier—before he realized it was a postman.

He was in his middle twenties, a long-haired, bespectacled street type obviously working the Christmas overflow for a few dollars to supplement what he earned at some honest job downtown. And now he stood with his back to the wall, letter box receptacles behind him, a double-tiered unit set flush with the wall and referred to, in postal parlance, as a gang box unit. The old women had caught him as he'd begun to disperse the mail. His postal key on its long chain was still inserted in the lock of the master door of the upper tier. The master door had been pulled down but before he could begin to drop mail into the receptacles from above they had swamped him. Now he was pinned flat.

Bird edged around the mob, stood half-concealed by a marble pillar, and tried to decide whether to help the postal official or not. His mind cast back over all the *do not roll, fold, crush, crease, or bend* mail that he had received rolled, folded, crushed, creased, and bent. Also dropkicked. In the moment of hesitation, the postman screamed, "Ladies, ladies! I'm not going to deposit this mail till you all get the hell away from me! Please!"

There was panic in his face, and his voice labored to sound commanding, but there was a discernible crack in every syllable. The old women pressed closer for a moment, swaying in on him like telegraph vines aching for a message; spittle and madness were everywhere. Then, abruptly, there was a chilling sound that filled the lobby. It came from nowhere and everywhere, according to tradition. A voice as menacing, as sepulchral, as a cry for revenge from beyond the grave. It rose above the babble and its timbre held the vibrations of supernatural authority (though Bird detected a faint croaking far back in the glottis). WHO KNOWS WHAT EE-VIL LUUURKS IN THE HEARTS OF GRUBBY, VENAL OLD WOMEN WHO WEAR SUPPORT HOSE? THE SHUHADOW KNOWS! And then there was a chilling laugh that rose and rose and spiraled and soared and twisted like smoke from a pillaged city; a laugh that penetrated marble and steel and human flesh and froze the thoughts in the brain. One of the lenses of the postman's eyeglasses cracked.

Bird did not move. The old women, many of them clutching their cats, did not move. The postman did not move. Then, slowly, with fear, with the caution of a lemming herd brought to awareness at the final fatal moment that it was about to tumble over a cliff, the throng moved back gingerly. They cleared a space around the petrified postman.

"What the hell kind of a nuthouse *is* this?" he mumbled, lens shards tumbling down one cheek. There was no answer. So he began to tremble. GET ON WITH IT,

NITWIT, the voice said, and it was a command not to be ignored. The postman pulled loose the key from the master door, inserted it in the lower tier door, opened the metal plate, and began very quickly depositing Social Security checks in their proper receptacles. Bird watched; not the postman, or the old women huddling together, but the darker corners of the lobby. He thought he detected movement, a swirl of smoke, a whisper of dark cloth, an eddy of wind, a substanceless substance coming in his direction.

Finally, the postman finished his chores, locked the tier doors, and bolted through the mob and out the open front door, into the winter chill, even as the old women surged forward. Bird thought of the scene in *Zorba the Greek* where the old ladies wait for Bouboulina to die so they can confiscate her possessions: black-clad creatures crouched in bright-eyed mercilessness. They rushed the gang boxes and opened them hurriedly, withdrawing the checks that would permit them to have one meal of hamburger and onions tonight instead of canned pet food. One by one, then in clots, then in large groups, then again one by one, they rushed away from the mailboxes, clutching their cats, bedroom slippers making whispering sounds against the marble floor. Doors slammed and the sounds of skeletal shufflers climbing the stairs were all that remained . . . save for one old woman.

She stood in front of her open mailbox, her stick-thin hand inside the aperture, feeling, feeling. Her hand came up empty. Her check was not there. The beneficent government had fucked up. Tears stood in her tired eyes. Her body slumped into an exhausted S. Her shoulders trembled. She dropped her cat. It slipped around her feet and looked up at her. Bird felt helpless; he clenched his teeth; an auto graveyard junk compacter squeezed his insides. Who had brought this old woman to this place, this condition? It wasn't just age and being useless and unwanted, it was some entropic force, some nameless conspiracy of inarticulate inhumanity that reduced people to being open bird mouths, raw nerve ends, naked animals, husks deprived of visions, flesh waiting to rot. It wasn't just that some bureaucratic fiefdom had slipped a cog. That could happen. No system is perfect. It was that this lined and discarded creature had been brought to a final state of subsistence where one day's delay of her check could render her helpless and terrified.

At that moment, Cordwainer Bird swore that if he could purge his soul of the hatred for the particular group that had crushed *his* soul so effectively, if he could bring *them* to their knees, he would devote the rest of his life to wrecking these other conspiracies of corporate and governmental complexity whose only purposes in life were to preserve and maintain power at the level they'd attained and to beat down human beings to the *service* of the systems.

He remembered a quote from Brendan Behan. "I respect kindness to human beings first of all, and kindness to animals. I don't respect the law; I have a total irreverence for anything connected with society except that which makes the roads safer, the beer stronger, the food cheaper, and old men and women warmer in the winter, and happier in the summer." It was a flawed philosophy, and there were parts of it Bird did not subscribe to—there were too many roads already, and not enough land unflawed by concrete—but the tone was there; the tenor was right; the message was clear. Yes, from this moment on he would be considerably more than a writer, or a Fury bent on reclaiming his soul for personal reasons. From this moment on he would take up the mantle of Uncle Kent and Uncle Bruce Hagin, who had gone under the name G-8 when he had fought with his Battle Aces; and to some extent—though with greater sanity—Uncle Richard Wentworth, The Spider.

From this moment on the Bird would fly against the *new* forces of evil in the world.

His reverie was shattered by the shouting of the toothless old woman. Frustrated beyond endurance, she shrieked her hatred of the impossibly gigantic forces that had brought her low. As she scuffled back toward the door to the corridor down which her bleak room lay, she cursed them, without knowing who they were. She gummed her words. "God damn the Post Office! God damn the Social Security Administration!" She reached the door to the corridor and kicked it open with strength Bird could not have suspected lay in such a fragile body. The door banged against the inner wall of the corridor and hung there on its pneumatic door-closer. She staggered down the corridor toward her room, the cat padding at her heels. "God damn you Government! God damn you Herbert Hoover! God damn you Franklin Delano Roosevelt! God damn you Harry S Truman! God damn you Dwight D. Eisenhower! God damn you John F. Kennedy, may you rest in peace! God damn you Lyndon Baines Johnson! God damn you, God damn you, God damn you Richard Shit Nixon! God damn you Gerry Ford! God damn you Jimmy Carter." Bird's view of the old woman was steadily being narrowed as the door closed with a sigh, but in the final instant before it closed completely he saw her shove open the door to her room, the cat got underfoot, she kicked it viciously, sending it out of sight through the inner doorway, and the last thing he heard, in an anguished howl, was, "God damn you . . . God!"

Bird stood trembling uncontrollably.

Then he heard a faint cackling beside him.

He was alone in the lobby.

"Uncle Kent?" he asked the emptiness, looking around.

"Huh? Who's that?" The voice came out of nowhere.

"It's me, Uncle Kent. Cordwainer."

"Who? What? Are you The Black Master? Zemba? The Cobra? Who sent you? I have weapons, I still have weapons!"

"It's *me,* Uncle Kent . . . your nephew, Cordwainer Bird."

"You mean: it's *I,* not *me.* Oh, you. What the hell're you doing skulking around here? You out of a job again? I always told your momma you'd amount to nothing."

"Uh, listen, Uncle Kent, I need your help."

"Just what I thought, you little turd. Tryin' to make another touch, eh? Well, forget it. I snitched my Social Security check before those damned old biddies could get at him. Heh heh, filched it right out of that damned hippie's mailbag. Didn't even see me workin', did you? Heh, did you?"

"No, Uncle Kent, you were very subtle. I never saw a thing."

"Damned right you didn't. I'm as good as I ever was. I can *still* cloud men's minds so they cannot see me! Wish it worked as well on those be-damned cats. One of the little monsters pissed up my pant leg."

Bird could hear the sound of fabric rustling, as of someone shaking a leg. Still he could see no one.

"How's chances we go upstairs to your room and talk, Uncle Kent?" Bird suggested. "I don't need any money; I'm working on a case and I need some advice."

"Well, why didn't you say so; you take the elevator. I'll just fly up."

"You can't fly, Uncle Kent."

"Oh. Yeah, yeah, right, I forgot. Okay, we'll *both* take the elevator."

"Uh, Uncle Kent?"

"What now? Boy, you have become one be-damned nuisance, always asking stupid questions, why is the grass green, how many grains of sand in the Gobi, how high's the moon."

"You once told me how many grains of sand there were in the Gobi."

"I did? Hmmm. Well, what is it this time? Can't it wait till we take the elevator upstairs and get settled?"

"Uncle Kent, this building doesn't *have* an elevator."

"It doesn't, that's peculiar. I could have sworn it had an elevator. What floor do I live on?"

"The tenth."

"Well, you take the elevator, and I'll just fly up."

"I knew this Bird fellow had been a tv writer who punched a lot of producers because they *allegedly* altered his work, but as far as I knew for *certain*, he was just another of those hack sci-fi writers. We were doing a book of his called *Where Do You Hide the Elephant in a Spaceship?* It was a paperback original, a bunch of his stories. George, his editor, was off to the National Book Awards in Washington, D.C. and I got a call from this Bird nut, and he wanted to see the galleys of his book before it was printed. Well, for God's sake, I'm an *executive editor,* not some lackey; so I told him I couldn't be bothered sending out galleys to just *any* one who called up and demanded them. Then he started screaming that he was the *author* and he used the vilest language I've ever heard. Why, I didn't even know such things *could* be done with a vacuum cleaner. So I just hung up on the little twerp; I mean, I had a handball court reserved at the Club, I couldn't be hanging around the office all day listening to that kind of abuse! After all, I'm an *executive editor!* How did *I* know the copyediting had been farmed out to one of our 100 Neediest Cases at the Menninger Foundation? It wasn't *my* fault the book was set in Urdu."

Excerpt from diary notes of the late Skippy Wingwalker, former Executive Editor, Avon Books, New York; used as source material in the New York magazine article, "Portrait of a Publishing Punk: The Four-Storey Swandive of Li'l Skippy; Did He Jump or Was He Eased Out of the Industry?" by Aaron Latham; *16 February 1976*

Kent Allard's room was bare. Spartan. The walls had been painted dead white. So had the ceiling and floor. Also the inside of the door to the corridor and the inside of the empty clothes closet. Also the windows. Light from the bitter winter's day outside barely filtered through the paint.

The Shadow had once told his nephew he liked it that way. "Spend so damned much time in the dark, hanging out in alleys and doorways, always sitting shivering on fire escapes, jumping out be-damned windows, never really had a chance to get to use a door in my adult life, I want it white in here. White!" His nephew understood the urgencies of Uncle Kent's declining years. He never thought it odd.

Now they sat on the floor, facing each other, cross-legged. Bird had a vagrant wish that Uncle Kent would put at least a stool or campaign chair in the room, but the old man had acquired his abilities in the Orient, and he practiced self-denial, even at the age of eighty-one. Bird put the wish out of his mind; it was the least he could suffer, to get some help from this once-great champion of Good and Truth and Decency.

"You still ticked-off at me for now showing you how to cloud men's minds?" The Shadow asked.

"No, Uncle Kent. I understand."

"Heh. *Sure* you do! *Sure* you do! Every time I showed someone I trusted how to do it, he turned into a creep. That be-damned Oral Roberts, for instance, and his buddy, what's his name, Willy Graham . . . *Billy* Graham! That's it, Billy Graham! Pukers, both of 'em. But they sure can cloud men's minds. Don't do too bad with women's minds, neither. And what about those Watergate tapes. Mind-clouding if I ever saw it! If I was fifty again, hell, if I was *sixty* again, even *seventy*, by damn! I'd have had them Ehrlichburger and Haldeburger by the heels." He paused in his ranting and looked at his nephew. "Cordwainer? What the hell are you doing here? Did you learn to cloud men's minds? I never saw you come in."

"We came in together, Uncle Kent. I need your help." He hurriedly added, to forestall a familiar conversation, "I don't need any money. I need some advice and some good solid Shadow-style deductive thinking about a clue."

"A clue! By God and Street and Smith, a *clue!* Feed it to me, boy! Just drop it on me! Let me have it! A clue, by damn, a clue! I *love* clues." And he began coughing.

Bird slid across the floor and clapped the old man on the back. After a few minutes the coughing subsided, Kent Allard wiped the tears out of his eyes, pushed his tongue back into his mouth, and whispered, "I'm fine. Just fine. What's this clue you've got?"

Quickly going over the events of earlier that day, the insidious placement of his latest book in Brentano's crypt-like basement, the attack by Mrs. Jararacussu and her thugs, the revelation of the clue to their whereabouts, the seek-&-destroy team that had butchered the unfortunate pawn Jararacussu, the escape . . . Bird capped the recapitulation with a repeat of the whispered words that had been the last gesture of *their* mind-slave, Mrs. Jararacussu. "She said: 'You'll find them under the lady—' and she was cut off in mid-sentence. There was more. What does it mean to you, Uncle Kent? You know New York better than anyone."

"Well, Billy Batson knows the subway system better'n me, but I know everything else, that's for certain."

"So what does it mean to you?"

"Pornography, that's what it means to me, boy! Under the lady, indeed. That's what's wrong with the world today, too damned much smut. Why, when I was your age, Margo Lane and I had a nice, clean, decent relationship. I'd take her out to Steeplechase Park every once in a while and we'd go in the tunnel of love, and that was as close as *we* ever got to all this jiggery-pokery."

"Whatever happened to Margo Lane, Uncle Kent?"

He looked bitter. "She ran off with Bernard Geis."

He would talk no more about it, so Bird let it drop.

"I don't think it was a smutty reference, Uncle Kent. I think she was talking about a location. What does 'under the lady' bring to mind besides pornography?"

The old man thought for a moment. His tongue slipped out of his mouth.

Suddenly, his face lit up. His weary old eyes sparkled. "By damn!"

Cordwainer sat forward. "What've you got?"

"It *wasn't* Bernard Geis, it was one of his Associates."

Cordwainer slumped back. It was no use. The old man simply couldn't keep his thoughts together. He started to get up. "Well, thanks, anyway, Uncle Kent."

The Shadow stared up at him. "Where the hell you think you're going, boy? I haven't told you the location yet!"

"But . . . I thought . . ."

"You thought the old man simply couldn't keep his thoughts together, didn't you?"

Cordwainer sat down again. He looked humbled.

A soft smile came to the old man's face. "Well, I'm a bit fuzzy, nephew, that's for certain. You don't have to be kind about it. I know. It's hard being old and useless, but I love you, you little twerp, and I'm not so fuddled I don't know you've been getting my ring out of hock all these years. So I owe you a big one. And I'm going to tell you something that no one else knows. But it's the answer to your problem."

Cordwainer stared intensely at his uncle. There was an ineffable sadness in the old man's face that he had never before seen. And The Shadow began to speak.

"It was, oh, I guess the summer of 1949, just after I finished the case of 'The Whispering Eyes,' when Margo started *nuhdzing* me about getting married. Well, I was set in my ways, I wasn't home much, she was always complaining about my coming in and out through the windows, and I just couldn't see it working out. So we started tapering off. That went on for about eight years. We did things slower in those days. Then Geis started up that gawdawful ballyhoo press of his in 1958, with non-books by Art Linkletter and those other mushbrains, and Margo had been doing some public relations work for him, and damned if she didn't meet one of his Associates, a clown named Bruce Somethingorother. Started seeing him on the sly. When I found out about it, she was already pretty much under the spell of all that glamour and glitter. She was out every night doing The Twist and hanging around with all the people we'd spent years whipping and imprisoning."

He was staring at the white floor, now turning gray as the dim daylight faded into dusk outside.

"I found myself getting jealous. It never happened before. I . . . I never really knew how much she meant to me. She was always just good old Margo Lane, friend and companion; we used to do the town when I was in my Lamont Cranston disguise; she looked really terrific in an evening gown. . . ."

He paused to collect his thoughts. It was almost dark in the empty room now, but Bird thought he saw tears in the old man's eyes.

"I trailed them one night. They went to a secret place

where they met with others in the publishing business, and there was . . . there was . . ." He found it difficult to even speak the words. Then he straightened, snuffled loudly, and said, "There was an orgy. I slipped in and . . . and . . . dealt with them."

He stopped.

Cordwainer stared, not believing what he had heard. Then he whispered, "You killed . . . Margo Lane . . . ?"

The old man nodded. He started to flicker in Cordwainer's sight, as though trying to find some hiding place in the power of his invisibility. But he found the courage to stay visible, firmed up and said, "They were in a secret lair built under a lady. That was when I retired. I wasn't fit to carry the battle to evildoers any longer. I was one of them."

Cordwainer waited.

"The lady is the lady with the lamp. Whoever it is you're after, nephew, they've taken over the hideout under the Statue of Liberty. It's the only thing that makes sense."

They sat that way for a while.

Finally, Cordwainer Bird stood, placed a hand on the old man's shoulder, and said, "They've corrupted thousands of good people, Uncle Kent. I'll make good for you. And for Margo Lane."

He started for the door. The old man's voice stopped him. "Who are they, Cordwainer? Who are they, these utterly evil corrupters of truth and good? The Mafia, the military-industrial complex, the telephone company?"

"Far worse, Uncle Kent." And for the first time he spoke *their* name. "They're the New York Literary Establishment, dedicated to polluting the precious bodily fluids of all right-thinking readers and anyone else they can sink their diseased fangs into."

He opened the door. Turning back, he saw the old man vaguely, sitting on the floor alone and helpless, there in the final darkness. "But they've ruined their last writer, Uncle Kent. They've published their last non-book. Now they will feel the claws of . . . the Bird!"

And he was gone. In the silence of the white room there was only the pathetic whisper of an old man crying for times that were gone, never to be reclaimed.

> "In one evening, the entire New York literary scene was decimated. The unknown avenger who left only a single black raven's wing feather found his victims and meted out what some have called a peculiarly appropriate kind of justice for each one. Editor Michael Korda was found on a bridle path in Central Park, crushed beneath his horse. Tom Congdon, the Doubleday editor who cobbled up *Jaws,* was discovered nearby in the Central Park Weather Station pond, gummed to death by a school of minnows. Jason and Barbara Epstein of *The New York Review of Books* were found manacled to the wall of their posh apartment, hopelessly insane from having been forced to listen to a Dwight Macdonald lecture playing over and over on a tape loop. Elaine Kaufman of Elaine's Saloon was found stretched out on the bread-cutting board at Nick Spagnolo's restaurant, stuffed to bursting with *chicken al limone.* John Leonard and Harvey Shapiro, the former and the current editors of *The New York Times Book Review* had been stripped naked, put in a storage shed where the *Times* stockpiled its newsprint rolls, and had—on threat of what terrible fate we'll never know—been forced to fight it out with deadly pica rulers. Neither survived. But it was a massacre on Liberty Island, in a secret crypt beneath the Statue, that was most violent and terrible."
>
> Excerpt from a news
> story by Pete Hamill,
> *The Village Voice;*
> *10 February 1976*

The little man with the robin's-egg blue eyes and the straight black hair stood on the deck of the Upper New

York Harbor ferry, watching the Statue of Liberty grow closer. He stood near the prow, knowing that in a few minutes he would be diving overboard, knowing that he would be swimming toward a fate and a future that destiny had marked for him.

His thoughts fled backward. To the days in Hollywood and the terrible experiences with illiterate producers, cowardly network officials, tasteless censors, rapacious studio negotiators. To the day when he had done the awful deed that had sent him forever from the Coast and scriptwriting.

He dwelled on the foolish innocence that had led him to believe writing science fiction books was the answer, the release, the freedom. To the disillusionment. And then the attempt to break into what they called "the mainstream" of American literature. To the way they had held him down, paid him insulting advances, buried his books with terrible cover art and a two-thousand-copy sale to libraries. He thought of it all . . . the publisher who now lay on a slab in the morgue . . . the butchered book buyer hanging from a Rodin sculpture . . . the editor thrown from a fourth-floor window . . . and what lay ahead.

But the time for being beaten and used was gone. Now he was committed. What lay ahead, in all its finality and vengeful bloodletting . . . could not be avoided. They had gone too deep, had entrenched themselves too well. If even The Shadow had been broken by them, it would take a younger, stronger, less squeamish, *new* kind of avenging angel to set things right. The list was long, and only a few of them would be there, under the Statue. There would be more days, and more encounters.

But all that was in the future. The first step was *now!*

As the ferry neared the island, the little man stepped to the railing in the darkness, lifted himself, stood poised for a moment, then dropped smoothly and swiftly into the foul waters of New York Harbor, into the maelstrom of a destiny that would certainly be recorded by other writers, perhaps better writers, but writers who would know that Cordwainer Bird was their guardian angel.

Introduction to Seeing

It's Terry Carr, the anthologist again. He's to blame.

I get in terrible trouble through Terry's good offices and good intentions. Frequently. This time it was with "Seeing."

Terry called me one day a couple of years ago and said he was doing a collection of original stories that embodied the horror theme, but set in the future. And future horrors, he suggested, would be very different from those we know today. He asked me to write a story for the book, and said it would be published as a trade hardback by Little, Brown in 1977.

So I dwelled on the problem for a while—the problem of conceiving something not only universally horrible but wholly extrapolative—and decided Terry was wrong. Fear is universal, and what frightens us can be broken down into identifiable categories. Fear of closed-in places, fear of heights, fear of being burned or disfigured; snakes, spiders, pain of all kinds, fear of being ridiculed, drowning, fear of rejection. The usual chamber of horrors. And those would be present in any future time, even as they were throughout the past.

Now the problem resolved itself into my being able to write convincingly about something that frightened and horrified *me*. Unfortunately for my problem, none of the above give me even a moment's upset. I love cave crawling and tight places don't bother me in the least. I have climbed up the face of several buildings on sandblasting cables and once made a brief, precarious living hanging upside down in a painter's cradle, slathering rust-resistant paint on the underside of the Brooklyn-Manhattan Bridge; heights don't distress me. I won't stick my hand in a flame like a well-known Watergate conspirator, but fire doesn't send me into paroxysms of panic. I've hunted cottonmouth and water moccasin and once lopped the head off a knockwurst-thick rattler in my very own backyard here in Los Angeles, so that tells you how much I fear snakes. Same goes for spiders and other creepy crawlies. I have a very high pain threshold—which is why I usually look like a pile of mud when I come out the other side of a street fight—I just keep working even as I'm being pummeled—and as for disfigurement, well, I wasn't Paul Newman to start with, ain't my good looks that makes me the terrific little charismatic figure I are . . . so that takes care of *that*. I can swim, I've been rejected by experts (not to mention four divorces), and as for being ridiculed, well, when you're prepared to accept the core fact that you're an asshole, as I long ago accepted it about myself . . .

So what scares me?

Contact lenses.

I'd rather not discuss this, thank you.

Kathryn LorBiecki told me that we breathe through our eyes as well as our pores, and that having something laid over the cornea was, to me, like suffocating. She might be correct. I don't know. All I know is that the thought of things in my eyes paralyzes me. And when I realized that, I had the horror . . . but not the story.

So then I dreamed up the idea of eyes that could see in new and strange ways. The eyes of a mutant. Rare eyes, that would be valuable. And then I remembered Burke and Hare, the Irish laborer and his accomplice who, in the late 1820s, smothered people to provide bodies for sale to Dr. Knox of the Edinburgh School of Anatomy. They were the most famous body snatchers in history, and figures of darkness who seemed just right for my horror story. Which led me to the concept of an illicit traffic in mutant eyes, forever eyes. And that led me to the woman who had such eyes, and her personal torment, and then the Knoxdoctor who would *buy* the eyes, and the customer who would be able to pay a fabulous price for such a black market item . . .

And there it was.

So I began writing, trying to maintain the image of eyes throughout. (Consider the way I've described the spaceport.)

And when it was done I sent it off to Terry for *The Ides of Tomorrow*, and he was delighted enough with it to also pick it for his annual "best sf stories of the year" collection.

But. Trouble.

Little, Brown decided to issue it as a "young adult" book from their juvenile division, rather than as an adult trade book. And here was this utterly horrific story filled with dark and terrible visions being put into the hands of tots and acne-festooned teens.

The Virginia Kirkus Service—a review service circulated within the publishing industry, previewing new books—made this wonderful comment about the story:

"Nine stories, both original and horrible—so much so that one might wonder why they weren't pegged as adult. The opener, by the vaunted Harlan Ellison, tells, in the hyper-kinetic mode and diffusely pornographic sensibility which are his trademarks, of a peculiarly grisly sort of eye transplant."

Great. Just great.

Delighted to find out that my trademark is a diffusely pornographic sensibility. Whatever *that* means.

Well, at any rate, I seem to have achieved the level of horror I was groping for, in my peculiarly diffused pornographic and hyperkinetically modal way. Cha cha cha.

Clearly, all that is left for me, my career as a serious writer having been blighted by association with Terry Carr and the nameless pervert at Little, Brown who (I'm sure with utmost and diffusely pornographic intent) slid this story out of the adult category and into the paws of children . . . is a future in kiddie porn.

Great. Just great.

•

". . . take a walk some night on a suburban street and pass house after house on both sides of the street each with the lamplight of the living room, shining golden, and inside the little blue square of the television, each living family riveting its attention on probably one show; nobody talking; silence in the yards; dogs barking at you because you pass on human feet instead of on wheels. You'll see what I mean, when it begins to appear like everybody in the world is soon going to be thinking the same way and the Zen Lunatics have long joined dust, laughter on their dust lips."

Jack Kerouac, *The Dharma Bums*

Seeing

"I remember well the time when the thought of the eye made me cold all over."

Charles Darwin, 1860

"Hey. Berne. Over there. Way back in that booth . . . see her?"

"Not now. I'm tired. I'm relaxing."

"Jizzus, Berne, take a look at her."

"Grebbie, if you don't synch-out and let me get doused, I swear I'll bounce a shot thimble off your skull."

"Okay, have it like you want it. But they're gray-blue."

"What?"

"Forget it, Berne. You said forget it, so forget it."

"Turn around here, man."

"I'm drinking."

"Listen, snipe, we been out all day looking . . ."

"Then when I tell you something from now on, you gonna *hear* me?"

"I'm sorry, Grebbie. Now come on, man, which one is she?"

"Over there. Pin her?"

"The plaid jumper?"

"No, the one way back in the dark in that booth behind the plaid. She's wearing a kaftan . . . wait'll the lights come around again . . . *there!* Y'pin her? Gray-blue, just like the Doc said he wanted."

"Grebbie, you are one beautiful pronger."

"Yeah, huh?"

"Now just turn around and stop staring at her before she sees you. We'll get her."

"How, Berne? This joint's full up."

"She's gotta move out sometime. She'll go away."

"And we'll be right on her, right, Berne?"

"Grebbie, have another punchup and let me drink."

"Jizzus, man, we're gonna be livin' crystalfine when we get them back to the Doc."

"Grebbie!"

"Okay, Berne, okay. Jizzus, she's got beautiful eyes."

From extreme long shot, establishing; booming down to tight closeup, it looked like this:

Viewed through the fisheye-lens of a Long Drive vessel's stateroom iris, as the ship sank to Earth, the area surrounding the pits and pads and terminal structures of PIX—the Polar Interstellar Exchange port authority terminus—was a doughnut-shaped crazy quilt of rampaging colors. In the doughnut hole center was PIX, slate-gray alloys macroscopically homogenized to ignore the onslaughts of deranged Arctic weather. Around the port was a nomansland of eggshell-white plasteel with shock fibers woven into its surface. Nothing could pass across that dead area without permission. A million flickers of beckoning light erupted every second from the colorful doughnut, as if silent Circes called unendingly for visitors to come find their sources. Down, down, the ship would come and settle into its pit, and the view in the iris would vanish. Then tourists would leave the Long Driver through underground slidewalk tunnels that would carry them into the port authority for clearance and medical checks and baggage inspection.

Tram carts would carry the cleared tourists and returning Long Drive crews through underground egress passages to the outlets beyond the nomansland. Security waivers signed, all responsibility for their future safety returned to them, their wit and protective devices built into their clothing the only barriers between them and what lay aboveground, they would be shunted into cages and whisked to the surface.

Then the view reappeared. The doughnut-shaped area around the safe port structures lay sprawled before the newly arrived visitors and returnees from space. Without form or design, the area was scatter-packed with a thousand shops and arcades, hostelries and dives, pleasure palaces and food emporiums. As though they had been wind-thrown anemophilously, each structure grew up side by side with its neighbors. Dark and twisting alleyways careened through from one section to the next. Spitalfields in London and Greenwich Village in old New York—before the Crunch—had grown up this way, like a jungle of hungry plants. And every open doorway had its barker, calling and gesturing, luring the visitors into the maw of unexpected experiences. Demander circuits flashed lights directly into the eyes of passersby, operating off retinal-heat-seeking mechanisms. Psychosound loops kept up an unceasing subliminal howling, each message striving to cap those filling the air around it, struggling to capture the attention of tourists with fat credit accounts. Beneath the ground, machinery labored mightily, the occasional squeal of plasteel signifying that even at top-point efficiency the guts of the area could not keep up with the demands of its economy. Crowds flowed in definite patterns, first this way, then that way, following the tidal pulls of a momentarily overriding loop, a barker's spiel filling an eye-of-the-hurricane silence, a strobing demander suddenly reacting to an overload of power.

The crowds contained prongers, coshmen, fagin brats, pleasure pals, dealers, pickpockets, hustlers, waltzers, pseudo-marks, gophers, rowdy-dowdy hijackers, horses, hot slough workers, whores, steerers, blousers of all ages, sheiks, shake artists, kiters, floaters, aliens from three hundred different federations, assassins and, of course, innocent johns, marks, hoosiers, kadodies, and tourists ripe for shucking.

Following one such tidal flow of crowd life, down an alley identified on a wall as Poke Way, the view would narrow down to a circular doorway in a green one-storey building. The sign would scream THE ELEGANT. Tightening the angle of observation, moving inside, the place could be seen to be a hard-drinking bar.

At the counter, as the sightline tracked around the murky bar, one could observe two men hunched over their thimbles, drinking steadily and paying attention to nothing but what their credit cards could buy, dumbwaitered up through the counter to their waiting hands. To an experienced visitor to the area, they would be clearly identifiable as "butt'n'ben" prongers: adepts at locating and furnishing to various Knox Shops whatever human parts were currently in demand.

Tracking further right, into the darkness of the private booths, the view would reveal (in the moments when the revolving overhead globes shone into those black spaces) an extremely attractive, but weary-looking, young woman with gray-blue eyes. Moving in for a tight closeup, the view would hold that breathtaking face for long moments, then move in and in on the eyes . . . those remarkable eyes.

All this, all these sights, in the area called WorldsEnd.

Verna tried to erase the memory with the oblivion of drink. Drugs made her sick to her stomach and never accomplished what they were supposed to do. But chigger, and rum and bowl could do it . . . if she downed them in sufficient quantities. Thus far, the level had not been even remotely approached. The alien, and what she had had to do to service him, were still fresh in her mind. Right near the surface, like scum. Since she had left the safe house and gone on her own, it had been one disaster after another. And tonight, the slug thing from . . .

She could not remember the name of the world it called its home. Where it lived in a pool of liquid, in a state of what passed for grace only to those who raised other life forms for food.

She punched up another bowl and then some bread, to dip in the thick liquor. Her stomach was sending her messages of pain.

There had to be a way out. Out of WorldsEnd, out of the trade, out of the poverty and pain that characterized this planet for all but the wealthiest and most powerful. She looked into the bowl and saw it as no one else in The Elegant could have seen it.

The brown, souplike liquor, thick and dotted with lighter lumps of amber. She saw it as a whirlpool, spinning down to a finite point of silver radiance that spun on its own axis, whirling and whirling: a mad eye. A funnel of living brilliance flickering with chill heat that ran back against the spin, surging toward the top of the bowl and forming a barely visible surface tension of coruscating light, a thousand-colored dome of light.

She dipped the bread into the funnel and watched it tear apart like the finest lace. She brought it up, soaking, and ripped off a piece with her fine, white, even teeth—thinking of tearing the flesh of her mother. Sydni, her mother, who had gifted her with this curse, these eyes. This terrible curse that prevented her from seeing the world as it was, as it might have been, as it might be; seeing the world through eyes of wonder that had become horror before she turned five years old. Sydni, who had been in the trade before her, and her mother before *her;* Sydni, who had borne her through the activities of one nameless father after another. And one of them had carried the genes that had produced the eyes. Forever eyes.

She tried desperately to get drunk, but it wouldn't happen. More bread, another bowl, another chigger and rum—and nothing happened. But she sat in the booth, determined not to go back into the alleys. The alien might be looking for her, might still demand its credits' worth of sex and awfulness, might try once again to force her to drink the drink it had called "mooshsquash." The chill that came over her made her shiver; brain movies with forever eyes were vivid and always fresh, always now, never memories, always happening *then.*

She cursed her mother and thought the night would probably never end.

An old woman, a very old woman, a woman older than anyone born on the day she had been born, nodded her head to her dressers. They began covering her terrible nakedness with expensive fabrics. She had blue hair. She did not speak to them.

Now that he had overcome the problems of pulse pressure on the association fibers of the posterior lobe of the brain, he was certain the transplanted mutations would be able to mold the unconscious cerebral image of the seen world into the conscious percept. He would make no guarantees for the ability of the recipient to cope with the flux of the external world in all its complexity—infinitely more complicated as "seen" through the mutated transplant eyes—but he knew that his customers would hardly be deterred by a lack of such guarantees. They were standing in line. Once he had said, "The unaided human eye under the best possible viewing conditions can distinguish ten million different color surfaces; with transplants the eye will perceive ten *billion* different color surfaces; or more," then, once he had said it, then he had them hooked. They . . . *she* . . . would pay anything. And anything was how much he would demand. Anything to get off this damned planet, away from the rot that was all expansion had left of Earth.

There was a freehold waiting for him on one of the ease-colonies of Kendo IV. He would take passage and arrive like a prince from a foreign land. He would spin out the remaining years of his life with pleasure and comfort and respect. He would no longer be a Knoxdoctor, forced to accept ghoulish assignments at inflated prices, and then compelled to turn over the credits to the police and the sterngangs that demanded "protection" credit.

He needed only one more. A fresh pair for that blue-haired old harridan. One more job, and then release from this incarceration of fear and desperation and filth. A pair of gray-blue eyes. Then freedom, in the ease-colony.

It was cold in Dr. Breame's Knox Shop. The tiny vats of nutrients demanded drastically lowered temperatures. Even in the insulated coverall he wore, Dr. Breame felt the cold.

But it was always warm on Kendo IV.

And there were no prongers like Grebbie and Berne on Kendo IV. No strange men and women and children with eyes that glowed. No still-warm bodies brought in off the alleys, to be hacked and butchered. No vats with cold flesh floating in nutrient. No filth, no disgrace, no payoffs, no fear.

He listened to the silence of the operating room.

It seemed to be filled with something other than mere absence of sound. Something deeper. A silence that held within its ordered confines a world of subtle murmurings.

He turned, staring at the storage vats in the ice cabinet. Through the nearly transparent film of frost on the see-through door he could discern the parts idly floating in their nutrients. The mouths, the filaments of nerve bundles, the hands still clutching for life. There were sounds coming from the vats.

He had heard them before.

All the voiceless voices of the dead.

The toothless mouths calling his name: *Breame, come here, Breame, step up to us, look at us, come nearer so we can talk to you, closer so we can touch you, show you the true cold that waits for you.*

He trembled . . . surely with the cold of the operating room. *Here, Breame, come here, we have things to tell you: the dreams you helped end, the wishes unanswered, the lives cut off like these hands. Let us touch you, Dr. Breame.*

He nibbled at his lower lip, willing the voices to silence. And they went quiet, stopped their senseless pleading. Senseless, because very soon Grebbie and Berne would come, and they would surely bring with them a man or a woman or a child with glowing blue-gray eyes, and then he would call the woman with blue hair, and she would come to his Knox Shop, and he would operate, and then take passage.

It was always warm, and certainly it would always be quiet. On Kendo IV.

Extract from the brief of the Plaintiff in the libel suit of 26 Krystabel Parsons v. Liquid Magazine, *Liquid Newsfax Publications, LNP Holding Group, and 311 unnamed Doe personages.*

from *Liquid Magazine* (uncredited profile):

Her name is 26 Krystabel Parsons. She is twenty-sixth in the line of Directors of Minet. Her wealth is beyond measure, her holdings span three federations, her residences can be found on one hundred and fifty-eight worlds, her subjects numberless, her rule absolute. She is one of the last of the unchallenged tyrants known as power brokers.

In appearance she initially reminds one of a kindly old grandmother, laugh-wrinkles around the eyes, blue hair uncoiffed, wearing exo-braces to support her withered legs.

But one hour spent in the company of this woman, this magnetism, this dominance . . . this force of nature . . . and all mummery reveals itself as cheap disguise maintained for her own entertainment. All masks are discarded and the Director of Minet shows herself more nakedly than anyone might care to see her.

Ruthless, totally amoral, jaded beyond belief with every pleasure and distraction the galaxy can provide, 26 Krystabel Parsons intends to live the rest of her life (she is one hundred and ten years old, and the surgeons of O-Pollinoor, the medical planet she caused to have built and staffed, have promised her at least another hundred and fifty, in exchange for endowments whose enormity staggers the powers of mere gossip) hell-bent on one purpose alone: the pursuit of more exotic distractions.

Liquid Magazine managed to infiltrate the entourage of the Director during her Grand Tour of the Filament recently (consult the handy table in the front of this issue for ready conversion to your planetary approximation). During the time our correspondent spent with the tour, incidents followed horn-on-horn in such profusion that this publication felt it impossible to enumerate them fully in just one issue. From Porte Recoil at one end of the Filament to Earth at the other—a final report not received as of this publication—our correspondent has amassed a wealth of authenticated incident and first-hand observations we will present in an eleven-part series, beginning with this issue.

As this issue is etched, the Director of Minet and her entourage have reached PIX and have managed to elude the entire newsfax media corps. *Liquid Magazine* is pleased to report that, barring unforeseen circumstances, this exclusive series and the final report from our correspondent detailing the mysterious reasons for the Director's first visit to Earth in sixty years will be the only coverage of this extraordinary personality to appear in fax since her ascension and the termination of her predecessor.

Because of the history of intervention and censorship attendant on all previous attempts to report the affairs of 26 Krystabel Parsons, security measures as extraordinary as the subject herself have been taken to insure no premature leaks of this material will occur.

Note Curiae: Investigation advises subsequent ten installments of series referred to passim foregoing extract failed to reach publication. Entered as Plaintiff Exhibit 1031.

They barely had time to slot their credits and follow her. She paid in the darkness between bursts of light from the globes overhead; and when they were able to sneak a look at her, she was already sliding quickly from the booth and rushing for the iris. It was as if she knew she was being pursued. But she could not have known.

"Berne . . ."

"I see her. Let's go."

"You think she knows we're onto her?"

Berne didn't bother to answer. He slotted credits for both of them and started after her. Grebbie lost a moment in confusion and then followed his partner.

The alley was dark now, but great gouts of blood-red and sea-green light were being hurled into the passageway from a top-mixer joint at the corner. She turned right out of Poke Way and shoved through the jostling crowds lemming toward Yardey's Battle Circus. They reached the mouth of the alley in time to see her cut across between rickshas, and followed as rapidly as they could manage through the traffic. Under their feet they could feel the throbbing of the machinery that supplied power to WorldsEnd. The rasp of circuitry overloading mixed faintly with the clang and shrieks of Yardey's sonic come-ons.

She was moving swiftly now, off the main thoroughfare. In a moment Grebbie was panting, his stubby legs pumping like pistons, his almost-neckless body tilted far forward, as he tried to keep up with lean Berne. Chew Way opened on her left and she moved through a clutch of tourists from Horth, all painted with chevrons, and turned down the alley.

"Berne . . . wait up . . ."

The lean pronger didn't even look back. He shoved aside a barker with a net trying to snag him into a free house and disappeared into Chew Way. The barker caught Grebbie.

"Lady, please . . ." Grebbie pleaded, but the scintillae in the net had already begun flooding his bloodstream with the desire to bathe and frolic in the free house. The barker was pulling him toward the iris as Berne reappeared from the mouth of Chew Way and punched her in the throat. He pulled the net off Grebbie, who made idle, underwater movements in the direction of the free house. Berne slapped him. "If I didn't need you to help carry her . . ."

He dragged Grebbie into the alley.

Ahead of them, Verna stopped to catch her breath. In the semidarkness her eyes glowed faintly; first gray, a delicate ash-gray of moth wings and the decay of Egypt;

then blue, the fog-blue of mercury light through deep water and the lips of a cadaver. Now that she was out of the crowds, it was easier. For a moment, easier.

She had no idea where she was going. Eventually, when the special sight of those endless memories had overwhelmed her, when her eyes had become so well adjusted to the flash-lit murkiness of the punchup pub that she was able to see . . .

She put that thought from her. Quickly. Reliving, that was almost the worst part of *seeing*. Almost.

. . . when her sight had grown that acute, she had fled the punchup, as she fled *any* place where she had to deal with people. Which was why she had chosen to become one of the few blousers in the business who would service aliens. As disgusting as it might be, it was infinitely easier with these malleable, moist creatures from far away than with men and women and children whom she could see as they . . .

She put that thought from her. Again. Quickly. But she knew it would return; it always returned; it was always there. The worst part of *seeing*.

Bless you, Mother Sydni. Bless you and keep you.

Wherever you are; burning in tandem with my father, whoever he was. It was one of the few hateful thoughts that sustained her.

She walked slowly. Ignoring the hushed and urgent appeals from the rag mounds that bulked in the darkness of the alley. Doorways that had been melted closed now held the refuse of WorldsEnd humanity that no longer had anything to sell. But they continued needing.

A hand came out of the black mouth of a sewer trap. Bone fingers touched her ankle; fingers locked around her ankle. "Please . . ." The voice was torn out by the roots, its last film of moisture evaporating, leaves withering and curling in on themselves like a crippled fist.

"Shut up! Get away from me!" Verna kicked out and missed the hand. She stumbled, trying to keep her balance, half turned, and came down on the wrist. There was a brittle snap and a soft moan as the broken member was dragged back into the darkness.

She stood there screaming at nothing, at the dying and useless thing in the sewer trap. "Let me alone! I'll kill you if you don't leave me alone!"

Berne looked up. "That her?"

Grebbie was himself again. "Might could be."

They started off at a trot, down Chew Way. They saw her faintly limned by the reflection of lights off the alley wall. She was stamping her foot and screaming.

"I think she's going to be trouble," Berne said.

"Crazy, you ask me," Grebbie muttered. "Let's cosh her and have done with it. The Doc is waiting. He might have other prongers out looking. We get there too late and we've wasted a lot of time we could of spent—"

"Shut up. She's making such a hell of a noise she might've already got the police on her."

"Yeah, but . . ."

Berne grabbed him by the tunic. "What if she's under bond to a sterngang, you idiot?"

Grebbie said no more.

They hung back against the wall, watching as the girl let her passion dissipate. Finally, in tears, she stumbled away down the alley. They followed, pausing only to stare into the shadows as they passed a sewer trap. A brittle, whispering moan came from the depths. Grebbie shivered.

Verna emerged into the blare of drug sonics from a line of top-mixers that sat horn-on-horn down the length of Courage Avenue. They had very little effect on her; drugs were in no way appealing; they only intensified her *seeing*, made her stomach hurt, and in no way blocked the visions. Eventually, she knew, she would have to return to her coop; to take another customer. But if the slug alien was waiting . . .

A foxmartin in sheath and poncho sidled up. He leaned in, bracing himself with shorter appendages against the metal sidewalk, and murmured something she did not understand. But the message was quite clear. She smiled, hardly caring whether a smile was considered friendly or hostile in the alien's mind. She said, very clearly, "Fifty credits." The foxmartin dipped a stunted appendage into the poncho's roo, and brought up a liquid shot of an Earthwoman and a foxmartin without its shield. Verna looked at the liquid and then away quickly. It wasn't likely the alien in the shot was the same one before her; this was probably an example of vulpine pornography; she shoved the liquid away from her face. The foxmartin slid it back into the roo. It murmured again, querulous.

"One hundred and fifty credits," Verna said, trying hard to look at the alien, but only managing to retain a living memory of appendages and soft brown female flesh.

The foxmartin's fetching member slid into the roo again, moved swiftly out of sight, and came up with the credits.

Grebbie and Berne watched from the dimly shadowed mouth of Chew Way. "I think they struck a deal," Grebbie said softly. "How the hell can she do it with something looks like that?"

Berne didn't answer. How could people do *any* of the disgusting things they did to stay alive? They *did* them, that was all. If anyone really had a choice, it would be a different matter. But the girl was just like him: She did what she had to do. Berne did not really like Grebbie. But Grebbie could be pushed and shoved, and that counted for more than a jubilant personality.

They followed close behind as the girl with the forever eyes took the credits from the alien and started off through the crowds of Courage Avenue. The foxmartin slid a sinuous coil around the girl's waist. She did not look at the alien, though Berne thought he saw her shudder; but even from that distance he couldn't be certain. Probably not: a woman who would service *things*.

Dr. Breame sat in the far corner of the operating room, watching the movement of invisible life in the Knox Shop. His eyes flicked back and forth, seeing the unseen things that tried to reach him. Things without all their parts. Things that moved in liquid and things that tried to crawl out of waste bins. He knew all the clichés of seeing love or hate or fear in eyes, and he knew that eyes could reflect none of those emotions without the subtle play of facial muscles, the other features of the face to lend expression. Even so, he *felt* his eyes were filled with fear. Silence, but movement, considerable movement, in the cold operating room.

The slug alien was waiting. It came up out of a belowstairs entranceway and moved so smoothly, so rapidly, that Berne and Grebbie froze in a doorway, instantly discarding their plan to knife the foxmartin and prong the girl and rush off with her. It flowed up out of the dark and filled the twisting passageway with the wet sounds of its fury. The foxmartin tried to get between Verna and the creature; and the slug rose up and fell on him. There was a long moment of terrible sucking sounds, solid matter being turned to pulp and the marrow being drawn out as bones caved in on themselves, filling the lumen with shards of splintered calcium.

When it flowed off the foxmartin, Verna screamed and dodged away from the mass of oily gray worm oozing toward her. Berne began to curse; Grebbie started forward.

"What the hell good can you do?" Berne said, grabbing his partner. "She's gone, dammit!"

Verna ran toward them, the slug alien expanding to fill the passageway, humping after her like a tidal wave. Yes, yes, she had *seen* that crushed, empty image . . . *seen* it a thousand times, like reflections of reflections, shadow auras behind the reality . . . but she hadn't known what it meant . . . hadn't *wanted* to know what it meant! Servicing aliens, as perverted and disgusting as it was, had been the only way to keep sane, keep living, keep a vestige of hope that there was a way out, a way off Earth. Yes, she had seen the death of the foxmartin, but it hadn't mattered—it wasn't a *person,* it was a creature, a thing that could not in sanity have sex with a human, that *had to have* sex with a human, in whatever twisted fashion it found erotic. But now even that avenue was closing behind her . . .

She ran toward them, the slug alien making its frenzied quagmire sounds of outrage and madness, rolling in an undulant comber behind her. Grebbie stepped into her path and the girl crashed into him, throwing them both against the wall of the passageway. Berne turned and ran back the way he had come. An enormous shadow, the slug alien, puffed up to three times its size, filled the foot of the passage.

Berne saw lights ahead, and pounded toward them.

Underfoot, he felt a rumbling, a jerking of parts and other parts. There was a whining in his ears, and he realized he had been hearing it for some time. Then the passageway heaved and he was hurled sidewise, smashing face first into the melted window of a condemned building. He flailed wildly as the metal street under him bucked and warped, and then he fell, slamming into the wall and sliding down. He was sitting on the bucking metal, looking back toward the foot of the passage, when the slug alien suddenly began to glow with blue and orange light.

Verna was lying so close to the edge of the creature that the heat it gave off singed her leg. The fat little man she'd run into was somewhere under the alien. Gone now. Dead. Like the foxmartin.

But the slug was shrieking in pain, expanding and expanding, growing more monstrous, rising up almost to the level of second-storey windows. She had no idea what was happening . . . the whining was getting louder . . . she could smell the acrid scent of ozone, burning glass, boiling lubricant, sulfur . . .

The slug alien glowed blue, orange, seemed to be lit from inside, writhed hideously, expanded, gave one last, unbelievable sucking moan of pain and *burned.* Verna crawled away on hands and knees, down the egress passage, toward the light, toward the shape of a man just getting to his feet, looking dazed. Perhaps he could help her.

"The damned thing killed Grebbie. I didn't know what was happening. All at once everything was grinding and going crazy. The power under the streets had been making lousy sounds all night, I guess it was overloading, I don't know. Maybe that filthy thing caused it somehow, some part of it got down under the sidewalk plate and fouled the machinery, made it blow out. I think it was electrocuted . . . I don't know. But she's here, and she's got what you need, and I want the full amount; Grebbie's share and mine both!"

"Keep your voice down, you thug. My patient may arrive at any moment."

Verna lay on the operating table, watching them. *Seeing* them. Shadows behind shadows behind shadows. All the reflections. *Pay him, Doctor,* she thought, *it won't mat-*

ter. He's going to die soon enough. So are you. And the way Grebbie bought it will look good by comparison. Good bless and keep you, Sydni. She could not turn it off now, nor damp it with bowl, nor hide the images in the stinking flesh of creatures from other worlds of other stars. And in minutes, at best mere moments, they would ease her burden; they would give her peace, although they didn't know it. *Pay him, Doctor, and let's get to it.*

"Did you have to maul her?"

"I didn't maul her, damn you! I hit her once, the way I hit all the others. She's not damaged. You only want the eyes anyhow. Pay me!"

The Knoxdoctor took credits from a pouch on his coverall and counted out an amount the pronger seemed to find satisfactory. "Then why is she so bloody?" He asked the question as an afterthought, like a surly child trying to win one final point after capitulating.

"Creep off, Doc," Berne said nastily, counting the credits. "She was crawling away from that worm. She fell down half a dozen times. I told you. If you're not satisfied with the kind of merchandise I bring you, get somebody else. Tell me how many other prongers could've found you a pair of them eyes in gray-blue, so quick after a call?"

Dr. Breame had no time to form an answer. The iris dilated and three huge Floridans stepped into the Knox Shop, moved quickly through the operating room, checked out the storage area, the consultation office, the power bins, and came back to stand near the iris, their weapons drawn.

Breame and Berne watched silently, the pronger awed despite himself at the efficiency and clearly obvious readiness of the men. They were heavy-gravity-planet aliens, and Berne had once seen a Floridan put his naked fist through a plasteel plate two inches thick. He didn't move.

One of the aliens stepped through the iris, said something to someone neither Berne nor the doctor could see, and then came back inside. A minute later they heard the sounds of a group moving down the passage to the Knox Shop.

26 Krystabel Parsons strode into the operating room and waved her guard back. All but the three already in the Knox Shop. She slapped her hands down to her hips, locking the exo-braces. She stood unwaveringly and looked around.

"Doctor," she said, greeting him perfunctorily. She looked at the pronger.

"Greetings, Director. I'm pleased to see you at long last. I think you'll find—"

"Shut up." Her eyes narrowed at Berne. "Does this man have to die?"

Berne started to speak, but Breame quickly, nervously answered. "Oh, no; no indeed not. This gentleman has been most helpful to our project. He was just leaving."

"I was just leaving."

The old woman motioned to one of the guards, and the Floridan took Berne by the upper arm. The pronger winced, though the guard apparently was only serving as butler. The alien propelled Berne toward the iris, and out. Neither returned.

Dr. Breame said, "Will these, uh, gentlemen be necessary, Director? We have some rather delicate surgery to perform and they can . . ."

"They can *assist.*" Her voice was flat as iron.

She dropped her hands to her hips again, flicking up the locking levers of the exo-braces that formed a spiderweb scaffolding around her withered legs. She strode across the operating room toward the girl immobilized on the table, and Breame marveled at her lack of reaction to the cold in the room: he was still shivering in his insulated coverall, she wore an ensemble made of semitransparent, iridescent flow bird scales. But she seemed oblivious to the temperature of the Knox Shop.

26 Krystabel Parsons came to Verna and looked down into her face. Verna closed her eyes. The Director could not have known the reason the girl could not look at her.

"I have an unbendable sense of probity, child. If you cooperate with me, I shall make certain you don't have a moment of regret."

Verna opened her eyes. The Director drew in her breath.

They were everything they'd been said to be.

Gray and blue, swirling, strange, utterly lovely.

"What do you see?" the Director asked.

"A tired old woman who doesn't know herself well enough to understand that all she wants to do is die."

The guards started forward. 26 Krystabel Parsons waved them back. "On the contrary," she said. "I not only desire life for myself . . . I desire it for you. I'm assuring you, if you help us, there is nothing you can ask that I will refuse."

Verna looked at her, *seeing* her, knowing she was lying. Forever eyes told the truth. What this predatory relic wanted was: everything; who she was willing to sacrifice to get it was: everyone; how much mercy and kindness Verna could expect from her was: infinitesimal. But if one could not expect mercy from one's own mother, how could one expect it from strangers?

"I don't believe you."

"Ask and you shall receive." She smiled. It was a terrible stricture. The memory of the smile, even an instant after it was gone, persisted in Verna's sight.

"I want full passage on a Long Driver."

"Where?"

"Anywhere I want to go."

The Director motioned to one of the guards. "Get her a million credits. No. Five million credits."

The guard left the Knox Shop.

"In a moment you will see I keep my word," said the Director. "I'm willing to pay for my pleasures."

"You're willing to pay for my pain, you mean."

The Director turned to Breame. "Will there be pain?"

"Very little, and what pain there is, will mostly be yours, I'm afraid." He stood with hands clasped together in front of him: a small child anxiously trying to avoid giving offense.

"Now, tell me what it's like," 26 Krystabel Parsons said, her face bright with expectation.

"The mutation hasn't bred true, Director. It's still a fairly rare recessive—" Breame stopped. She was glaring at him. She had been speaking to the girl.

Verna closed her eyes and began to speak. She told the old woman of *seeing*. Seeing directions, as blind fish in subterranean caverns see the change in flow of water, as bees see the wind currents, as wolves see the heat auras surrounding humans, as bats see the walls of caves in the dark. Seeing memories, everything that ever happened to her, the good and the bad, the beautiful and the grotesque, the memorable and the utterly forgettable, early memories and those of a moment before, all on instant recall, with absolute clarity and depth of field and detail, the whole of one's past, at command. Seeing colors, the sensuousness of airborne bacteria, the infinitely subtle shadings of rock and metal and natural wood, the tricksy shifts along a spectrum invisible to ordinary eyes of a candle flame, the colors of frost and rain and the moon and arteries pulsing just under the skin; the intimate overlapping colors of fingerprints left on a credit, so reminiscent of paintings by the old master Jackson Pollock. Seeing colors that no human eyes have ever seen. Seeing shapes and relationships, the intricate calligraphy of all parts of the body moving in unison, the day melding into the night, the spaces and spaces between spaces that form a street, the invisible lines linking people. She spoke of *seeing,* of *all* the kinds of seeing except. The stroboscopic view of everyone. The shadows within shadows behind shadows that formed terrible, tortuous portraits she could not bear. She did not speak of that. And in the middle of her long recitation the Floridan guard came back and put five million credits in her tunic.

And when the girl was done, 26 Krystabel Parsons turned to the Knoxdoctor and said, "I want her kept alive, with as little damage as possible to her faculties. You will place a value on her comfort as high as mine. Is that clearly understood?"

Breame seemed uneasy. He wet his lips, moved closer to the Director (keeping an eye on the Floridans, who did not move closer to him). "May I speak to you in privacy?" he whispered.

"I have no secrets from this girl. She is about to give me a great gift. You may think of her as my daughter."

The doctor's jaw muscles tensed. This was, after all, *his* operating room! *He* was in charge here, no matter how much power this unscrupulous woman possessed. He stared at her for a moment, but her gaze did not waver. Then he went to the operating table where Verna lay immobilized by a holding circuit in the table itself, and he pulled down the anesthesia bubble over her head. A soft, eggshell-white fog instantly filled the bubble.

"I must tell you, Director, now that she cannot hear us—"

(But she could still *see,* and the patterns his words made in the air brought the message to her quite distinctly.)

"—that the traffic in mutant eyes is still illegal. Very illegal. In point of fact, it is equated with murder; and because of the shortage of transplantable parts, the MediCom has kept it a high crime; one of the few for which the punishment is vegetable cortexing. If you permit this girl to live you run a terrible risk. Even a personage of *your* authority would find it most uncomfortable to have the threat of such a creature wandering loose."

The Director continued staring at him. Breame thought of the unblinking stares of lizards. When she blinked he thought of the membranous nictitating eyelids of lizards.

"Doctor, the girl is no problem. I want her alive only until I establish that there are no techniques for handling these eyes that she can help me to learn."

Breame seemed shocked.

"I do not care for the expression on your face, Doctor. You find my manner with this child duplicitous, yet you are directly responsible for her situation. You have taken her away from whomever and wherever she wished to be, you have stripped her naked, laid her out like a side of beef, you have immobilized her and anesthetized her; you plan to cut out her eyes, treat her to the wonders of blindness after she has spent a lifetime seeing far more than normal humans; and you have done all this not in the name of science, or humanity, or even curiosity. You have done it for credits. I find the expression on your face an affront, Doctor. I advise you to work diligently to erase it."

Breame had gone white, and in the cold room he was shivering again. He heard the voices of the parts calling. At the edges of his vision things moved.

"All I want you to assure me, Dr. Breame, is that you can perform this operation with perfection. I will not tolerate anything less. My guards have been so instructed."

"I'm perhaps the only surgeon who *can* perform this

operation and guarantee you that you will encounter no physically deleterious effects. Handling the eyes *after* the operation is something over which I have no control."

"And results will be immediate?"

"As I promised. With the techniques I've perfected, transfer can be effected virtually without discomfort."

"And should something go wrong . . . you can replace the eyes a second time?"

Breame hesitated. "With difficulty. You aren't a young woman; the risks would be considerable; but it *could* be done. Again, probably by no other surgeon. And it would be extremely expensive. It would entail another pair of healthy eyes."

26 Krystabel Parsons smiled her terrible smile. "Do I perceive you feel underpaid, Dr. Breame?"

He did not answer. No answer was required.

Verna saw it all and understood it all. And had she been able to smile, she would have smiled; much more warmly than the Director. If she died, as she was certain she would, that was peace and release. If not, well . . .

Nothing was worse than life.

They were moving around the room now. Another table was unshipped from a wall cubicle and formed. The doctor undressed 26 Krystabel Parsons and one of the two remaining Floridans lifted her like a tree branch and laid her on the table.

The last thing Verna saw was the faintly glowing, vibrating blade of the shining e-scalpel, descending toward her face. The finger of God, and she blessed it as her final thoughts were of her mother.

26 Krystabel Parsons, undisputed owner of worlds and industries and entire races of living creatures, jaded observer of a universe that no longer held even a faint view of interest or originality, opened her eyes.

The first things she saw were the operating room, the Floridan guards standing at the foot of the table staring at her intensely, the Knoxdoctor dressing the girl who stood beside her own table, the smears of black where the girl's eyes had been.

There was a commotion in the passageway outside. One of the guards turned toward the iris, still open.

And in that moment all sense of *seeing* flooded in on the Director of Minet. Light, shade, smoke, shadow, glow, transparency, opacity, color, tint, hue, prismatics, sweet, delicate, subtle, harsh, vivid, bright, intense, serene, crystalline, kaleidoscopic, all and everything at once!

Something else. Something more. Something the girl had not mentioned, had not hinted at, had not wanted her to know! The shadows within shadows.

She *saw* the Floridan guards. *Saw* them for the first time. Saw the state of their existence at the moment of their death. It was as if a multiple image, a strobe portrait of each of them lived before her. The corporeal reality in the front, and behind—like endless auras radiating out from them but superimposed over them—the thousand images of their futures. And the sight of them when they were dead, how they died. Not the action of the event, but the result. The hideous result of having life ripped from them. Rotting, corrupt, ugly beyond belief, and all the more ugly than imagination because it was *seen* with forever eyes that captured all the invisible-to-normal-eyes subtleties of containers intended to contain life, having been emptied of that life. She turned her head, unable to speak or scream or howl like a dog as she wished, and she *saw* the girl, and she *saw* the doctor.

It was a sight impossible to contain.

She jerked herself upright, the pain in her withered legs barely noticeable. And she opened her mouth and forced herself to scream as the commotion in the passageway grew louder, and something dragged itself through the iris.

She screamed with all the unleashed horror of a creature unable to bear itself, and the guards turned back to look at her with fear and wonder . . . as Berne dragged himself into the room. She *saw* him, and it was worse than all the rest, because it was happening *now,* he was dying *now,* the vessel was emptying *now!* Her scream became the howl of a dog. He could not speak, because he had no part left in his face that could make a formed sound come out. He could see only imperfectly; there was only one eye. If he had an expression, it was lost under the blood and crushed, hanging flesh that formed his face. The huge Floridan guard had not been malevolent, merely Floridan, and they were a race only lately up from barbarism. But he had taken a long time.

Breame's hands froze on the sealstrip of the girl's tunic and he looked around her, saw the pulped mass that pulled itself along the floor, leaving a trail of dark stain and viscous matter, and his eyes widened.

The Floridans raised their weapons almost simultaneously, but the thing on the floor gripped the weapon it had somehow—amazingly, unpredictably, impossibly—taken away from its assassin, and it fired. The head of the nearest Floridan caved in on itself, and the body jerked sidewise, slamming into the other guard. Both of them hit the operating table on which the Director of Minet sat screaming, howling, savaging the air with mortal anguish. The table overturned, flinging the crippled old woman with the forever eyes to the floor.

Breame knew what had happened. Berne had not been sent away. It had been blindness for him to think she would leave *any* of them alive. He moved swiftly, as the remaining Floridan struggled to free himself of the corpse that pinned him to the floor. The Knoxdoctor had the e-scalpel in his hand in an instant, palmed it on, and threw himself atop the guard. The struggle took a moment, as Breame sliced away at the skull. There was a muffled sound of the guard's weapon, and Breame staggered to his feet, reeled backward, and crashed into a power bin. Its storage door fell open and Breame took two steps into the center of the room, clutching his chest. His hands went inside his body; he stared down at the ruin; then he fell forward.

There was a soft bubbling sound from the dying thing that had been the pronger, Berne, and then silence in the charnel house.

Silence, despite the continued howling of 26 Krystabel Parsons. The sounds she made were so overwhelming, so gigantic, so inhuman, that they became like the ticking of a clock in a silent room, the thrum of power in a sleeping city. Unheard.

Verna heard it all, but had no idea what had happened. She dropped to her knees, and crawled toward what she thought was the iris. She touched something wet and pulpy with the fingertips of her left hand. She kept crawling. She touched something still-warm but unmoving with the fingertips of her right hand, and felt along the thing till she came to hands imbedded in soft, rubbery ruin. To her right she could faintly hear the sound of something humming, and she knew the sound: an e-scalpel, still slicing, even when it could do no more damage.

Then she had crawled to an opening, and she felt with her hands and it seemed to be a bin, a large bin, with its door open. She crawled inside and curled up, and pulled the door closed behind her, and lay there quietly.

And not much later there was the sound of movement in the operating room as others who had been detained for reasons Verna would never know, came and lifted 26 Krystabel Parsons, and carried her away, still howling like a dog, howling more intensely as she saw each new person, knowing eventually she would see the thing she feared seeing the most. The reflection of herself as she would be in the moment of her dying; and knowing she would still be sane enough to understand and appreciate it.

From extreme long shot, establishing; trucking in to medium shot, it looks like this:

Viewed through the tracking devices of PIX's port authority clearance security system, the Long Drive vessel sits in its pit, then slowly begins to rise out of its berth. White mist, or possibly steam, or possibly ionized fog billows out of the pit as the vessel leaves. The great ship rises toward the sky as we move in steadily on it. We continue forward, angle tilting up to hold the Long Driver in medium shot, then a fast zoom in on the glowing hide of the ship, and dissolve through to a medium shot, establishing the interior.

Everyone is comfortable. Everyone is watching the planet Earth drop away like a stained-glass window through a trapdoor. The fisheye-lens of the stateroom iris shows WorldsEnd and PIX and the polar emptiness and the mottled ball of the decaying Earth as they whirl away into the darkness.

Everyone sees. They see the ship around them, they see one another, they see the pages of the books they read, and they see the visions of their hopes for good things at the end of this voyage. They all see.

Moving in on one passenger, we see she is blind. She sits with her body formally erect, her hands at her sides. She wears her clothing well, and apart from the dark smudges that show beneath the edge of the stylish opaque band covering her eyes, she is a remarkably attractive woman. Into tight closeup. And we see that much of her grace and attractiveness comes from the sense of overwhelming peace and containment her features convey.

Hold the closeup as we study her face, and marvel at how relaxed she seems. We must pity her, because we know that blindness, not being able to see, is a terrible curse. And we decide she must be a remarkable woman to have reconciled such a tragic state with continued existence.

We think that if we were denied sight, we would certainly commit suicide. As the darkness of the universe surrounds the vessel bound for other places.

"If the doors of perception were cleansed everything would appear to man as it is, infinite."

William Blake, *The Marriage of Heaven and Hell,* 1790

Introduction to The Boulevard of Broken Dreams

Another thing that disturbs me about the rise of illiteracy in this country: Readers, the few who remain, have had their intellectual taste bastardized so systematically that for many people there is an inability to read anything subtler than one of those dreary gothic novels or something by Harold Robbins. "Quick reads" such as *Jaws* and *Oliver's Story* become the level at which readers can grasp entertainment. Indirection, careful omission of explicits, subtlety go by the boards.

I've found more and more frequently these days that even fairly intelligent people reading good books come to the end of a story with a quizzical expression on their faces. Unless they have been told with nailed-down precision that John dies in the fire and Joan marries Bernice and the secret message in the codex was that we are all alien property, many readers have no idea what the point of the story might have been.

Such has been the case with the short story you are about to read. It demands knowledge of a well-known historical fact. A common fact that every immigrant to this country before 1955 knew as well as . . . well, as well as his own name. I suppose I could say that this story is about the guilt of the survivor and *tell* you the fact you need to know . . . but I won't.

I won't, because I think if you care enough to want to know what this story says (and it says something about which I care passionately), then you will ask your Lithuanian grandmother or your Russian uncle or your Polish grandpoppa. Or anyone who went through the horror of World War II in Europe.

And perhaps the quote below will help, or at least alarm you. God, I hope so, otherwise we're in deep trouble.

•

"Those who cannot remember the past are condemned to repeat it."

George Santayana, *The Life of Reason*

The Boulevard of Broken Dreams

The demitasse cup of thick, sludgy espresso stopped mid-way between the saucer and Patrick Fenton's slightly parted lips. His arm froze and he felt cold; as if beads of fever-sweat covered his forehead. He stared past his luncheon companions, across the tiny French restaurant, through the front window that faced onto East 56th Street, eyes widened; as the old man strode by outside.

"Jesus Christ!" he said, almost whispering in wonder.

"What's the matter?" Damon said, looking worried.

Fenton's hand began to shake. He set the cup down very carefully. Damon continued to stare at him with concern. Then Katherine perceived the luncheon had come to a halt and she looked back and forth between them. "What's happening?"

Fenton pulled his napkin off his lap and wiped his upper lip. "I can't believe what I just saw. It couldn't be."

Damon shoved his plate away and leaned forward. He had been the only one Fenton had communicated with during the month in the hospital; they were good friends. "Tell me."

"Forget it. I didn't see it."

Katherine was getting impatient. "I don't think it's

nice to play these nasty little word games. Just because I'm facing the kitchen and you're not, is no reason to taunt me. What *did* you see, Pat?"

Fenton sipped water. He took a long pause, then said, "I was a clerk at the Nuremberg trials in forty-six. You know. There was an officer, an *Oberstleutnant*. Johann Hagen. He was in charge of the mass grave digging detail at Bergen-Belsen. He did things to women and small boys with a pickax. He was hung in June of 1946. I was there. I saw him hang."

Damon stared across at his old friend. Fenton was in his early sixties, almost bald now, and he had been sick. "Take it easy, Pat."

"I just saw him walk past that window."

They stared at him for a moment. Damon cleared his throat, moved his coffee cup, cleared his throat again. Katherine continued chewing and looked at each of them without speaking. Finally, when the light failed to fade from Fenton's eyes, she said, "You must be mistaken."

He spoke softly, without argument. "I'm not mistaken. You don't see a man hang and ever forget his face."

Damon laid a hand on Fenton's wrist. "Take it easy. It's getting dark. A resemblance, that's all."

"No."

They sat that way for a long time, and Fenton continued to stare out the window. Finally, he started to speak, but the words caught in his throat. He gasped and moaned softly. His eyes widened at something seen outside on the sidewalk. Damon turned with difficulty—he was an extremely fat man, a successful attorney—and looked out the window.

Katherine turned and looked. The street was thronged with late afternoon crowds hurrying to get inside before the darkness that promised rain could envelop them. "What now?" she said.

"Another one," Fenton said. "Another one. Dear God, what's happening . . . ?"

"What do you mean: another one?"

"Katherine," Damon said snappishly, "shut up. Pat, what was it?"

Fenton was holding himself, arms wrapped around his body like a straitjacket. "Kreichbaum." He said the name the way an internist would say *inoperable*. "From Treblinka. They shot him in forty-five. A monster; bonfires, furnaces, fire was his medium. They shot him."

"Yes? And . . . ?" Katherine let the question hang.

"He just walked by that window, going toward Fifth Avenue."

"Pat, you've got to stop this," Damon said.

Fenton just stared, saying nothing. Then, after a moment, he moaned again. They didn't turn, they just watched him. "Kupsch," he said. Softly, very softly. And after a few seconds, he said, "Stackmann." Shadows deepened in the little French restaurant. They were the only ones left dining, and their food had grown as cold as the tablecloths. "Oh, God," Fenton said, "Rademacher."

Then he leaped to his feet, knocking over his chair, and screamed, "What kind of street *is* this?!"

Damon tried to reach across to touch him, to get him to sit down, but Fenton was spiraling toward hysteria. "What kind of day is this, where am I? They're dead, all of them! They went to the gallows or the wall thirty years ago. I was a young man, I saw it, all of it . . . what's happening here today?"

They tried to stop him as he pushed past them and ran out into the street.

It was almost totally dark now, even in late afternoon.

As though charcoal dust had been softly sifted down over the city. Crowds moved past him, jostling him. Only the pale purple glow of the dead Nazi war criminals who walked slowly past him provided illumination.

He saw them all, one by one, as they walked past, strolling in both directions, free as the air, saying nothing. hands empty, wearing good shoes.

He tried to grab one of them, Wichmann, as he came by. But the tall, dark-haired Nazi shrugged him off, smiled at the yellow armband Fenton wore, smiled at the six-pointed star on the armband, and shoved past, walking free.

"Changed at Ellis Island!" Fenton screamed at Wichmann's retreating back. "I had nothing to do with it!"

Then he saw the purple glow beginning to form around him.

The street became night.

Introduction to Strange Wine

A dear man who wrote under the name "H. H. Hollis" died in a Houston hospital a week or two ago as I write this. The wife of a good friend of mine, a young woman, very young, went in for an exploratory and they opened her up and took a look and closed her up again and just shook their heads. She'll not be with us long. So young, and talented. Joe Oles's son had happen to him what happened to Willis Kaw's son in this story. It's what they mean when they say a "*real* tragedy." A guy I've known for over twenty years hit a snowy patch on a Michigan road last December and missed missing a telephone pole by less than a foot. It cost him his life.

There's a scene out of a Kerouac novel in which a guy goes to visit a famous poet, and he asks him, "What's it all about? What's the secret of life, man? Is there an answer?"

And the poet thinks about it for a moment, and purses his lips in contemplation—because that's a big one—and he goes to the window and looks out at the city. And finally he turns around and says, "You know, there's an awful lot of bastards out there."

I'll be *damned* if I can make any sense out of life. It gets more complex the longer I keep breathing. And everything I thought I knew for sure keeps coming up for grabs, keeps changing and shifting like one of those oil-seep toys you can buy that change color and shape from moment to moment depending on how you hold it. Most of the time it seems to be an insane universe, filled with pain. Then, every once in a bit, some moment of joy or love or true friendship presents itself, and you get the strength to maintain, to go on a little longer.

Maybe that's what it's all about. Maintaining.

Hell, I don't know. Maybe there *is* a better life. And maybe *this* is the better life. What a pisser *that'd* be!

•

"Only a few go mad.
The sky moves in its whiteness
Like the withered hand of an old king.
God shall not forget us.
Who made the sky knows of our love."

Kenneth Patchen, "The Snow is Deep on the Ground"

•

"The story of the one-legged messenger is that his other leg is walking on the far side of death. 'What seems to be over there?' they ask him. 'Just emptiness?' 'No,' he says. 'Something before that, with no name.' "

W. S. Merwin, "Nothing Began as It Is"

Strange Wine

Two whipcord-lean California highway patrolmen supported Willis Kaw between them, leading him from the cruiser to the blanket-covered shape in the middle of the Pacific Coast Highway. The dark brown smear that began sixty yards west of the covered shape disappeared under the blanket. He heard one of the onlookers say, "She was thrown all that way, oh it's awful," and he didn't want them to show him his daughter.

But he had to make the identification, and one of the cops held him securely as the other went to one knee and pulled back the blanket. He recognized the jade pendant he had given her for graduation. It was all he recognized.

"That's Debbie," he said, and turned his head away.

Why is this happening to me? he thought. *I'm not from here; I'm not one of them. This should be happening to a human.*

"Did you take your shot?"

He looked up from the newspaper and had to ask her to repeat what she had said. "I asked you," Estelle said very softly, with as much kindness as she had left in her, "if you took your insulin." He smiled briefly, recognizing her concern and her attempt to avoid invading his sorrow, and he said he had taken the shot. His wife nodded and said, "Well, I think I'll go upstairs to bed. Are you coming?"

"Not right now. In a little, maybe."

"You'll fall asleep in front of the set again."

"Don't worry about it. I'll be up in a little while."

She stood watching him for a moment longer, then turned and climbed the stairs. He listened for the sounds of the upstairs ritual—the toilet flushing, the water moving through the pipes to the sink, the clothes closet door squeaking as it was opened, the bedsprings responding as Estelle put herself down for the night. And then he turned on the television set. He turned to Channel 30, one of the empty channels, and turned down the volume control so he did not have to hear the sound of coaxial "snow."

He sat in front of the set for several hours, his right hand flat against the picture tube, hoping the scanning pattern of the electron bombardment would reveal, through palm flesh grown transparent, the shape of alien bones.

In the middle of the week he asked Harvey Rothammer if he could have the day off Thursday so he could drive out to the hospital in Fontana to see his son. Rothammer was not particularly happy about it, but he didn't have the heart to refuse. Kaw had lost his daughter, and the son was still ninety-five percent incapacitated, lying in a therapy bed with virtually no hope of ever walking again. So he told Willis Kaw to take the day off, but not to forget that April was almost upon them and for a firm of certified public accountants it was rush season. Willis Kaw said he knew that.

The car broke down twenty miles east of San Dimas, and he sat behind the wheel, in the bludgeoning heat, staring at the desert and trying to remember what the surface of his home planet looked like.

His son, Gilvan, had gone on a vacation to visit friends in New Jersey the summer before. The friends had installed a freestanding swimming pool in the back yard. Gil had dived in and struck bottom; he had broken his back.

Fortunately, they had pulled him out before he could drown, but he was paralyzed from the waist down. He could move his arms, but not his hands. Willis had gone East, had arranged to have Gil flown back to California, and there he lay in a bed in Fontana.

He could remember only the color of the sky. It was a brilliant green, quite lovely. And things that were not birds, that skimmed instead of flying. More than that he could not remember.

The car was towed back to San Dimas, but the garage had to send off to Los Angeles for the necessary parts. He left the car and took a bus back home. He did not get to see Gil that week. The repair bill was two hundred and eighty-six dollars and forty-five cents.

That March the eleven-month drought in Southern California broke. Rain thundered down without end for a week; not as heavily as it does in Brazil, where the drops are so thick and come so close together that people have been known to suffocate if they walk out in the downpour. But heavily enough that the roof of the house sprang leaks. Willis Kaw and Estelle stayed up one entire night, stuffing towels against the baseboards in the living room; but the leaks from the roof apparently weren't over the outer walls but rather in low spots somewhere in the middle; the water was running down and triculating through.

The next morning, depressed beyond endurance, Willis Kaw began to cry. Estelle heard him as she was loading the soaking towels into the dryer, and ran into the living room. He was sitting on the wet carpet, the smell of mildew rising in the room, his hands over his face, still holding a wet bath towel. She knelt down beside him and took his head in her hands and kissed his forehead. He did not stop crying for a very long time, and when he did, his eyes burned.

"It only rains in the evening where I come from," he said to her. But she didn't know what he meant.

When she realized, later, she went for a walk, trying to decide if she could help her husband.

He went to the beach. He parked on the shoulder just off the Old Malibu Road, locked the car, and trotted down the embankment to the beach. He walked along the sand for an hour, picking up bits of milky glass worn smooth by the Pacific, and finally he lay down on the slope of a small, weed-thatched dune and went to sleep.

He dreamed of his home world and—perhaps because the sun was high and the ocean made eternal sounds—he was able to bring much of it back. The bright green sky, the skimmers swooping and rising overhead, the motes of pale yellow light that flamed and then floated up and were lost to sight. He felt himself in his real body, the movement of many legs working in unison, carrying him across the mist sands, the smell of alien flowers in his mind. He knew he had been born on that world, had been raised there, had grown to maturity and then . . .

Sent away.

In his human mind, Willis Kaw knew he had been sent away for doing something bad. He knew he had been condemned to this planet, this Earth, for having perhaps committed a crime. But he could not remember what it was. And in the dream he could feel no guilt.

But when he woke, his humanity came back and flooded over him and he felt guilt. And he longed to be back out there, where he belonged, not trapped in this terrible body.

"I didn't want to come to you," Willis Kaw said. "I think it's stupid. And if I come, then I admit there's room for doubt. And I don't doubt, so . . ."

The psychiatrist smiled and stirred the cup of cocoa. "And so . . . you came because your wife insisted."

"Yes." He stared at his shoes. They were brown shoes, he had owned them for three years. They had never fit properly; they pinched and made his big toe on each foot feel as if it were being pressed down by a knife edge, a dull knife edge.

The psychiatrist carefully placed the spoon on a piece of Kleenex, and sipped at his cocoa. "Look, Mr. Kaw, I'm open to suggestion. I don't want you to be here, nor do you *want* to be here, if it isn't going to help you. And," he added quickly, "by *help* you I don't mean convert you to any world view, any systematized belief, you choose to reject. I'm not entirely convinced, by Freud or Werner Erhard or Scientology or any other rigor, that there is such a thing as 'reality.' Codified reality. A given, an immutable, a constant. As long as what someone believes doesn't get him put in a madhouse or a prison, there's no reason why it should be less acceptable than what we, uh, 'straight folks' call reality. If it makes you happy, believe it. What I'd like to do is listen to what you have to say, perhaps offer a few comments, and then see if *your* reality is compatible with *straight folks'* reality.

"How does that sound to you?"

Willis Kaw tried to smile back. "It sounds fine. I'm a little nervous."

"Well, try not to be. That's easy for me to say and hard for you to do, but I mean you no harm; and I'm really quite interested."

Willis uncrossed his legs and stood up. "Is it all right if I just walk around the office a little? It'll help, I think." The psychiatrist nodded and smiled, and indicated the cocoa. Willis Kaw shook his head. He walked around the psychiatrist's office and finally said, "I don't belong in this body. I've been condemned to life as a human being, and it is killing me."

The psychiatrist asked him to explain.

Willis Kaw was a small man, with thinning brown hair and bad eyes. He had weak legs and constantly had need of a handkerchief. His face was set in lines of worry and sadness. He told the psychiatrist all this. Then he said, "I believe this planet is a place where bad people are sent to atone for their crimes. I believe that all of us come from other worlds; other planets where we have done something wrong. This Earth is a prison, and we're sent here to live in these awful bodies that decay and smell bad and run down and die. And that's our punishment."

"But why do *you* perceive such a condition, and no one else?" The psychiatrist had set aside the cocoa, and it was growing cold.

"This must be a defective body they've put me in," Willis Kaw said. "Just a little extra pain, knowing I'm an alien, knowing I'm serving a prison sentence for something I did, something I can't remember; but it must have been an awful thing for me to have drawn such a sentence."

"Have you ever read Franz Kakfa, Mr. Kaw?"

"No."

"He wrote books about people who were on trial for crimes the nature of which they never learned. People who were guilty of sins they didn't know they had committed."

"Yes. I feel that way. Maybe Kafka felt that way; maybe he had a defective body, too."

"What you're feeling isn't that strange, Mr. Kaw," the

psychiatrist said. "We have many people these days who are dissatisfied with their lives, who find out—perhaps too late—that they are transsexual, that they should have been living their days as something else, a man, a woman—"

"No, no! That isn't what I mean. I'm not a candidate for a sex change. I'm telling you I come from a world with a green sky, with mist sand and light motes that flame and then float up . . . I have many legs, and webs between the digits and they aren't fingers . . ." He stopped and looked embarrassed.

Then he sat down and spoke very softly. "Doctor, my life is like everyone else's life. I'm sick much of the time, I have bills I cannot pay, my daughter was struck by a car and killed and I cannot bear to think about it. My son was cut off in the prime of his life and he'll be a cripple from now on. My wife and I don't talk much, we don't love each other . . . if we ever did. I'm no better and no worse than anyone else on this planet and *that's* what I'm talking about: the pain, the anguish, the living in terror. Terror of each day. Hopeless. Empty.. Is this the best a person can have, this terrible life here as a human being? I tell you there are better places, other worlds where the torture of being a human being doesn't exist!"

It was growing dark in the psychiatrist's office. Willis Kaw's wife had made the appointment for him at the last moment and the doctor had taken the little man with the thinning brown hair as a fill-in, at the end of the day.

"Mr. Kaw," the psychiatrist said, "I've listened to all you've said, and I want you to know that I'm very much in sympathy with your fears." Willis Kaw felt relieved. He felt at last someone might be able to help him. If not to relieve him of this terrible knowledge and its weight, at least to tell him he wasn't alone. "And frankly, Mr. Kaw," the psychiatrist said, "I think you're a man with a very serious problem. You're a sick man and you need intense psychiatric help. I'll talk to your wife if you like, but if you take my advice, you'll have yourself placed in a proper institution before this condition . . ."

Willis Kaw closed his eyes.

He pulled down the garage door tight and stuffed the cracks with rags. He could not find a hose long enough to feed back into the car from the tail pipe, so he merely opened the car windows and started the engine and let it run. He sat in the back seat and tried to read Dickens' *Dombey and Son,* a book Gil had once told him he would enjoy.

But he couldn't keep his attention on the story, on the elegant language, and after a while he let his head fall back, and he tried to sleep, to dream of the other world that had been stolen from him, the world he knew he would never again see. Finally, sleep took him, and he died.

The funeral service was held at Forest Lawn, and very few people came. It was a weekday. Estelle cried, and Harvey Rothammer held her and told her it was okay. But he was checking his wristwatch over her shoulder, because April was almost upon him.

And Willis Kaw was put down in the warm ground, and the dirt of an alien planet was dumped in on him by a Chicano with three children who was forced to moonlight as a dishwasher in a bar and grill because he simply couldn't meet the payments on his six-piece living room suite if he didn't.

The many-legged Consul greeted Willis Kaw when he returned. He turned over and looked up at the Consul and saw the bright green sky above. "Welcome back, Plydo," the Consul said.

He looked very sad.

Plydo, who had been Willis Kaw on a faraway world, got to his feet and looked around. Home.

But he could not keep silent and enjoy the moment. He had to know. "Consul, please . . . tell me . . . what did I do that was so terrible?"

"Terrible!" The Consul seemed stunned. "We owe you nothing but honor, your grace. Your name is valued above all others." There was deep reverence in his words.

"Then why was I condemned to live in anguish on that other world? Why was I sent away to exist in torment?"

The Consul shook his hairy head, and his mane billowed in the warm breeze. "No, your grace, no! Anguish is what *we* suffer. Torment is all *we* know. Only a few, only a very few honored and loved among all the races of the universe can go to that world. Life there is sweet compared to what passes for life everywhere else. You are still disoriented. It will all come back to you. You will remember. And you will understand."

And Plydo, who had been, in a better part of his almost eternal life of pain, Willis Kaw, *did* remember. As time passed, he recalled all the eternities of sadness that had been born in him, and he knew that they had given him the only gift of joy permitted to the races of beings who lived in the far galaxies. The gift of a few precious years on a world where anguish was so much less than that known everywhere else.

He remembered the rain, and the sleep, and the feel of beach sand beneath his feet, and ocean rolling in to whisper its eternal song, and on just such nights as those he had despised on Earth, he slept and dreamed good dreams.

Of life as Willis Kaw, life on the pleasure planet.

Introduction to The Diagnosis of Dr. D'arqueAngel

I'm particularly proud of having written this story. Not that it's an earthshaker or the most inspired narration I've ever lucked into, but because *I* wrote it and neither Ray Bradbury nor Frank Herbert did.

That may seem a weird thing to say, but on a day several years ago when Frank and Ray and I wound up all together on the same lecture platform, and we were kicking around ideas and memories of our childhood, I popped this idea—"How about a story in which there's a doctor who gives you periodic injections of death, so you build up a tolerance to it, and cannot die?"—and all three of us rolled our eyes and said WOW!

And we all three vowed, in front of that huge audience, to write the story, and it was to be a race to see who could get it set down on paper first.

And three or four years went by, and none of us did it; and then one day I remembered the idea and plopped down behind this very typewriter at which I now sit, and in nine straight hours of typing I wrote this story.

I sent a copy to Frank and I sent a copy to Ray.

They haven't responded. You think they're mad at me?

•

"Ordinarily my ratio of concerns is something like this: Fifty per cent work and worry over work, 35% the perpetual struggle against lunacy, 15% a very true and very tender love for those who have been and are close to me as friends and as lover. But [sometimes] the ratio changes to something like this: Work and worry over work, 89%; struggle against lunacy (partly absorbed in the first category) 10%; very true and tender love for lover and friends, 1%. A stranger would doubt this, but you have known me and observed me for a long time. Surely you see how it is!"

Tennessee Williams

The Diagnosis of Dr. D'arqueAngel

The word beautiful simply did not do her justice. She was quantum leaps beyond merely beautiful. Exquisite, perhaps: carried to the nth degree. She sat behind her desk and Romb hoped she wouldn't stand up; he wasn't at all sure he could handle an unobstructed view of her, full length. She was purely the most breathtaking human being he had ever seen. He thought she would look perfect standing on a pedestal in Thrace somewhere.

"You're staring, Mr. Romb," she said. Gently. With amusement.

He felt his face grown warm. He was in his thirties, very slick, good moves—and he wasn't used to being embarrassed by women. It was usually the other way around. "Oh, excuse me, Doctor; I was thinking about what you said. Then it is possible?"

"Oh, yes. It's possible. It *can* be done. But it comes at a premium, of course."

"I expected as much," Romb said. He had vague feelings of danger: contracts signed in blood, loss of immortal soul, less nameable tremblings. He wore tinted aviator glasses and his hair had been styled by an Italian. His suit had been purchased in Savile Row. "Just *how* much is the question."

"Ten percent of what you realize."

"I have no idea how much that might be."

"Payment deferred. I can wait. My patients are unfailingly grateful. I've never had to sue for collection."

"Patients? You've used these treatments before."

"Occasionally. When the circumstances have been, er, extraordinary, shall we say. A high degree of confidentiality is, of course, imperative."

He thought about that for a moment. *Imperative* was as inadequate as *beautiful*. He had come to the office of Dr. D'arqueAngel as a final act of desperation. He had heard whispers among a strange group of his acquaintances who were involved with witchcraft . . . a silly bunch of people, really, but on occasion he found them amusing. And they had been talking about her one evening at what they called their "coven," though it was more like a social tea for overage singles than a coven as he had read about such things. The whispers had been incomplete, hardly specific; but if what they said about her was accurate, she might be the answer to his nightmarish dilemma.

Simply stated, it didn't *sound* all that desperate:

Charles Romb wanted to murder his wife.

The actuality of the situation, however, was a quantum leap beyond desperate. Beyond nightmarish. It was, simply stated, a life sentence in a living Hell.

"Mr. Romb?"

He realized he had been staring again. These lapses into preoccupation had been coming more and more frequently. He had been staring into the middle distance, thinking about Sandra, thinking how monstrous his even *being here* seemed in retrospect. But he *had* come here, he *was* sitting across the Saarinen desk from her, and he *had* confided his desire . . . to a total stranger.

An exquisite, disturbing stranger he had heard about only in whispers.

"I'm sorry. I still can't believe I'm here saying these things to you. The whole idea is so crazy . . . but I'm so damned miserable . . ."

"I understand perfectly, Mr. Romb. You can be completely open with me." She didn't say it, but the unspoken next sentence was certainly, *You can trust me; I'm a doctor.*

"But it works?" He felt like a fool pressing her; she had already said it worked, had said it several times.

"Oh, it works very well indeed. As well as snake venom. Same principle, really." She steepled incredibly slim fingers. He watched her hands in fascination.

"I'm not sure I understand that."

"Consider," Dr. D'arqueAngel said, "if you were to be injected with infinitesimal doses of, say, the venom of the black mamba—*Dendroaspis polylepis*—every other day for a year or two, with the dosage increasing just slightly with each inoculation; by the end of the second year if you were on a visit to, say, Zaire, and you were struck by a black mamba, instead of almost instant paralysis and death within seconds, you might become very ill . . . but you wouldn't die. Your tolerance level would have been built up so your system would fight the venom. Do you understand the parallel to my treatments?"

He understood. But could not believe it.

"And that's how you'll keep me from dying? You'll give me periodic injections of snake venom?"

She smiled, a mysterious and entrancing smile. "No, Mr. Romb: I'll give you periodic injections of death."

"That's unbelievable. It's impossible. Look: I'm going to do it, I'm going to have you give me the treatments; no matter what; I'm just about at the end of my sanity, so I'm *going* to do it. No matter what. But tell me the truth. If it's a con job, if it's just craziness, then tell me. I know that sounds loony, but even if you tell me it's all a made-up story, I'll make the deal and I'll pay you what you ask." He heard himself speaking and knew it sounded hysterical, lunatic, stupid in the extreme. And he knew he couldn't stop, knew the thin line of concern that ran vertically between his eyebrows when he was on the edge this way, was there now. But he couldn't help himself.

"Mr. Romb," she said, getting up and coming around the desk, "it's real, it works, I won't tell you it's a myth, because I can do it. You can trust me."

And she leaned down and took his face in her exquisite hands and she brought her incredible face to his and she kissed him deeply.

He felt his stomach drop away. He was light-headed and unable to breathe. For the first time in his life he felt blood pulsing in parts of his body he'd never even known had the power to send back such messages to his spinning brain. The touch of her mouth on his had stunned and awed him.

And instantly the thought of being kissed by Sandra flooded in on him.

He tried to speak, to ask her why she had done that, why she had withered his soul with a kiss, this unbelievably beautiful woman with the power, the power, the *power* to stave off death! But only sounds came. His hands moved in aimless patterns. Sounds, dumb sounds, helpless and lost.

"It works," she said again, whispering the words close to his face. The scent of her skin was warm and swift and strange.

"But . . ."

He wanted to ask her how it was possible, how she could put death in a needle and send it into someone's bloodstream.

She seemed to sense what he wanted to know. But she

didn't answer the unspoken question. She held his face and she stared at him and then she said, "It doesn't matter how I've done it. Can you understand that? If you've come to me, and told me what you wouldn't dare tell anyone else, then you'll never need to know *how* I've done it. Just that I've done it, and no one else can duplicate it. I've found the secret. The process that distills the essence of death, to fractionate it, to create the antitoxin for death."

Her touch was cool and his skin beneath her fingers felt as though it was being carbonated, shot full of minute bubbles of energy. "Who are you?" he whispered, barely able to control his trembling.

"I'm your doctor," she said. "Shall we begin your treatments now?" And she kissed him forever once more.

When he pulled into the driveway and the gates swung closed behind the Bentley, he saw Sandra standing on the portico, waiting for him. The usual nausea welled up in him. She was always waiting for him. And it was in moments like these, with her loving arms merely instants away from his flesh, that he despised himself most.

He knew he had no one to blame for his nightmare but himself. A lifetime of believing merely being pretty and being smooth entitled him to ease and plenty had put him where he was. Pretty, he had met Sandra and pursued her. Smooth, he had known every thrust and vector of the dance of desire, and he had caught her. Pretty, he had conned his way into the family; and smooth, he had conned his way into her father's corporation. Smoothly, prettily, he had worked his way up in the superstructure of an international conglomerate and—patiently—which entailed considerable amounts of both qualities—he had waited for the old man to die. Now he was fully and wholly in the burning center of the nightmare. No less smooth, no less pretty than he had ever been. But now in the molten core of hell, burning endlessly.

He had everything patience and several other qualities could buy. Wealth, position, security, freedom, material possessions . . . and Sandra.

Sandra, who loved him. More than life itself, Sandra *loved* him. First thing in the morning, himself mirrored in her eyes, she loved him. Last thing at night, the smoke of undiminished passion clouding those loving eyes, she adored him the more. Endless touches, caresses, murmurings of ardor; and always the paralyzing, certain knowledge that tomorrow she would love him a little more than today; and the day after tomorrow more than the day before. Certain, paralyzing knowledge: as one with the venom of the black mamba: instant paralysis, death within seconds.

The idea of death became the only sanity in his lunatic nightmare burning hell of an existence.

Sandra's death.

By poison. By gunshot. By swift sweet steel. By fire, incinerated, reduced to ashes and the ashes scattered over the private lake that formed the eastern border of the family estate.

All this, as Sandra grew in his windshield eye, and he grew in the eyes of his loving wife.

And one thing more. The touch of the lips of Dr. D'arqueAngel. Still with him, even as the serum she had injected into his arm was with him.

It would, she had said, produce a small death. He need not worry.

Before he could step out of the Bentley, Sandra was there, opening the door, leaning in to kiss him. His stomach did not drop away; it merely heaved. He did not grow light-headed nor was his breathing impaired. A splitting headache *did* make itself felt, however; and as for breath, hers made him ill. The touch of her mouth on his was an abomination.

And the worst part was that there was absolutely nothing wrong with her. She was fine, she was just simply fine, he *knew* that. It was all of his own making, all the abhorrence. *And he wanted her dead.* No less than dead. Gone. Dead. Out of his life. Out of the world. Dead.

"Where have you been, darling? I've been waiting for hours. I called the Elliots and begged off. It would've been dreary anyhow. Wouldn't you much rather just spend a quiet, cozy evening at home with me . . . ?"

Dead! Only one thought, a frozen bit of survival in the molten core of hell. Dead!

And in bed that night, as she moved beneath him, demanding her daily ration of his life-essence, she heard him murmur, as if from far away, "Who are you?" and she put her moist mouth beside his oddly warm and distressingly warm ear and she said, "I'm your wife."

And in the night, he had a small heart attack; the shortest, tiniest punch of a thrombosis. But he did not die. It was a little death.

The office of Dr. D'arqueAngel was dimly lit from hidden banks of rose-tinted lights behind the moldings of the walls. He lay on her wide couch and ran his left hand down the length of her pale body, learning for just a moment the mythic contours and timeless silkiness.

In the seven months of his treatments, he had become drunk with the sight and touch of her. There was always an injection, of course; but there was also—always—the hour of insensate passion. And he had grown stronger as the months went by. More strongly able to sustain the life with Sandra—against the time when she would be gone. And stronger in his relationship with the doctor. She said very little, but her need for his body had hardly required vocalizing. Now he felt like his old self again: dominant with women, secure, smooth. And extremely pretty.

She moved out from under his hand and stood up. The sight of her, stretching in the semidarkness, sent waves of expectation through him. But in a moment, even though she was naked, he knew her professional manner was in the ascendant.

"Your system is quite remarkable, Charles."

"Oh? And how is that?"

"You've come along at almost twice the normal speed of past patients. I'd say your tolerance is at the level of others who have been under treatment for thirteen months."

"Who are these others?"

"Now, now, Charles. Let's not go into that again. You know what professional ethics forbid my talking about. But tell me about the most recent deaths."

In seven months he had *not* died from a serious tumble down three flights of stairs, a knifing by a mugger in the underground parking lot of his office building, inhaling a dose of virulent pesticide left uncapped by an inept gardener, drowning in his club's swimming pool when he dove too deep and struck his head on the bottom, several dozen coronary thromboses, and a bout with the flu that had dropped into pneumonia.

"I woke up in the middle of the night about a week ago and found I couldn't breathe. My lungs seemed to have collapsed. It was horrible."

"Yes, that one's fairly common. And what else?"

"Some punk kids were playing on the freeway overpass, dropping rocks on the cars. A big one came through the windshield and damned near brained me. Opened a huge gash in my right temple. There was blood all over the car."

"How long to heal?"

"About an hour."

"Startling. Absolutely startling. Yes, I'd put you at thirteen months. I think your treatments should be coming to an end in a few weeks."

Terror gripped his heart. It was like a giant fist squeezing through his rib cage. "I'll still see you after . . . after she's . . ."

"We'll see," was all she said. The way a mother would speak to a child who wanted to stay up past his bedtime. We'll see.

"Three weeks, Charles. I'm certain we're only talking about three weeks."

"Then you'll have ten percent of everything I inherit."

"I'm not thinking about that."

"I hope not," he said, and reached for her with a commanding manner. She came to him again, but there was very little of subservience in her surrender.

And later she put the needle into his arm and pressed the hypodermic plunger and sent the gray, swirling mixture that she said was the essence of death into his body.

He decided to do it the most direct way possible. In a way no one could ever question. So there would never be even the slightest whisper of gossip that Charles Romb had murdered his wife to gain control of her father's fortune. (Nor that Charles Romb had been driven by an excess of love to eradicate the creature who loved him so slavishly.)

On the first night of heavy rain, he insisted they go out to a movie. She wanted to stay home and give him a massage. He insisted and on the canyon road he suddenly swerved the Bentley and sent it thundering through the guard rails and into space. The car turned lazily and struck at stand of young, newly planted spruces, tearing out an even dozen before rolling past, over the rim of the plateau.

The Bentley dropped another hundred feet, impacted front end-on, flipped over onto its roof, crushing the top into the body, slid another fifty feet and came to rest on the tennis court of a wealthy hotel caterer who had moved up into the canyon as protection from the burglars and rip-off artists who flourished in the center of the city.

Romb had made certain not to turn off the ignition when he drove through the guard rails. The impact of the crash ruptured the gas tank as he'd known it must, and the Bentley suddenly exploded with flames.

Sandra had no doubt died at the first crunch of car against timber. The caterer's twenty-year-old son, a beach lifeguard during the summer months, threw himself and an asbestos lounging pad into the family swimming pool, and using it as protection, rushed the wreck. He managed to drag Charles Romb's dead body from the mangled and still smouldering debacle, sustaining third and second degree burns over one-fifth of his body.

Sandra was dead on arrival at the hospital.

Charles Romb was dead on arrival as well.

No one could have been more surprised than the intern on duty when, mere moments after he had pronounced the charred and broken remnant called Charles Romb dead, the body moaned, twisted on its stretcher, and began calling for its doctor.

But nowhere in the medical callbook or in the Yearbook of the American Medical Association could he find a Dr. D'arqueAngel.

"You've healed nicely, Charles," she said.

He reached for her, but she motioned him to the seat on the other side of her desk.

"It was god-awful," he said. He had some difficulty speaking. There were still bandages covering half his face, with patches of rejuvenating flesh still puckering under them.

"Yes, I know. It usually is. But you'll be totally well again in a few months. It was very wise of you to get yourself transferred to a private nursing home. The startling nature of your recovery, back from the dead, might well have caused some comment."

He stared at her, waiting. He knew she was holding something back.

"You're wondering when I'm going to ask for a settlement of accounts, aren't you?" She went around the desk, moving smoothly, and sat down. She motioned to the chair opposite once again. "Do sit down, Charles. We have a few things to discuss."

Romb shrugged out of his topcoat with some difficulty, wincing with pain. He tossed the coat on the wide couch and sat down. Yes, they had things to discuss. Now that he was free of Sandra, and a millionaire estimated at thirty times over, he felt his former awe of the mysterious Dr. D'arqueAngel greatly reduced. It was about time she learned precisely who held the power reins in what he planned as a very long, very pleasurable relationship.

"Listen," he said, crossing his legs, making certain the creases in his pants were straight, "I've decided to move the head office of my corporation to Bermuda; I like the climate there. I'll want you to come with me, of course."

She did not smile.

"Why settle for ten percent when you can have all of what I own? We can share it equally. I'll give you the kind of life you've always dreamed about."

She did not smile.

"We're in this together," he said, with a touch of meaning he intended as gentle menace. "I'm not sure what the law would be concerning your treatments, but I don't think either of us would want the other running around without some, uh, check on our activities."

She did not smile.

"Well? Say something."

She did not smile, but reached into a drawer of the desk and turned something, probably a rheostat, because the light dimmed to that half-dusk she always provided when they made love. In the semidarkness her face lost definition and all he could see clearly were her eyes . . . which now, for the first time, seemed incredibly old and wise.

"Don't be ridiculous, Charles. I have my practice."

"You'll have to close down your practice."

"I think not."

"I have no intention of signing over ten percent of my holdings to you."

"That won't be necessary. It was never necessary. That was merely a false estimate I knew you would consider the correct sort of payment for my services. My bill is totaled in quite a different coin."

Something unhuman and shadowy slithered through Charles Romb's mind.

"I think you'll decide to keep your offices here in the city, Charles; and I think you'll decide to be on call whenever I want you."

"And what makes you think that?"

"Here is something you ought to see." She reached into the drawer again, and he heard a switch click. A portion of the wall behind the desk folded away accordionlike, and he was staring at a screen. She worked with switches and dials in the drawer, and the screen lit up and began to hold a series of very clear slide photographs. "You've been curious about my other patients. Here is one of them. A very dear friend of mine named Philip." He recognized the man on the screen as a best-selling novelist who had not published anything new in several years.

The slides clicked on and off the screen in rapid succession. The first shot showed the novelist as a hardy young man in his late twenties. The second slide showed him seemingly two years older, slightly stooped. The third slide showed him with a touch of gray in his thick mop of hair, and his right hand was thrust into his pants pocket, apparently balled up. The slides clicked on and off much faster, and each one showed the young man in progressively more aged and physically decrepit stages of life. They seemed to blur as she ran them faster and faster, and the young man became an old man and the old man became a withered figure and the withered figure became a caricature of life, bent and twisted and clearly in constant pain. When the final slide was gone, and the screen was a square of bright light, Dr. D'arqueAngel worked her switches and the screen went off, the wall unpleated, and she was sitting there staring at him.

She was smiling.

"What's that supposed to mean?" Romb asked. But he was afraid he knew.

"Those are time-lapse photographs taken of my friend Philip."

Trembling, Romb softly asked, "How far apart? Two years each? Three? Five?"

"Every twenty minutes," she said.

Charles Romb heard, quite distinctly, somewhere in the universe, an escape-proof steel trap spring shut with a deadly clang.

"You see, Charles, everyone needs love. I'm sure you know that better than most people. Some need more love than others; Sandra, for one example. Others need hardly any; you, for another example. I need quite a lot. I'm a very demanding woman, Charles. I have to be. Not only is it my nature, but one finds as one grows older, much older, very much older, that attractive lovers seem to want equally attractive lovers. Life can be very lonely for the old and the ugly."

He was about to say, *But you're neither, you shouldn't have any problem finding thousands who would pay to make love to you,* but before he could speak he saw her eyes. They did not seem to belong in that exquisite face. They belonged in the face of a creature awesomely ancient and withered.

"I'd like you to meet Philip," Dr. D'arqueAngel said, still smiling. She pressed a button in the desk drawer and a door Romb had never noticed before slid smoothly into the wall and something barely human crutched its way into the room. In the half-light Charles Romb could barely make out the definition of body and features, but it was obviously the popular novelist, grown hideously old and wretched. He dragged himself through the doorway and took only two steps before his rotted lower limbs failed to support him. He fell, and began to crawl toward the woman.

When he reached her, he laid his head in her lap and she stroked his head as one would a faithful lapdog.

"The treatments must be continued, Charles. Otherwise I'm afraid the remissive process begins in something under a year. Deterioration accelerates and is impressively rapid and total."

Romb could not speak. The sight of the novelist groveling for a caress was loathsome—and fascinating.

"I practice preventative medicine, Charles. On my own behalf. The distillate of death has to come from *somewhere*. And from my own point of view even more important, the antitoxin. The merest fractionate of the essence that has the most salutary effects on preserving one's youth." She made a negligible gesture as if what she was about to say didn't really mean much: "Since I have no call for it, I use it myself."

Hoarsely, Romb asked, "How many of us are there?"

She named a captain of industry, a prominent actress, the owner of a successful chain of parking lots, a television newscaster with his own late-night talk show, that year's leading presidential candidate from the party out of office, a husband and wife team of diplomats assigned to the United Nations, a famous criminal lawyer given to courtroom theatrics, and a leading nightclub comedian. "My patients form a small but sturdy community of donors. Each supplies the others. Very carefully calibrated amounts of life, to stave off death, Charles. Not too much, not too little, each time; the balance is so delicate. Periodically I have to find a few more strong sources of supply, such as yourself. But when one of my, er, friends grows recalcitrant, threatens to tip the balance, well, I'm afraid in the interests of the common good I have to exercise a degree of corporal punishment. I withhold treatments."

She stroked the novelist's head meaningfully.

"After that, I'm afraid the patient can be maintained only at the level of deterioration that obtains when the treatments are resumed."

There was not, Romb realized, nearly enough smoothness or prettiness in the possible world.

"Give up this idea of Bermuda, Charles. I think you would find the climate most disagreeable . . . very quickly. And give up the idea of dispensing your love elsewhere; we need all you can give, you see. Stay here in the city with all of us. We'll treat you well, and with only the slightest inconvenience, a daily office call for your donation and your injection, you'll live to be, oh, I'd say two or three hundred years old."

The novelist whimpered in pain.

"I need love, Charles. Quite a lot of love. Love, as I'm sure you've heard said, keeps you young and happy."

In the semidarkness Charles Romb sat frozen in his chair considering two or three hundred years with a small death on each day of that time. He sat staring across at the ancient eyes of Dr. D'arqueAngel, dreading the moment when her secret flesh would touch his. Unparalleled love was to be his future. For a very long time. And the only sounds in the room were the husky, sensuous breathing of the shadowed woman, and the whimpers of the creature at her feet.

From the burning core of his molten hell Charles Romb screamed. *Sandra!* he screamed, in the silence of his soul. But from the terrible darkness of that place there was no answer, no answer at all.